I0670843

Eagle Spotted,
Message Decoded

Siddhartha Choudhary

First published in India 2010 by **Frog Books**
an imprint of **Leadstart Publishing Pvt Ltd**
1 Level, Trade Centre
Bandra Kurla Complex
Bandra (East) Mumbai 400 051 India
Telephone: +91-22-40700804
Fax: +91-22-40700800
Email: info@leadstartcorp.com
www.leadstartcorp.com / www.frogbooks.net

Marketing Office:
Unit: 122 / Building B/2
First Floor, Near Wadala RTO
Wadala (East) Mumbai 400 037 India
Phone: +91-22-24046887

US Office:
Axis Corp, 7845 E Oakbrook Circle
Madison, WI 53717 USA

Copyright @ Siddhartha Choudhary

All rights reserved. No part of this publication may be
reproduced, stored in or introduced into a retrieval system, or
transmitted, in any form, or by any means (electronic, mechanical,
photocopying, recording or otherwise) without the prior written
permission of the publisher. Any person who does any
unauthorised act in relation to this publication may be liable to
criminal prosecution and civil claims for damages.

ISBN No: 978-93-80154-36-7

Publisher and Managing Editor: Sunil K Poolani
Books Editor: Sadhvi Sharma
Design Editor: Mishta Roy

Typeset in Book Antiqua
Printed at Repro India Ltd, Mumbai

Price — India: Rs 295; Elsewhere: US $14

To my wife, **Nidhi**. *This is for you…*

About the Author

Siddhartha Choudhary, a graduate from Marine Engineering & Research Institute, Calcutta, India, spent three years of his life working as a marine engineer on board oil tankers. He quit sailing in 2002 and joined IIM Ahmedabad (2003-05) to pursue the Post Graduate Programme. He then worked as a Product Manager with Monsanto and Johnson & Johnson.

This is his first book and he can be contacted at siddhartha.choudhary@gmail.com

1

Polished Shoes

The old man had a blank look on his face. He was sitting on a wooden bench, with a glass in hand. He gazed into space expressionless. As he took another sip he closed his eyes and then opened them slowly as if emerging from a deep slumber. He moved the steaming glass away from his mouth and rested it on his lap. He still stared into the oblivion but his eyes weren't cold anymore and his posture seemed straightened. I looked at the tin plated board that was hanging above him. It said, 'Raju Lakshmi Tea Centre' painted in motley colours. On the right side of the board was a painting of Amitabh Bachchan, which would have been perfect for a hair-cutting salon; funny that this had never occurred to me before, on the numerous occasions that I had had several glasses of tea here. Apart from the old man there were around a dozen people outside the stall. There was a *mualvi*, a *pandit*, a *sardarji*, and a few young guys. My gaze drifted to the person dressed in dark grey trousers and neatly ironed white shirt standing outside the shop with a glass in his hand. He was carrying a laptop bag on his shoulders. He took a cigarette from the stall owner and lit it using the flame from a small lamp hung at the stall. He took a deep breath and blew out the smoke almost immediately. He then hurriedly took a sip from the glass. I wanted to be there, sipping tea and smoking, not having to worry about work...just enjoying the moment and the cold weather. And whenever I was in Raju's shop I would always spend a good moment looking at the lamp. Like other lamps, it burnt on kerosene, but I had never seen such a unique lamp before. It was very small and dusty but looked as if it belonged to the Mughal period. The greenish-blue colour of the base looked like the colour of the deepest sea. I quickly turned around to catch a glimpse of the lamp for the last time. I could still see the shop in the rear-view mirror; all these completely different people at Raju's tea stall looked one as they sipped the hot beverage. They all had the same lost look as they sipped from their respective glasses. Had their forefathers been here, they too would have worn the same expression; the art of tea drinking in India has been the same for ages. It is an Indian 'thing', an activity that belies economic and cultural boundaries.

Our vehicle stopped in front of the *paan* shop. I could see the usual bunch of guys hanging around. I looked at them chattering and laughing. I knew their future was bleak but I sort of envied their present. As I crossed the shop, I waved a 'hi' to the owner. I didn't remember talking to him though I landed there almost every night after dinner. I would quietly smoke my after dinner quota of cigarettes, have some mint and go home.

I went to the adjacent cubicle to buy stationery for my trip. I came out in five minutes, stopped, and turned around to look at the grocery store. The owner was a peculiar guy; you would always find him dusting the place down. He never looked at his customers. His eyes, instead, searched for an area to dust next. He wasn't visible from where I was standing but I could see the cloth moving on the front shelf. I straightened myself and felt a tad stupid about wanting to catch a glimpse of him. I was going to miss even the seemingly inconsequential people, who unconsciously had become a part of my life in Ranchi.

My boring and purposeless life had begun to suddenly appear perfect. We were on the way to the airport and it was too late to realise what I wanted- I wanted to stay here and I was not prepared for this change. It was a cold January morning and my future appeared colder.

I took my place in the backseat and said, "Papa, I got it. I'm ready for the trip now." I looked enviously towards Sonu, who was sitting next to me. He was in the first year of an IT engineering college. He didn't have much to study, had many friends, and a lot more free time. He had absolutely no idea about what he wanted to do in life. There was good chance of him actually ending up doing absolutely nothing. He had no ambitions, no zeal to try out different things, and no inkling to make an impact on the world. I failed to understand why, despite all this, he still seemed much happier than I ever could be!

I nudged him and said, "I am more comfortable than you are." He could hardly move his legs. Neither could I.

He responded coolly, "Yup, but I am taller than you are and I'm more famous."

I shook my head mockingly and rolled my eyes. "And you would take longer than any person to get a B.E. degree," I snapped.

"Ha, you'll see. I'll be in the top ten per cent of the class."

I started laughing, while he tried hard to keep his deadpan expression.

A different conversation was ensuing in the front of the car, where my parents were talking animatedly. My mother was making matters difficult by sobbing intermittently. I have never really liked goodbyes, and I just wanted to get over with this part ASAP. I was not even thinking of what lay ahead. I had a long journey for that. I looked out of the window, "All those familiar faces and structures...out here lay my comfort zone," I thought.

I had spent my childhood and adolescence here. For four years I had been away from Ranchi. After completing my engineering degree just three months ago, I had returned, only to leave again. I had an offer from C.O.S Corporations, a US based company listed in the NYSE, which had a fleet of 50 sea-going vessels (oil tankers and chemical carriers). C.O.S. Corp provided transportation services in the international shipping markets.

The three months in Ranchi were great—no study, no assignments and no more exams. Besides, all I had to do was to workout in the morning, eat, play tennis and snooker, meet friends…and in the time remaining, just laze around doing absolutely nothing.

The best part of my day was she…

I remembered the day I saw her for the first time. It was just after I had returned to Ranchi. Winter had not set in yet and there was only that slight chill in the evenings. My evenings were spent playing lawn tennis with my friend Garu. As I drove down to Garu's home, the evening appeared different. The roads were covered with fallen leaves and twigs. The wind in my face and hair felt refreshing. I took a deep breath; the smell around me was a blend of eucalyptus trees, rose petals and dry wood. I entered the locality and turned in the lane opposite school. I crossed the tennis courts, reached Garu's apartment building, parked my bike and ran up two storeys before I was at Garu's doorstep. I could hear his footsteps and whistling as he came to open the door. For him the best part of *his* day had just begun.

"Let's go for a smoke before tennis today." He always insisted on that.

I said in an irritable tone, "*Yaar*, why do we always have to discuss this? We will play first, go for a fag later."

"*Chal na yaar*! I wait all day for you to come over and that's when I smoke."

"Ok *baba*. Let's smoke first."

We went by the tennis court. Nobody was around that early; the sun was still bright. We went out the colony's gates to visit the *paan* shop next to the road. It was a small cubicle structure, just enough for the owner to squeeze in. He would usually be seen standing outside his shop. He would sit inside only when someone asked him to prepare a *paan*, as it was only then that he required reaching out for the ingredients, which he had carefully stored inside a white cylindrical box. There were around seven makeshift shops that had sprung up here as soon occupants moved into the newly built colony there. I looked around…there was one bicycle repair shop, one fast food stall, one electrical shop, two vegetable shops and one stationary shop. Of course, all these shops had come up illegally. The *paan* shop owner saw us coming and he had our milds ready for us.

We smoked while discussing Garu's future. I said, "You need to give some thought to what you want to do in life."

He wasn't too comfortable talking about it, but I could see his life was going nowhere. I continued, "You have wasted three years because of NDA (National Defence Academy). You enrolled for engineering through correspondence last year. Are you still pursuing that course?"

Garu replied with a straight face, "Yes, of course. I've already cleared the second year exam."

I knew he was lying. He always did. The engineering books on his desk had not changed for a year. I doubted if he had read even one of them seriously.

I looked at him as he smoked. He didn't care about anything. He had absolutely no worries in life. He had a peculiar way of looking at you; he would bend his head low while his eyes looked up at you. It was a somewhat Mario Puzo gangster-look, except that he looked really stupid. He trimmed his moustache with scissors; he wanted to look clean-shaven but still wanted to avoid the guilt of shaving the moustache off completely. As far back as I could remember, he had always sported a crew cut; the hairstyle had come up from the day my school friends and I decided that we would join the army.

There was something else which had been bothering me for a while and I pointed it out rather bluntly, "Your hair is cut so short. You shouldn't be applying gel. As it is, all of that is going to your scalp. You will start losing your hair."

He dragged another puff not bothered by what I was saying. His mind was on the tennis match we had to play with our usual opponents. "We will beat the twins today. They always beat us because of a lack of co-ordination between us."

I said coldly, "We lose because they screw us totally in your serve, your unique 'under-hand' serve!"

"In underhand, the ball at least reaches the other side. If I start serving like you, I'll make all double faults..."

I just stared at him as he enjoyed his cigarette.

We started playing after 15 minutes. The twins were happy to see us. We were the best opponents they had ever played against. For any tennis opponent we were moral boosters and entertainers. Whenever a fast shot would come in from the other side, Garu's priority was not to return it, but to save himself from getting hurt.

A shot whizzed past Garu, who looked as if he had seen a ghost.

I was pepping him up, "You need to stay focused! We still can win this match...it's my serve next."

He had his excuse ready, "I didn't see the ball! It was way too fast...I am just a human being!"

The score read 6-3, 6-4, 4-2 [40-15] in favour of the twins. Garu was to pick the serve. And as expected an Ace it was! The game score: 5-2.

I was to serve next.

I threw the ball in the air, and from the corner of my eyes, I noticed a figure standing on the third floor of a building, which was around 20 feet from the court. I hit the ball real hard for an Ace! I couldn't help but steal glances at the figure standing there.

After the second consecutive ace I approached Garu and asked him, "Who is she?"

He looked at me with disgust, "What's wrong with you? We are in the middle of a game where our asses are being whipped royally by the twins and you come here and ask me about a girl!"

I shrugged and said, "Why are you over-reacting?" and with that started walking back to my side of the court.

I was mid-way when Garu said, "You don't want to know her. She is still in school and not your type."

I turned around and exclaimed, "School!"

The twins were looking at us with disgust.

Garu was signalling me to serve and when I didn't, he said, "Class 12."

I was not done with the conversation yet, "Oh, she's a kid..."

Garu looked at the twins and then at me helplessly, "I think the twins would throw us out of the court..." and then added, "I thought you said we can still win this match! Can you forget the girl and concentrate on the match?"

The other four services of mine were double faults. We lost the match.

Garu wasn't talking to me. We came out of the court and passed by her house. I looked up. She was looking at me. "Not a bad looking girl", I thought, but quickly reminded myself that she was too young. She should be concentrating on her studies now and I ought to get my mind off her.

Garu was talking about something. I asked, "I didn't hear you...what were you saying?"

"She called me yesterday."

I thought I knew who he was talking about but I wanted to confirm, "Who called you?"

"Anoushka."

"Who's Anoushka?"

"The girl you were staring at a few seconds back."

I felt stupid. I said slowly, "She called *you*? So she is interested in you..."

"No. She was enquiring about you. I gave her your number."

I could not hide my excitement as I said, "What? I don't understand!"

Garu didn't like my reaction too much. He said, "My advice is that you stay away from her. She's not the stable kinds. I heard she is going around with somebody."

"Why are you telling me that? What difference would that make to me?" I shrugged.

"Guess she will call you. Gave your home number."

"You should have given her my cell number!"

"I thought it didn't matter!"

"Hello! What if mom picks up?"

He smiled wickedly, "That's the idea!"

I looked at him unbelievably, "You sick bastard. You don't want her to connect with me! Anyway I'll get even with you tomorrow. Gotta rush, Manish must be waiting..."

I was on the way to the club. I would spend my evenings there playing snooker with fellow members. This part of the locality was away from the main road. The narrow road was lined with eucalyptus and mango trees. The trees must have been planted decades ago. I looked at the duplex row houses and envied the senior employees who lived in this area. The trees perfectly complemented the roads and the night sky, which was visible in the midst of the dense foliage. It seemed as if all the elements of nature perfectly blended with each other in this part of town; everything looked so perfect — the sight, the smell and the sound. And yet, I couldn't help but notice that I was alone. The surroundings were so beautiful that they seemed surreal and... even frightening. I could see shadows moving behind the shrubs, the tree branches, it seemed, were closing in on me. The place had suddenly become darker and colder. I accelerated, hoping that the engine didn't die suddenly. I could see the club now, and the engine was still running.

I went inside the old iron gate of the club and parked my bike near the entrance. It was good to be back in the light and re-assuring to see people. The snooker room was on the first floor. It was visible from where I had parked the bike. I looked at the huge windows. I could see the lights were on, which meant that there was somebody playing. The lights that I could see were not the ceiling lights but the special lights above the snooker table. I guessed Manish was there already. I ran inside the glass doors and took a right towards the stairs. I didn't want to wait too long for my turn. There was only one table and sometimes there would be around five people waiting for their turn. I crossed the table-tennis room on my right and the open-air badminton courts on my left. I ran up the stairs and crossed the library before I reached the snooker room. Manish was there, playing with Bilal. I was happy to see that there was nobody else there...

Bilal was not a professional marker; his father used to work at the club before him and he had taught Bilal how to use the cue. He wasn't interested in studies, so his father had requested the management to give him the job after he retired. Bilal was around 45 and was unmarried. He had no other job apart from the one at the club from five to ten in the evening. He wore the same shirt and trousers throughout the week and would change after his weekly off, which was on Monday.

I had learnt to play at a pool table and obviously I had learnt all the wrong moves. Bilal taught me the basics of how to hold the cue and hit the ball; he taught me since he didn't want me to tear the expensive cloth on the table. I learnt the intricacies of the game watching Bilal and Manish play.

I looked at Manish play his shot. He was deeply concentrating as he bent over to take the black ball. He looked towards the right. I knew he was thinking of placing the cue ball next to the red near the centre after he potted the black. He hit, the black went in and the cue ball got placed exactly were it should have been. He took the red and then the blue. He was way ahead in this game and on his current run he had scored 80 points already.

Manish wasn't aware that I was already there. I went behind him and thumped my feet on the ground with force. The sudden vibration on the floor disturbed him and he mis-cued. Manish looked confused, then looked in Bilal's direction and then right and left, and back towards Bilal as if expecting an explanation from him. Bilal looked in my direction, smiled slyly and shamelessly added the foul points to his tally. Manish immediately turned around and saw me. His expressions changed to an 'Ah...I know what happened', looking like Inspector Clouseau who had just had a startling revelation on the case. He moved his fist in the air as he moved towards me.

"Case cracked", I thought as I stood straight with a wooden face. I raised my hands in front of my body shrugging as if asking 'What?'

He was pointing his index finger at me while nodding his head. He moved his fist in the air as he moved towards me. I looked at him quizzically and shrugged as if asking 'what'. He pointed at me, and nodded his head as if he knew I was to blame. I raised my hands above my head while shaking my head. He smiled and opened his mouth to make a sound, 'Uh...' I smiled back, admitting to my act by bending forward with folded hands. He was almost the same height as I, fairer than I was and he had a moustache. His moustache looked totally out of place on his thin face and lean body. I thought of perhaps telling him to trim it. I had a wild thought; what if he trimmed his moustache to look like that of Hitler, he would look exactly like the German leader... only that Manish would be taller and exactly the opposite in nature.

I started laughing thinking about the facial similarity. Manish raised his eyebrows, and raising his arms in the air enquired as to why I was laughing. I raised my hands in the air and spelt out 'Adolf Hitler' using my fingers. He had a confused look on his face. I next pointed my finger to his moustache and used my index and middle fingers to imply the movement of scissors. He started laughing. Even as he laughed the only sound he managed was a faint 'Aaaggghhh'.

Manish was born like this; he couldn't speak nor could he hear. He had gone to a special school as a kid, had learned computers as an adult, and was now working in the same organisation as my father. He was doing much better in life than most of us. It was difficult to communicate with him but I thoroughly enjoyed our discussions.

Manish always had something to converse about, while I was the silent types. He had started playing at the club when he was in school. He was a favourite with the other players.

After the game was over Bilal looked at me and said, "It would not last."

I was taken aback by his statement. I got down from where I was sitting, went to choose a cue, applied chalk on it and asked him, "What won't last?"

I had heard him say this before, "Stay away from women and you will remain stress free and happy."

I exclaimed, "How do you know? Is it that obvious?"

He just smiled. It was my turn. I played a pathetic short, moved away from the table and asked Bilal, "I know you have enough clothes to wear a fresh pair daily.

But you don't...is it because you want to avoid female attention?"

He laughed for a while and then looked at me and said, "You still expect an answer?"

I nodded. He then said, "I don't see the need to change my clothes frequently. I take shower when I really want to. I don't just want to do a duty."

After the game, Manish and I moved towards the balcony, walking past the stairs in the opposite direction. We crossed the old bar. The lights were out and the doors locked. I stood by the huge windows and looked inside. The cobwebbed sofa and bar stools, dusty and mouldy carpet and empty bar gave a completely different picture to what it used to be years ago. I had heard stories from Bilaal and Manish about the fine group of gentlemen who frequented this place. They would play billiards and then go on to have a round of scotch with their friends. People would discuss anything and everything — from politics to spirituality, from marriage to live-in.

Bilaal was a self taught man; he observed and heard these gentlemen. They were his window into life. With time, however, the patrons changed. One day a rowdy group in the bar got involved in a fight, a person was stabbed and with that the bar was put under lock. The club had changed and for the oldies there was one more reason not to be there. All this had its effect on Bilaal too — he transformed, his medium which connected him to the world was there no more. His life changed, the club was just a job now, and the new members for him were the reason for the sad turn his life had taken. Only Manish reminded him of the good old days.

I followed Manish to the huge balcony where we often smoked after the game. Manish was pointing towards the bar and signalling something, which I didn't get. With the cigarette dangling in between his lips he extended his left palm towards me and moved his right index finger on the palm. I followed the movement; he was writing 'Britishers' on it.

This bar, in fact the entire club was made by the Britishers.

There was nobody else in the billiards room so Bilaal came out and joined us. I couldn't help but ask him, "This club was made by Britishers?"

He smiled as if he was one of them, "Yes, the ceiling fan in the billiards room was installed 110 years ago and there's been no maintenance ever since. The ball bearings are working fine even today. The billiards table was made back then with the finest quality wood. You cannot find such a fine piece of work anywhere in India. Even the gate at the entrance has been there for ages."

I whistled. Manish stood there nodding. It seemed he knew the story already.

I couldn't believe it, "110 yrs!"

Bilaal was smiling, "My great great grandfather used to be the marker then...for the Britishers."

I couldn't believe it. I looked at Bilaal's shabby clothes and imagined what his forefather would have worn a century back—a spic n span uniform. But then I realised that I was in worn-out jeans, a sweaty sweatshirt and very dirty sneakers myself.

I wondered, "What would Naveen and Sachin be doing now?" and then thought, "I should have been there with them. Wearing a uniform and polished shoes...feeling on top of the world..." But there I was in that old club, hanging out with survivors and feeling like a loser.

Chasing Trouble

Two days went by and nothing changed. We were still losing in tennis everyday and she would stand at the same place watching us play.

The following morning Garu called at 10. It was unusual to get a call from him this early.

I asked him, "All well?"

"Anoushka just left her place with her mom and they are on a pedal rickshaw and they are heading towards your locality. I want you to see her up close before you speak to her on the phone or do something stupid," Garu instructed me.

"Thanks buddy. I'm on my way," I said, and rushed out, telling my mother that I would be back in ten minutes.

I started my bike. I assumed they were going out of the locality and for that they would have to come towards my home, which was at the other end. There were two ways they could've taken — the road which led to the school or the one which led to the CET office (while coming from Garu's colony the road divided into two at the stadium — one road to the school and the other to the office and they met again at the roundabout, which was around 200 metres from my home). I decided to turn towards the office route — this one was shorter hence the most preferred by the rickshaw-*walas*. There was not a soul in sight. I slowed down near the stadium. I waited for sometime anxiously but nothing happened.

I thought, "I may have reached here too soon, the rickshaw would take time."

After waiting for what seemed like hours I set off towards the school. I had gone around fifty feet when I saw a rickshaw. I could see from behind the backs of two women sitting in it—a petite frame wearing a T-shirt and the other heavier built one wearing a sari. It had to be them! My heart was beating faster as I approached the rickshaw; I slowed down as I contemplated my next move. Her mom was with her so I thought I would play it down, just make my presence felt and carry on. I honked when I was about to cross the rickshaw and then I slowed down and turned my head to see the passengers...it wasn't her! On top of that the sudden honking had startled them—the young girl looked like she was about to have a heart attack while the old lady seemed like she wanted to break my neck with her bare hands. I hit the accelerator and made a quick exit.

I drove back to my home my mind preoccupied with the wasted effort. I had almost reached home and was about to take a right to enter the lane when my phone rang. I applied the brakes suddenly because of which the engine died on me.

It was Garu's call. He asked, "What happened?"

I said irritably, "Nothing... I didn't find her..."

"Oh, so what's your plan now?"

"No plans. Will watch HBO...listen I'm still on the road...will call you when I reach home." With that I kicked the engine into action and turned my head around to throw a casual glance at the road before I crossed it. I was taken aback by the pair of eyes looking at me so deeply, imploring me to acknowledge their existence as if it were a matter of life and death. I closed my eyes for a wee bit longer as I tried to come to terms with what was happening; the rickshaw had just appeared from nowhere! I looked towards her again. She was still looking at me; she had even forgotten that her mom was sitting next to her. Her mom was staring at me with contempt.

She wanted to protect her daughter from me. I felt uncomfortable so I looked away for a while and then stole another glance at her before they crossed me. It all happened so fast yet somehow it felt that I had seen everything in slow motion. The moment seemed like a PowerPoint presentation where the slide advancement had been set to a very slow speed.

She turned back and kept looking at me, as long as I was visible to her. I stood on the roadside holding my bike long after she was gone. If Garu hadn't called that very moment, I probably would have missed her. I knew it was a sign that there was something about to happen between the two of us. I just knew that this was a life changing moment for me.

Later in the day I was still thinking about the incident...the expression in her eyes meant something else...the more I thought about it the more certain I was that there was some connection between us.

I gave Garu a call in the afternoon, "I saw her."

"So, how was it? I mean now you know that she isn't your type, right?"

"What is my type? How can I decide that now? I was never interested in her so how does it matter?"

"Smart decision. You deserve a better girl..."

"Let me make something clear. I am not interested because she's too young, not because I think she is not good enough! And what do you mean by that anyway?"

"Hmmm so you like her."

"No! Alright, *maybe* I like her...come on, she's not that bad! Don't you worry...I'm not going to have a fling with her. I will tell her that she ought to study and forget about having anything to do with me...obviously, I'm enjoying the attention."

"Don't fall for her. She is trouble, believe me."

"I wouldn't have been able to see her today if you hadn't called. If I do fall for her, you would be one of the reasons!"

Sonu was listening to all the conversation. He was as usual lying in bed. He only liked one work and that was 'no work'.

He said after a few hours, "What's up? Why do you have that funny expression on your face?"

"Shh...you idiot. Come out there's something I need to know." And then in the same breath I shouted, "Ma, we both are in the garden..."

She shouted back, "I don't know what you are upto today! You still have to finish the work in the bank! Tomorrow bank would be open for half a day and day after it would be closed!"

"I'll do it Mom. Don't worry!"

She replied, "I'm not worrying! It's your work and I've reminded you ten times already so don't blame me later!"

I made a mental note of going to the bank next week and then pulled Sonu out of the bed and took him out in the garden.

He was complaining, "Where's the fire!"

"Do you know Anoushka?"

"Why?"

I said impatiently, "Can we not answer a question with a question...?"

"Ok fine then." And with that he started walking in.

I caught him by his arm and pleaded, "Why get sensitive *yaar*? Tell me about her."

"She's trouble."

"Elaborate!"

"That's all there is. Stay away from her. Doesn't have a good record."

I was feeling disappointed. I asked him, "Have you seen her?"

He just looked at me and then I realised my mistake- he knew every girl!

So I rephrased my question, "What's wrong with her?"

"For one she's too young. And then she I think is going around with someone. Then there was something ugly which happened in school between her and some guy...whole school knows about it. You don't wanna know about it! Did you get your answer?"

"Don't most good looking girls end up being known for all the wrong reasons?"

"No not all!"

"I saw her today. She doesn't look like the type who would get into trouble."

There was a silence for a while as we stared at each other and then he said as he sighed a long heavy one, "Why do you always get attracted to the wrong woman?"

"And how about you?"

"*Bhaiya* your history proves how nicely all your relationships have worked..."

"Hello! I'm not having a relationship. Not with her. She's not my type, you know."

"Only time will tell!" and with that he went inside.

A few hours later I and Sonu were watching a movie on HBO.

The phone rang and mom shouted, "Can someone pick up the phone? Can't even get to take a nap peacefully!"

I ordered him, "Go get it."

"You get it! I made the bed last night." He said coolly.

"Ok...fine! I'll beat the crap out of you if it's not for me. Pray that the phone isn't for you!"

He was least bothered by my threat.

"Hello?" I said angrily.

"Hello??" a soft voice answered from the other end.

My tone changed immediately, "Yes?"

"Siddhartha?" said the voice. I knew it was her.

"Yes...it is..." I said as my heart beat quadrupled.

"Anoushka here. I actually...ummm..."

"Hi! Anoushka! Yes...yes! God, so Garu wasn't lying...I'm Siddhartha, I play tennis everyday, near your home...how silly of me to say that." I said as I laughed like a fool.

"You are cute!"

There was silence for a while. The 'I am stupid' feeling hadn't passed yet.

She said, "So you are playing tennis again today?"

"Yes I am. Would you be there?" I said and almost immediately thought, "God what kind of conversation is that?"

"Yes of course. I like to see you play."

I probed, "Oh! You like tennis?"

"No...just your game."

I was smiling as I said, "Oh?"

"I like it when you are aggressive and like it when you are sad on losing the game. You seem like a nice kid..."

"Do you know how old I am?" I suddenly realised I wasn't supposed to be flirting with her.

"Nope. Where do you study?" she asked innocently.

"Listen Anoushka, I know you are too young. You are still in school. I have graduated and am about to start working."

"Oh! You don't look that old! I am young but I'm no fool. I understand everything," she retorted.

"Of course I am not that old...just that you are quite young."

"I want to talk to you."

"Ok. Go ahead."

"I meant meet you in person."

"Not such a good idea! This is Ranchi...everybody knows everybody!"

"I like you."

"Anoushka, you know nothing about me."

"I'll take my chances."

"Why are you doing this?"

"Because I feel for you. Besides, I've seen you for a moment and it wasn't enough. I want to meet you..."

I could refuse no further. Besides, my curiosity had been roused now, "Alright...where and when?"

"On my terrace."

"What?! Six families live in your building. Anybody could see us there. It is way too risky."

"Meet me at 4.30pm today," she said decisively.

I was not too comfortable with this. I reasoned, "Let us think about this. Maybe we can meet some..."

She cut me short, "Today, 4.30 pm...I have to go now. Bye..."

It was too big a risk...my parents would have killed me! I didn't know anybody in her building, which meant that as a new face, I would be even more conspicuous. There was only one logical solution, and it rang loud in my head – 'Don't go.'

Same evening I was telling my mother, "Ma, I gotta go early today."

"It's too sunny to be playing tennis now," she said, by now sure that there was something wrong with me.

"Yup Ma gotta meet Garu."

"What's happening?" she confronted me.

"No-nothing is happening. I am just going a little early, that's it," I replied trying to sound normal.

"Ma, ask him what time Garu comes back from his classes!" Sonu would always pick the choicest of moments to stick his neck out.

"Why don't you shut up? It's between mom and me."

"Fine, but I want to join you for tennis today. Ma, tell him to wait for me."

I had no time for this. I said impatiently, "I'm not waiting. I have already given time to Garu."

Sonu wasn't the one to give up easily. He retorted, "Yes, Garu the business tycoon, who is strict about punctuality, isn't it? And since when have you started being on time? Who are you going to meet? Tell me or I will go tell ma."

"You both should be sent to a zoo! Would you let me think? Now, where did I spend that Rs 750?" Maa walked in with a book. Ma always noted her expenses, but there was always a variation between cash in hand and her balance sheet in her books. Obviously the difference was always in the negative.

I was really angry with Sonu, "I am not taking you with me. You drive down Pa's car once he's home. I'm already late."

I reached the tennis court at 4.20 pm, parked my vehicle, and looked up at the balcony. She wasn't there. Several thoughts raced through my head as I walked towards the building, 'What should I do now? Can't call on her landline, for I don't have her number. I hope nobody is looking at me...what if I meet someone on the stairs? Where should I pretend to go?'

Nobody was around on the road, so I quickly got in and started climbing the stairs furtively. There were 3 floors in her building with 2 apartments per floor. She lived on the 3rd floor, which I slowly crossed and continued towards the roof. I moved up, there were doors both on my left and right side which led to the 2 common roofs shared amongst the 6 families. One roof was locked. I tried the unlocked door and peeped outside. She wasn't there. So I stayed put on the stairs feeling like a cornered rat.

I heard some noise from the floor below. I missed a beat. "If it's not Anoushka, I'm going to be in real big trouble", I thought.

I could hear footsteps clearly now — I peeped from around the corner. It was Anoushka! I was relieved, but immediately started feeling uneasy...I wondered what I was doing at this place. I was behaving like a thief and what I was doing didn't seem to be the right thing to do. There I was on a secret rendezvous with a complete stranger.

She was taller than I thought she was. I couldn't help but notice the grace with which she climbed the stairs. She was wearing cream coloured knee length cotton pants and a light blue sleeveless top. The strings of her pants were casually left untied and they dangled naughtily as she moved towards me. As she walked up the stairs I kept looking at her while trying to smile normally.

She had an oval face with soft contours around her cheek and chin. Her eyelashes were dense which gave a perfect outline to her perfect almond shaped eyes. She had just taken shower, and smelled of fresh lilies...her skin was radiating and her lips looked soft and moist. Her eyes were the most innocent pair I had ever seen. She was more beautiful than I had imagined. Maybe it wasn't such a bad idea to come meet her, I started thinking.

When I was out of my trance, I found her standing next to me. I could smell her perfume or the bodywash...whatever it was, it was intoxicating! Everything around me was going into rapid motion and then suddenly it all seemed surreal. Something was happening to me, as if I was being hypnotized...

I snapped out of it momentarily and managed a, "Hi Anoushka... so we finally meet."

She held my hand, looked me in the eyes and came real close. Her hands felt warm and soft but it wasn't the touch that took me totally by surprise. Any girl meeting someone for the first time would not be so bold unless she trusted him instinctively. She felt connected to me.

I knew what she was about to say next but I was afraid to hear it. She said the words I was dreading to hear, "I'm in love with you."

"What? How is that possible?" I wanted to feel unhappy about all this but I couldn't help but feel good.

"I don't want an answer. I just told you what I felt." She was now looking at my lips. I stayed very still as she closed in. I looked into her eyes and then her lips. She slowly withdrew and her gaze shifted towards my old Nike pair. I found my breath back and my pulse wasn't up the roof anymore.

She said softly, "Well... Sid do you like me?"

I didn't reply. I knew it was a trick question.

She looked at me as if reading my mind, "You know Siddhartha I've never ever been so sure about anything in life as I am right now."

I didn't know what to say, so I just smiled. She continued, "I've got a boring tuition class tomorrow, which I am planning to skip. We can spend time together, perhaps wander about a bit?"

"How do you normally commute for tuition?" I was wishing I had kissed her when I had the opportunity. She saw me looking at her lips and I quickly shifted my gaze back to her eyes.

"Oh the whole group travels in a rickshaw that my parents have hired." She had a hint of a smile on her face.

"Wouldn't he inform..." my lips were quivering with tension as I tried to resist the thought of grabbing her close to me.

"I'll take care of him. Don't worry. Pick me up outside the Main Entrance to our colony."

With that she came close, quickly planted a kiss on my cheeks. I don't know if she had done this on purpose but her kiss had faintly touched the edge of my lips. It was enough to understand what lay in store and quite less to make me want for more. While I stood there speechless and lost yet again, she was gone.

The Cricket Who Chose Not to Speak

I came out of Anoushka's building, afraid that somebody might see me coming out. I was thinking about my rendezvous the next day. What if people in town recognised my father's vehicle! Just then a jarring sound made me snap out of my thoughts. It was the phone. I immediately felt fortunate that it didn't go off while I was still in the building. All the residents would have turned up to see us perched outside the terrace. I took a deep breath and answered the phone.

"Siddhartha, where are you?" a familiar voice on the phone said.

"Vikram? How're you? Long time..."

Vikram said, "I called your home. Got this number from there."

I asked, "When are you getting on the ship?"

"In a month's time. I am joining the Indian Maritime Corporation. It has the biggest fleet in the country."

"I had no idea where you were. I thought you'd be sailing by now."

Vikram said nonchalantly, "Was generally whiling away my time. When are you joining?"

"In a few weeks. Listen, what are you doing in two hours? Let's meet, we'll talk then."

"Ok. I am going to be in the stadium today. That's where I spend my evenings. Meet me there. Bring cigarettes when you come. Am out of money."

"Sure, I'll do that. Stadium? What do you do there?"

"Meditate, smoke and enjoy. Come there and you'll know."

Vikram was my senior from college. He was one of those rare kinds who always did the opposite of what he was told to do, or least expected of him. He was very bright, but for him studies were a waste of time. He read voraciously about psychopaths, killers, psychological disorders and all things morbid. He always said that he could associate himself with all the characters in the books. There was something sinister about him.

The first time I met Vikram was at our college Annual fest. I was looking at the bulging biceps of Mr Herculix. This guy was six-feet-tall with a heavy build; he had beaten all the guys from our college in the arm wrestling championship. The guy was declared Mr Herculix and he was proudly roaming in the campus, four giggling girls by his side. They belonged to the Hotel Management Institute. We were envious of these guys who always managed to keep the company of some of the prettiest girls. We, on the other hand, belonged to an all-boys college. I saw the seniors coming in, visibly drunk. One of them, a thin guy was telling another, "Pankaj, screw this guy. What does he think? He can roam around here showing his biceps? And screw the bitches with him. Challenge him to an arm wrestling round."

I had seen Pankaj in the gym regularly. I wanted to watch this. Pankaj went up to this guy, "Buddy wanna arm wrestle me?"

Mr Herculix obliged with a smirk on his face.

A referee was rounded up...He checked their grips 1−2−3

The stud beat Pankaj in three seconds flat.

Pankaj got up looked at the thin guy with him and said, "Let's go Vikram. This guy's powerful."

Vikram ignored Pankaj's comment instead took on Mr Herculix, "Hey asshole, what do you think, you've become a champion? You think you're powerful? Do I look as powerful as you? But I'll show you what power is all about." He actually believed what he was saying. His facial muscles were tense, lips twisted in a vicious scowl, eyebrows raised and eyes fiery red. He looked like a tiger ready for his prey.

For a moment I saw the expressions on Mr Herculix's face change. He then looked at Vikram. As usual Vikram was dressed in a loose shirt in which he looked thinner than he actually was. He was good looking, not someone whose face reflected toughness. He had soft features except his eyes...his eyes were quite magnetic and intense. He was much shorter than I was, around 5' 7" and weighed around 60 kilos. He looked like a dwarf in front of the champion. Herculix too thought it was a joke.

Vikram took his position. He stared into the opponent's eyes, not once did he bat his eyelids.

The referee counted 1−2−3

I couldn't believe my eyes! Vikram took just two seconds to beat Mr Herculix! Suddenly the fizz had gone out of Mr Heculix's biceps.

"Do you want to try again?" said Vikram.

"Yes, I'll screw you this time," said Mr Herculix with a fake grimace.

1−2−3

Again, the same result, in an instant.

Vikram roared, "Want more asshole? Now fuck off from this college."

I couldn't believe my eyes. "How was this possible?" I thought.

I was thinking about this incident as I went into the stadium after my tennis game; he was sitting on the third row.

I lit a cigarette and offered him one.

We sat there for sometime, the silence was uncomfortable. I was meeting him after a year or so.

I knew I would be breaking the ice, "So..."

"Shhh..." he interrupted me before I could complete.

"What...?" I said softly.

"Can you hear the noise?"

I listened attentively to the sounds all around us for a few seconds. I then said, "Music? I guess it's Beethoven. Strange that somebody here would listen to..."

"Na, na. Pay attention...concentrate."

"Nope...nothing. I give up."

"Crickets...listen to those crickets."

"Ahhh...yes they're quite loud."

"Did you notice something?"

I listened to the crickets for a while before responding to his question, "Yes, when something passes by they become quite."

It was a pleasant evening. I could still hear the Beethoven, interspersed with other sounds — a popular soap played on someone's TV, some kids were playing behind us. There was nobody in the stadium at that hour but us. I looked at my watch. It was going to be 7.30 pm.

The sound of the crickets was almost deafening. There seemed to be several hundreds of them. Behind us were the stadium walls, surrounded by bushes. Whenever a vehicle passed on the road next to it, the crickets would go quiet. And then one would start chirping again, followed by the rest.

Vikram sat silently, so I asked, "Is it the same guy who starts the chirping first?"

"Yes." Vikram always spoke with such conviction that you would think he was a master of the subject. I envied him; he was smarter and physically tougher than I was.

Another vehicle zoomed by. There was silence again. And just like that, the chirping began again.

"Do you know why they make this noise?" Vikram said to me with an all-knowing air about him.

He saw me shrug, and continued, "It's a mating call."

"Why do you say so?"

"Because all insects and animals naturally behave in a certain way, which culminates into reproduction. It is their natural instinct to make the species survive." I was impressed.

He looked at me for a while and then kept puffing looking into the darkness.

He continued after a while, "The one with the best and loudest sound is the leader. He chirps to attract the female. The others are just followers who want to beat the leader. When a follower manages to attract maximum females he is the proven leader of the group and he replaces the previous one."

He continued his discourse, "...they make this noise at night because the female flies only then. Mostly to avoid predators...do you know why they become silent when a vehicle passes by?"

"I don't know, but I can guess – is it because they think there is no point shouting when there's already so much noise?"

He said, "Ha...they keep quiet because they are afraid of the loud noise."

I complained, "But, my point too sounds logical. When the female can't listen to their mating call, they rather keep shut then, right?"

"Aggression, huh? Let's fight it out."

I kept mum.

He continued, "Let us both try our methods to make the crickets shut up. Its past 8 and the traffic would be less. Here is what we do – when the crickets are singing we both will take turns to concentrate and communicate with them and convince them to stop chirping."

"How is that possible? Can we communicate with crickets?"

"Yes, we can."

I was thinking, "How does he know amazing things like these?"

And then I asked him, "Have you ever communicated with them before?"

"No. But I know it can be done. You just need to concentrate hard. Forget everything else...only the crickets should exist for you. When you reach that level you can connect with them mentally. It's the 1st part which is difficult. Concentration is the key. It's highly unlikely that you would be able to do it since it is your first time."

"You go first then." I thought it was a stupid game but then there was no point complaining to him.

"Ok," he closed his eyes and became real still. It was a moonlit night and I could partly see his face. He looked like a modern day sage. The task that we had set upon sounded impossible but somehow I felt he would be able to do it...20 minutes and he was still meditating. The crickets were loud enough, and no sign of his communication with them showed any effects. I could see a headlight on the other side of stadium. It was a bike and it turned right on the road near the bushes. The bike sped by and the crickets went silent.

Vikram opened his eyes completely pissed off, "Bloody shit! That was just when I was about to do it! I was almost there! It's your turn now!"

"I don't think I can...not sure what to do."

He lit another cigarette and said, "Try."

I felt like a dork participating in a sack race. I closed my eyes and breathed in. I could feel the cool breeze on my neck. The locality had become very quiet except the crickets. I was trying to relax and not think about how stupid this game was. A lot of thoughts started pouring in, 'I am supposed to meet Anoushka tomorrow. I'll take Papa's car...what if somebody recognises it! Some colleague of his would meet him in office the next day and say "I saw your son yesterday...in your car...with a girl..."'

I had to attune myself to the job at hand and for that I had to block these thoughts. I tried hard to concentrate. I heard someone's mobile phone ring and the theme of the popular news channel. "Focus on just the crickets...nothing else, only crickets..." I kept thinking to myself.

I could hear hundreds of crickets chirping... their noise started becoming louder – it seemed as if they were near to my ears. I could feel my eyeballs dancing in sync with the frequency of the chirps. Hundreds of lights began dancing in front of me, multicoloured and with the noise the colours changed. Sometimes they would become brighter and dim again with the noise. It was like slipping into a coma.

I had experienced something similar before. It was around 2 years back. I was still in college and was sitting in the East Wing of the Third Year student's dormitory with some batchmates. Juga had got a *'chillum'* (pipe) from a local rock n roll band who in turn had bought it from a coffee shop in Holland. We had grass from one of the best suppliers in Kolkata. His name was Munna and he lived around 300 metres from our college.

Juga was already high, "Munna wasn't there tonight...his hot wife was. She dresses herself in those revealing clothes whenever I go there."

"She's always dressed like that...," said casanova Kamal... "Munna wants her to be like that. Have any one of you gone to purchase after 10 pm?"

"I always go after 10," said the slyest of all Rajat, "...at that point either Munna is making out with her or she's lying in her bed half naked."

It was my first time with the chillum. It hit me instantly. I closed my eyes and started drifting away from the conversation... I could just hear the Roger Waters guitar play...at times the guitar music would change and become the noise of the rotating helicopter blades! So many lights ahead dancing around...I felt as if I was flying in a helicopter! I was holding tightly to the helicopter railing...I experienced a free fall...the blades were working overtime in the rough weather....we had begun to gain altitude...a free fall again...a sharp rise... I had never realised how amazing that guitaring was until that day. I was surprised that I could still clearly remember the trip!

I brought my mind back to the task at hand; I had to concentrate on just the crickets. My breathing had become slower. I was much more relaxed. The sound of the crickets was now very loud. It felt as if they had come near me. It seemed as if the crickets and I were slowly moving away from the world. I still could hear the noise of cars honking and a motorcycle speeding by but the noise came from very far away. I was moving away from these noises but the crickets remained close by. I had lost track of time. After a while it was just the crickets and me. There were no colours now... pitch dark and the noise of crickets. I felt weightless as if I was floating in the air. My body was still but I knew I was drifting ahead. It seemed like I was in very dark tunnel. I could see nothing ahead but I felt as if I knew I was moving in the right direction. The noise of the crickets had merged into one loud cricket's noise. However, now the noise wasn't near my ear. Where was it coming from- maybe from all over? It seemed like a technological marvel- the clarity was as good as if from a Bose' music system. It seemed as if the noise was coming from within me! It was loud but I wasn't listening to it through my ears. Though I was still in the air I'd stopped drifting now. My breathing was even slower; I didn't need too much air to survive in this tunnel. I guess the same way as I didn't need my ears to listen to the cricket.

"Siddhartha," the sudden voice didn't shake me up. I knew I was late and was expecting Vikram to wake me up.

"Let me concentrate, I think I am onto something..."

"You don't need to over here..." said the voice.

"I don't need to what over here?" I asked not too sure of whom that voice belonged to because it sounded like me.

I tried to look around in the dark, "Who's there?"

"No need to look around. You can't see me," said the voice.

I asked, "Who are you?"

"I am Poku. You were looking for me, here I am."

"I was looking for you? But I was trying to connect with a..."

"Cricket? So here I am, the spokesperson of the cricket community. I also work for the Cricket News Broadcasting Corporation (CNBC). I am in charge of corporate communications and am the VP Marketing and Sales."

"Huh? And what does your organisation, CNBC do?"

"It spreads news to the Cricket fraternity across India. You see, news is the biggest business for us."

"And what kinds of news do you broadcast and how?"

"Oh the usual stuff—politics, scandals, sports, administrational issues...you know the same stuff which you humans prefer. Why do you think we croak? We are built to spread the news around. There are other organisations too like consultancies, tour organisations, real estate groups, etc."

"Oh you are so much like us!"

"Yes, but we can't build stuff hence, we don't have IT, manufacturing, construction, etc. All our organisations were built around the fact that we have evolved communication skills. Ants are the best builders. Our society, however, isn't as hierarchical as theirs. We have a very flat structure, you know."

"Hmm..." I was impressed, "Why do they call you Poku?"

Poku answered, "Oh, I am the talkative kinds. Also, I am little crazy. They are very fond of me and they like calling me that...is that why you approached me?"

I came to the point, "Oh, I was just interested in knowing why you chirp. I thought you croak because it's a mating call."

Poku replied patiently, "Sex, that's what you humans can think about? We chirp because that's how we work. We don't have Television & Cable. We employ people and the message passes on by word of mouth."

"I'm sorry, I didn't mean to be rude. Then why is it that you become quiet when there's some noise."

"We become quiet only when we sleep. When there is disturbance, we switch over to a different frequency which is not audible to you. We call it the 'covert-con'."

I was impressed but it was all so unbelievable. But somehow it all made sense. I said, "I don't know what to say. I think we should call you one day to give us management *gyaan*."

He said with a sense of urgency in his voice, "Tell me, how can I help you?"

"I don't need help and how can you be of help?" I said doubtfully.

"It's not about who you think is capable of helping you. If you open your mind you can learn from everyone and everything. Are you afraid of the dark?"

"Not exactly...no... I'm just not too comfortable in the dark...maybe I am afraid."

"Why are you afraid?"

I was blabbering now, "Everyone is...maybe because we have not explored the dark. Maybe because we do not understand the dark. Maybe because we relate the dark to evil."

"The only thing you are afraid of is yourself."

I said defensively, "I love myself."

Poku ignored my statement and said, "When you close your eyes, your ears and your mouth you detach yourself from the world and then you communicate with yourself. In the dark your eyes cannot see the world, in the silence you cannot hear the world and since you are alone you do not speak."

I could see the connection.

He continued, "Hence in the dark you get connected with yourself. But you are afraid because you don't want to face your fears and weaknesses. And all your life you keep running away from them..."

He was making sense. I added, "And that's why I keep myself occupied with work or friends or TV so that I do not have to face myself? What do you suggest I should do?"

"Face you fears."

"How do I do that?"

Poku replied in a flat tone, "I do not have answers to that."

I persisted, "Shall I shut myself in a dark room?"

"Maybe..." the voice came, "If you are looking for answers, believe me you'll find a way. It's time for me to go."

"Poku, one last thing..."

"Yes?"

"If I tell you to do your conversation in 'covert-con' frequency for sometime, will you do that?"

"Why?"

"I don't know if it will help me...consider it a request from me."

I was losing his voice now. I could hear other voices too now.

"That is such a silly request..."

His voice was faint. I could hear the traffic now...
"Please!" I shouted.

He said something which wasn't audible.

"Siddhartha!" said a voice.

"Yes Poku." I said.

I realised my body was shaking and my senses were coming back to normal. I opened my eyes. I could see and feel. "What happened? Oh...Hi Vikram...!"

"It's been an hour and half. Do you know its 10.15 now?"

I said rubbing my eyes, "What? But I was only gone for 15 minutes ..."

"You have been sleeping for the last one and half hours."

I exclaimed, "Hey did you notice the crickets are quiet now!"

He smiled and said proudly, "Yea I know."

"You did it?" I asked him feeling disappointed.

He took a puff deep in thought. He was still looking at the night sky when he replied, "I tried waking you up but you weren't responding. So I thought I'll try and make them quiet myself. But you are a freak show man! How could you sleep in the stadium?"

"Well, I had a strange dream. It was about crickets..."

He immediately turned towards me. I was surprised to see he was interested. He said eagerly, "Oh? Do you want to talk about it?"

"Nah...not so interesting..." I knew he wouldn't understand, "But how did you manage to do it?"

"I just concentrated hard and proved myself to be more powerful than the other one. Once you defeat them, they oblige."

So I had fallen asleep, or so I thought.

CHAPTER

4

The Forbidden

I went about my next day following the same routine, but my mind always drifted back to the events of the previous evening. I wanted to think about Anoushka but I was actually thinking about Poku and what he had said to me.

I wanted to believe that it all had actually happened, but the truth was that it was only a dream.

I called Anoushka's home, "Anoushka? Hi...Siddh..."

"Yes I know it's you..."

"So I'll pick you up at 6, right? Outside the main entrance..."

"Change of plans."

I asked anxiously sensing trouble, "What?"

"I am not going for the tuition class. My parents are going out...so, come over to my place and we'll talk."

"Your place! I hope it's alright..."

"Yes of course it is alright. The front door will be locked so come in through the back door, Ok?"

I had spent the remainder of the day not thinking too much about going to her place. I had just shut it out of my mind lest I should go down the path of what was appropriate and what was not. But as soon as it was 5 pm I was thinking about why I had accepted the invitation.

By the time I had parked my bike outside her place my heart was pounding like a hammer. I started walking towards her home not too sure at all. I walked the three blocks wanting to just run away – it didn't feel right....

I convinced myself that I was just going there to have a conversation with her, but of course, in my heart I knew that I wanted more than that. There were a few people around. I looked ahead and was relieved to see nobody near her home. I ran up to the 3rd floor! I had forgotten that the front door was locked from the outside. I went to the backdoor. The door was open and I quickly went in. She was standing behind the door, looking at the floor, deep in thought. I wondered whether she too was having doubts about this meeting. To have reached here without getting caught was like a mission for me. And as it turned out, it was too much of a thrill too – I was sweating like a pig. She shut the door slowly. She still wasn't looking into my eyes...the silence and the infinite possibilities that the immediate future held made me very conscious of our togetherness.

She was wearing cycling shorts and a sleeveless top. The top was small and it was as if to remind me that she had an absolutely stunning figure. "Come in..." she whispered and turned around. Her top rested on her waist and I could make out the thin contours of her underwear. I immediately moved my gaze away searching for something inanimate. I mumbled, "Nice dining table".

She turned around and said, "What?"

I shook my head, "Nothing just admiring the furniture."

"Do you want water?" she asked.

"Huh? Oh...ya...yes sure." I said softly.

I went and sat on the sofa. She walked in with a glass in her hand. I wanted to ask her the name of the perfume she was wearing but I killed that urge. I was looking at her pretty face and trying hard not to overdo it. She walked slowly, like a dancer moving slowly on a soft romantic track. She sat at a distance, raised her arms to tie her hair. Her long slender arms behind her head, her thin beautiful fingers moving through her soft hair, her head slightly bent forward — the moment sent my heart apace. I became shifty. She was looking at me with a slight knowing smile.

She folded her legs and ran her hand over her shorts as if to titillate. We kept quiet for a while as I slowly sipped on that glass of water. She sensed my discomfort and strangely, that made her bolder. I knew she was looking at me now while I had my gazed fixed on the centre table.

"So, how are you?" she said softly.

"Am perfect, just great," I replied with a stupid grin.

"So do you workout? You have great chest and arms."

"Umm. Thanks, yes I do go to the gym."

"Siddhartha, do you know that I like you a lot? I find your face so attractive. You seem different from the guys I have seen," she said, looking at me fondly.

I was blushing now. I said, "You are a nice person too Anoushka. I am beginning to grow fond of you myself."

I was still holding the glass. She came close to take the glass away from my hands. Her fingers faintly brushed against mine and even that felt like magic. It reminded me of the kiss she had planted on my cheek the day before.

She took the glass and bent forward to reach the table in front of me. As she turned towards me, her long hair freed itself from the knot and fell over my legs. I did not move. She got up slowly, her breasts gently rubbing against my shoulder as she went towards the mirror. She then gently pulled her long tresses back and looked at me fondly...I smiled shyly. I was suddenly aware of how sensuous that moment was. My gaze travelled from her slender neck, down to her collar bone, and further down. She looked at me forbiddly with her playful glance.

"Anu you have got a nice frame...I 'm sure any man would want you in his arms for life..."

She moved towards me, bent forward maintaining eye contact. She gently touched the back of my hand saying, "I like the veins on your hand. It's so manly!"

I smiled like a baby.

She kept her soft warm hands on mine, lightly following the veins. She circled around the knuckles and moved her fingers towards mine. My smile had vanished by now. Our fingers were feeling each other playfully. I looked up into her eyes and time froze. I could now smell her breath. My lips reached out for hers and just then she turned away. My lips met with her cheeks. I opened my eyes surprised. I looked at her, puzzled.

"I want you to kiss me Siddhartha but I can't now..."

"What's wrong Noush?"

"Don't get me wrong...but we have just met and though I feel very strongly for you. The kiss would mean intimacy and I think let's not rush into it..."

"Yes, you are right..." I said hurtfully.

I started blabbering as I normally did when I didn't feel too good, "I understand Anoushka. But I think I should let you know that you have had a major impact on me. I want to spend time with you and know you. I was attracted to you when I looked at you standing there at your balcony. I wanted to be close to you when we met yesterday. And I like being near you now, watching you, feeling your presence. You are a pleasure to watch, and every movement of yours has this mesmerising elegance to it. Maybe I am..."

She kept looking at me with her eyebrows slightly twitched and with a childlike expression on her face. She said, "You didn't finish..."

"I think I am in love with you."

She kept looking at me for a while trying to read my thoughts. She remained quiet for sometime and then said, "I feel like I am going to drown into your eyes. They are so expressive. I feel like they are constantly talking to me. It is what attracts me to you."

Our eyes met again, but this time she looked into my eyes very boldly. Her gaze drifted to my lips... I moved closer to her and she fell into my arms. I kissed her on her face, not attempting to reach for her lips. She stood very still eyes closed tightly. Then I moved back. She opened her eyes looked at me smiling, came close and locked lips. She just made contact for a fraction of a second and went back. Her cheeks were red and her gaze was lowered. I moved closer to her, my fingers gently moving up and down her slender arms. We looked at each other. I moved closer again and kissed her neck, gently biting her. She was breathing heavily now; her hands were on my chest, her fingers gently digging in. And before I realised it, we were kissing passionately.

She stood up and led me to her bedroom.

She briefly stopped in front of the mirror and pulled me before her. Her hands moved up my stomach and chest. I was looking at her, her face red, eyebrows tense, breathing heavy and mouth open. She had no inhibitions anymore and we had both given in to each other.

"You've really got a great body," she purred in my ears.

I turned around and kissed her.

While we were kissing my hands moved over her breasts. She froze and then opened her eyes saying, "I shouldn't be doing this..."

I immediately moved my hands away saying, "Anu, I have to join my first job in two weeks. I will be on a ship. I am a marine engineer."

"Oh? Where would the ship be? You will keep coming here, right?"

"I'll have to go to the US. I will come back after seven months or so. Will you be alright...I'll be gone for a long time."

"Don't worry Sid, we will manage. I'm big enough to handle our relationship."

"Yes that I can see!" I said teasingly.

She pinched me on my arms.

I chased her to the sofa. She gave up and lay down. I bent over her and bit her gently on her neck. I slid her top up to kiss her around her navel. I tried to take it off but she held my hands tightly.

She was blushing as she said, "You know it's my first time..."

I promised not to look while she undressed. I could hear the clothes come off her body and I quivered. She then said, her voice hardly audible, "You may see me now..."

I opened my eyes slowly, my pulse racing by now.

Her clothes were on the floor. She had wrapped the curtains around her naked body.

I removed my T-shirt and jeans. I stood at a distance as she looked at me desirously. I made my move, reached for her hands as we locked lips. Slowly I moved my hands towards the curtain, pulling it away from her body. Her body was warm and her breathing very heavy. I moved my hands to her back holding her as my lips moved down to her neck and then further down, slowly caressing her breasts. Her knees gave way and I pulled her up, pushing her against the wall. My hands moved gently on her arms, her neck and her waist as I kissed her wildly.

Her locks danced against my flushed face, her arms were up in the air, her mouth partially open as she breathed out heavily. Her curves, her long legs shivered with ecstasy.

I whispered in her ears, "I want more of you," and with that I moved my hands around her waist and gently rolled down her underwear. She was in a state of complete abandon. I brought my right leg up to pull it all the way down, before she brought my naked body closer to hers. We kissed and pressed against each other, our bodies becoming one.

In the days that followed, we met secretly. I never made love to her. Deep down I knew she was too young to understand what was right for her; I wanted to give her time to realise whether she was ready for the relationship. While it was totally different for me...I was old enough to understand what was going on inside me, and I had developed a strong attachment to her.

CHAPTER

Where is He?

The car crossed the Hanuman temple and the airport was just down the turn. The place was so much a part of me.

"Life will be real tough for you *beta*. We had hoped that you wouldn't take this path. But...Oh, keep the tickets in your cabin bag; you'll need it at the entrance." Papa went on.

My chain of thoughts broke suddenly when I heard my father mention 'the tickets'. I realised I didn't have them! I bent forward to my mother and whispered in her ear, "Mom are the tickets with you?"

She shouted, "They were on the dining table! You didn't pick them up?"

I was frantically searching my pockets and the carry-on bags. Sonu was smiling.

Papa was mad with anger. He was still mumbling when we reached home. I rushed home, unlocked the door and ran towards the drawing room and voila there it was. The red coloured pages unfurling as I reached out for them as if the ticket didn't want to come to me...I took hold of it after a minor scuffle between us. I ran out holding the ticket high in the air as a champion would do while taking round of the stadium with the winning torch.

My father was still grumbling, "Can't even take care

of his ticket how will he manage alone on a ship! He takes things very lightly..." It was always like that. Whenever he had anything bad to tell me he would always go on the third person mode; he would talk to my mom about me as if I were not there at all.

Mom replied, "Why the fuss? We still have 2 hrs before his flight, we will reach at the airport in 10 minutes."

Father persisted, "But you never know what the traffic would be like..."

I thought, "Traffic in this sleepy town? We live in Ranchi not New York."

Father continued arguing with her, "Because of you, both of them have become irresponsible."

Out went Sonu's smile and in came Mom's sobbing.

I wanted to shout at them, to say "It's not about you, it's about me! Just imagine my life in a few days!" I had always known that it was going to be tough but the feeling had only begun to sink in now. I was stepping out of my comfort zone. I would have so many new responsibilities, and to make things worse, I had heard scary stories of people abandoning the ship in the very first month, unable to bear the tough life. I didn't want to be one of those. I wanted to be tough like Vikram, but I knew I wasn't. But I hoped to find some good people on board and felt that there was much to learn and experience. I wondered if I had made the right career decision. Mom was still sobbing...

She said in between sobs, "The *baba* told him he doesn't have to experience it."

I protested, "But he didn't say that Mom."

The *baba*...I had forgotten about him!

It happened around a month ago. I came home from the gym and was bragging to Sonu, "I lifted 200 pounds today."

"*Kitna fekta hai.* Not possible at all."

"I did, I lifted 35 kgs on each side."

He pointed out, "That's only 70 kg. What's wrong with your maths?"

"Dumbo, the bench press rod is 18kgs. You won't be able to lift even that!"

He ignored my statement and started a new conversation with mother, "Ma, what's for breakfast?"

Just then the doorbell rang.

I looked at Sonu and said sternly, "Go look who is there. Did you just hear the bell?"

My little brother was the cool guy; events surrounding him didn't seem to bother him. He replied, "I'm about to eat. Do you mind?"

I opened the door and saw a bearded man in his early forties. He was wearing a white *kurta* and white *dhoti*. His clothes were old but didn't look shabby. He had long hair. Despite his unkempt look there was something striking about him.

"There's nobody at home in case you want something from us. And I don't have any money." It was my usual excuse for strangers demanding alms at the door.

The stranger said, "I was just passing through this area. I was not supposed to come here..."

"But please come later on..."

He continued as if it was important for him to stop by, "I come here every year and go to Satellite colony. A devotee lives here and 10 more live in different parts of Ranchi."

"Why do you visit them?"

"I am from Shirdi. They are followers of Sai Baba and visit the temple every year."

"Oh the famous Sai baba temple at Shirdi."

I was amazed at myself. I would never converse with a stranger for even five seconds. In this part of the country most priests who visit homes are fakes.

"So when you visit the devotees, do you expect donations from them?" I couldn't believe I was continuing this polite conversation.

"I don't expect anything. They donate if they want to. The donations do help us with the upkeep though. We priests have no choice but to depend on contributions from outside. So, yes, one of the purposes of this visit is to collect donations from devotees."

"You said you were passing through..."

"Yes I visit Shridhar every year. He lives in the other

colony next to yours. I was walking by when I was pulled towards this house."

"Do you mean to say that you wouldn't be visiting the other houses in this apartment or the other six in front of our building?"

"No I had just come to meet Shridhar. Baba wanted me to visit your house. So here I am!"

I was confused about whether I should invite him in. It was ridiculous, inviting a stranger to home in Ranchi. Just the other day there was news of a *sadhu* who came in the house to perform some *puja*, lit something and the owners lost consciousness. They obviously were looted of almost everything.

"Please wait, I'll see if my mother wants to meet you."

Mom didn't trust anybody. She would have killed me if she knew that I was about to ask some stranger into our home.

"Mom, there's a priest on the door. He says he has come from Shirdi."

She came to the door and invited him to the house. Just like that!

"Shall I bring something to eat with the tea?" she asked courteously.

The saint declined politely, "No, today's my fast. I'll just have the tea."

I was looking at him and it seemed he knew exactly what was going through my mind. I wasn't expecting him to help me in anyway, yet I felt as if he knew something that could be of importance to me.

He smiled as he said, "I think you regularly dream of people chasing you. You are afraid and hiding and running..."

I replied immediately, "I am not afraid of anyone. And the constant dream that I get is me rising from bed every night as if my soul is getting away from my body and then I wake up with a start. It's more of my body rising in the air kind of a dream."

Though I actually used to have this floating dream quite often, I also had recurring bad dreams about people chasing to kill me. He was looking at me and smiling knowingly.

He then asked, "Son, do you believe in God?"

"Yes I do...I go to Hanumanji's temple...well I do know Sai Baba is great but actually have never been to his temple..."

"You may have heard of this before, God is a powerful source...you may choose to call him Hanuman or Sai baba or Allah or Christ. He lives inside each one of us."

I said impatiently, "Oh, I have heard that thousands of times. What does it even mean? God lives inside a killer too?"

He smiled again before he replied, "Yes. A killer does something bad because his perception of reality is different. He is not seeking out for the right answers or maybe he doesn't want to listen to the voice coming out from within. The voice from within, your intuitions, those are the signs from God. You can connect with God by connecting with your inner self."

I pleaded, "I don't understand why I can't be perfect and strong now? Can you teach me how to connect with God?"

"That will come with time."

"How will I know when the time has come?"

"You just have to watch out for the signals."

"What signals?"

He replied patiently, "They can be anywhere. It could be from anything...sometimes from such an inconsequential source that you may not even notice."

"Then how do I recognise if that is a particular sign which is telling me something?"

He closed his eyes as he said this, "Nobody can help you on this. You will feel that the world is trying to tell you something and whatever that is it should make sense for you...you need to set yourself free for that. We get chained by outside pressures and get too involved in the daily grinds of life and that increases the chances of you missing the signs, because in chasing those, you disconnect yourself from your innerself."

"In case a relevant sign appears and one fails to understand it? What happens then? Will some other sign come or is the chance gone forever?"

"Signs in different forms will keep coming till the time you either recognise it or till the time they stay relevant. Once the chance is gone with time it doesn't come back...but other opportunities will come again."

"Don't you think it is very complicated?"

"Yes it is. You can't keep looking for signs all the while. That would lead to paranoia and the whole purpose of life would get defeated. A child catches all the signals...he smiles when he gets a positive vibe from a stranger, he cries when he feels something isn't right...yet he enjoys life. Go back to being a child – live, work hard and listen to the inner voice."

"Do the signs come from within?"

Just then a sparrow came and sat on the window. He was looking at the bird as he said, "They can come from anywhere. The answers are within you. Signs are just like a bridge that connects the obvious with the 'not-so-obvious'...which connects the conscious with the sub-conscious. People who have attained the highest levels don't need the signs anymore...they get the answers from within."

The saint had mentioned something else too...

"You are going to take a long journey – it would be filled with hardships. Hence you should be prepared for that."

I asked eagerly, "Will I be successful? Will I complete the journey?"

He shook his heads slowly as he replied, "I don't have answers to these questions."

I was dejected as I said, "You don't?"

"Only one person would have answers to your problems..." he said looking at me.

"Me?"

He kept smiling.

I continued, "That's great. Then in that case may I ask you a question, at the expense of being rude?" I asked when he nodded, "When the answers lie within, why do we need God's help?"

"The world will stop needing me when it realises the solution lies within and I would love to see that day. But we all would still need God. Without Him the essence of our being stops to exist…"

"Ok, how do we connect with our inner self?"

"Praying is one of the ways…"

"What is your job then?"

"My job is to show the way. I am like the road sign — people lose their way, some find it without the signs and some find it faster with a little help. Today I was driven towards your home. Don't ask me why as I do not know."

"So you show the way by making people believe in Sai Baba?"

He smiled again, "Son, there are many paths which lead to Him. Nobody can force you or convince you to choose any one path…when you start believing, everything starts falling in place. I have not chosen to come here…it's His wish that I follow."

I wanted an answer desperately so I asked again, "Can you see the future?"

He smiled again — looking into his eyes, it seemed as if he had all the answers.

Maybe he took pity on me. He said, "You will be making a journey…it won't be easy. I see suffering ahead."

"*Baba* shall I not take the journey then?"

"That is a decision you should take. The man you are and the man you would become should be based on the path you choose."

"I understand that *baba*…suppose I do take the trip, what if even after the suffering there's nothing good that happens to me?"

He looked in my eyes and said, "You can never run away from the realities of life. Sufferings, pain and sadness are a part of life…Maybe I am telling you what you want to listen to. Maybe it's better for you to not take the trip. But I cannot change your future; I don't have the powers to do so. But I can tell you one thing, no matter which path you take, the outcome will be in your hands and that depends on how strong you are."

"You told me not to take the journey. Does that mean you think I am weak inside?"

"Child, like I said, I haven't told you anything. I say

what you believe. I have to go now. I am required elsewhere."

We were about to reach the airport. It was my mom's turn now, "I always stopped you from joining this career. I had stopped you right from the time you were applying for the written exam..."

"Mom, it was my decision and I'm sure that's the right path."

My father pitched in, "Now after four years of education you can't even work. Where will you get a job now?"

I kept quiet, mom continued as if my father had not said anything, "The *baba* meant that it wasn't the best job for you. Who will take care of you there? You will be so far from home!"

I had no other option but to take this trip because I wanted to prove to my parents and to myself that I had made the right choice. Within, however, I wasn't too sure. There were times I felt I wouldn't survive even a month there.

Foxtrot Oscar
'Comfort Zone'

We reached the airport and I had that much too familiar sinking feeling. So many signs were telling me that I would not be successful...so many reasons not to take this trip...

Everything at the airport seemed like a blur to me. It was my first international flight. After security procedures, the wait to board seemed endless. I finally boarded the flight to Frankfurt. Aboard the plane everything seemed to be moving in slow motion...the cockpit announcements seemed distant, the air hostesses ugly and rude, the in flight entertainment was pathetic and the leg room was worse than that in my father's small car. Everytime I would begin to sleep, the sad hostesses would bring in something to eat or to drink. I started passing on my food to my co-passenger. This guy owned a sex shop in Amsterdam. He described the different kinds of kinky toys available at his store. The most popular one among the girls this season was a toothbrush shaped like a penis; the head of the penis would go inside the mouth while the balls would rest inside the palm.

"The grip is good, so say my young customers!" he said, smiling as he gestured like he was giving a blow job. I looked around nervously and was relieved to see that nobody was paying attention to our discussion.

I told him, "I am an Engineer. I know how to make engineering designs. If you pay me well I can make interesting stuff...stuff as good as dick shaped toothbrushes."

He didn't like my offer too much. I feared I had offended him, so I added, "It was a joke. Your designs are totally out of this world."

He smiled and stuffed a croissant in his mouth as he said, "I make them myself. Been doing that since I was 13."

I was surprised. "Oh! That young! So you were exposed to adult stuff quite early...your wife must be really happy with you, eh?"

"My wife? Happy? With me?" he said as he moved his right hand in the air with disgust.

"You don't use your own toys? You must have learned a lot about love making and about how to satisfy a woman in bed."

"The only people I know how to make happy are my customers." His impromptu reply set me thinking...life's strange. The man who gives tips to young and old lovers about the art of love making had a sad love life.

I asked for another Budweiser. The beer was helping already; I had begun to enjoy the conversation with my new friend. Suddenly the flight didn't look that bad and the hostesses appeared friendly and beautiful. I turned around to see him enjoy the food. After he had finished eating he took out his card, "This is my shop's address and phone number. Visit me and I'll give you good toys for your girlfriend. She'll be occupied when you are away. I'll also give you a decent discount."

I smiled as I took his card. It was a masterpiece. At first glance the card's shape looked like that of a pair of binoculars but soon I knew what they were a pair of boobs; on observing closely I could see the nipples...they had been water-marked. The name of the shop "Divine Intersection" was written on top. On the side was a photograph of two dildos 'intersecting' each other at 90 degrees. His complicated name was written at the bottom of the card.

"Very innovative," I said looking impressed.

I don't know when I dozed off. I woke up with a start and looked at my watch. I had lost track of time. My friend was still eating. He was happy to see that I was awake. I smiled at him and looked at my watch again.

He understood my predicament- he looked at his watch and said, "40 minutes...that's how long you have been sleeping."

I groaned, "That's not long..."

"Where are you from?" he asked me.

"India."

"Yes, I guessed that. Where in India? Bombay?"

I fiddled with my seat belt as I replied, "No, actually I have lived in many different places in India. Was born in a city, which is in the eastern part of India, studied somewhere else...in Calcutta. Do you know Calcutta?"

He said vaguely, "Yes I think I've heard of the place."

"You seem to know about India. Have you been there?"

"A few times, my cousin has a shop in Jaipur."

"Oh great!"

"I have also travelled to Bombay, Trivandrum, Cochin, Pondicherry...how can I forget...Goa and...Delhi."

I was impressed. I said, "You have seen more of India than I have."

He asked, "Where are you going?"

"I'm going to US to join a ship. Sadly I don't get to see your beautiful country."

"A ship eh? That's a tough job! But you look like a tough guy, I'm sure you would do well."

I didn't say anything, just smiled politely. I felt uneasy — statements like those always worried me, and I had good reason to be too. In my final year of college, my batchmate who had a room next to mine asked me one day, "How do you manage to get 65 percent by just studying the night before exams? You sleep in class or are not there most of the time. You don't even cheat!"

"I just study around 70 percent of the course and that's enough to pass." I said proudly. Four weeks after this conversation, I flunked the Marine Electricity final year exam.

And then there was this girl in the school who approached me during lunch break one day, looked at me with a twinkle in her eyes and said, "You'd look great in uniform!" Everybody around me was sure that I would make it to the army easily. Only I didn't.

As I sat there worrying about my co-passenger's exceptional faith in me, I was transported back in time when my hopes of 'looking good in uniform' were dashed.

All those of us interested in joining the NDA had cleared the written exam and had received the call for the Service Selection Board (SSB), all except Garu. The initial stages of the SSB process were easy as they were written tests. The problems had begun when we moved on to the next set of tasks. I had struggled to get my views across in the Group Discussion. In the 'Military Planning Exercise' I somehow convinced the group to follow my plan. But midway we reached a dead end. This exercise had resulted in me losing all credibility with the group. I did well in both the group obstacles and the individual obstacles race but failed miserably in the extempore. I had always hated public speaking and that day was no different. Initially, the two minutes seemed like piece of cake, but when I started, I could speak for barely fifteen seconds. The other 105 seconds were spent standing in front of the assessors and my fellow competitors like a dork. They looked at me expectantly, hoping that it was only a calculated pause. They waited with bated breath, thinking that I was going to bowl them over with my next words. But the words never came. I stood there, paralyzed, and speechless.

The interview was the icing on the cake. When asked about the reason I wanted to join the army, I said what everybody had told me not to, "Sir, I want to serve my country." I was surprised I didn't tell him the actual reason, which was that I was fascinated with fighter planes and guns.

Abruptly came the question, "Oh that you can do even as an Engineer or a doctor, can't you?"

I found myself saying, "Sir, actually I've not prepared for the engineering entrance exam yet. I'll have to start doing it if I don't secure admission in the NDA." I knew then that my fate had been sealed.

He looked at me as if he wanted to slap me real hard, "So, do you mean to say you don't have to study much to join the National Defence Academy?"

"No sir, that's not what I meant. For engineering and medicine you require coaching classes and have to prepare extensively...sir, actually, we need to prepare for NDA too but not to that level..." I continued to dig my grave deeper.

"I see your point. The interview is over...and listen...if I were you I would start preparing for the engineering entrance exam," said the officer.

Naveen's ambition had been to be a doctor and Sachin's had been to join the NASA as an aeronautical engineer. Since they had been selected in the defence academy, they had thought it a waste of effort to prepare for the respective entrance exams. Suddenly their dream jobs had changed and with my great performance at the SSB, I had no option but to change my dream job too. So, reluctantly I prepared for the engineering entrance exams. Garu, who was most passionate about the defence forces in our group, could never even appear for the SSB interview. Despite six attempts, he could not clear the written exam. By that time Naveen and Sachin had finished their training at the NDA and had joined the Indian Military Academy, while I had entered the fourth year of college.

So four years since, here I was on way to work and so were the others...except Garu who remained in Ranchi.

Soon we made our descent. I had another eight hours before boarding my connecting flight to the US. I was sitting uncomfortably in a very comfortable seat, too conscious of my surroundings. My mind was in frenzy as I was thinking about so many things at the same time. I looked around; nobody was paying any attention to me... some casual glances at most. I wanted to freshen up but I couldn't get myself to get out of my seat lest I should attract attention of other passengers. I got up finally, looking around anxiously. I got some friendly glances. I felt a tad comfortable now, relieved that I wasn't terribly unwelcome here after all.

I could see the washroom sign far ahead. It was a huge airport, beautifully designed. I was on the first floor, walking on a wide carpeted area, glass walls on both sides. On my left I could see around seven aircrafts parked at the bay and behind them I could see the runaways. On my right I could see the city. Up ahead were the numerous duty free shops, eateries, coffee shops, cheese counters, liquor and chocolate shops...everything under the sun was available here. It took me around seven minutes to reach the loo. I peeped inside the toilet and was relieved to find jet spray attached on the toilet seat. I had used toilet paper before and they left me with a raw unclean feeling. Water, however, felt nice.

I walked about the airport whiling away my time. The whole setting at the airport was modern, cosy, methodical, convenient and very international.

I didn't have a friendly neighbour on my US leg. I spent my time watching movies and sleeping. Though the flight wasn't too comfortable I wanted it to last forever. It was the fear of the unknown that made me apprehensive about my arrival in this new country. Or perhaps it was my lack of confidence.

The flight landed in New York on time. I boarded a small 30 seater aircraft to a port on the eastern coast, a small town called Bucksport. Outside the airport I located the person with a placard in hand — 'MT Limar, Junior Engineer, Mr Siddhartha'. MT Limar was the name of the ship, MT stood for Motor Tanker. I was led to a BMW.

I moved towards the front door, the driver had a puzzled look on his face. I was on the wrong side.

"Oh I forgot, in our country the driver's seat is on the right side. I'm sorry."

He was smiling as he nodded his head, "Don't you want to sit in the back? It would be more comfortable."

"I'll enjoy the ride more from here," I said as I hopped in the seat next to him. How long is the ride?"

"About 2 hrs…" he said as he started the magnificent machine.

The ride was much more fun than the flight.

"Are the roads too complicated here? I mean any possibility of us not being able to locate the ship?" I was still hoping that I would never reach that dreaded ship.

The driver smiled and said, "First ship?" He continued when he saw me nodding, "I can understand how you feel. My first job was in a meat shop. I still remember the day…couldn't sleep at night. I would wake up every half an hour expecting the alarm to ring, would look at the watch, feel relieved and try to go back to sleep. When the alarm rang finally I was almost sick. It took me a lot of effort to get out of bed. I reached my workplace on time. It was a shabby stinking place with flies all over. I was given a half hour briefing of how to cut the meat. Well that was the job. I would cut meat all day…wanted to quit but couldn't because my family needed the money. I did this job for three fucking years. They promoted me to be in-charge of billing. It was a clean job, where I just had to deal with customer orders."

"Well, that's good. Shit gets over one day…"

"Yes, but you know, I was so used to the shitty job that I didn't enjoy the billing work."

"Oh?"

"Yup, I approached the owner and asked him for my previous job back."

"Huh? I don't understand."

He smiled and said, "Me neither…well that was a long time ago. We re-located after my father died. The point I wanted to make was that you will get used to your job. It takes a while but it settles down finally."

What he said set me thinking. It made sense. I had read in a survey that shipping was the toughest job in the world but then I realised there could be others that were tougher.

"Tell me something…" I asked, "Why did you choose this job?"

"Oh when we moved to Bucksport I went to the meat shops in the city for job. They didn't need a meat cutter...everything here is mechanised. Not like it was in the countryside. I worked there for a while but wasn't too happy in the clean environ I guess," he said with a chuckle. "I started driving my uncle's pick up truck...one thing led to another and I found this job."

"Hmm...your life has been interesting."

"Life *is* interesting. Where you from?" He asked nonchalantly.

"India...of course you know that. I studied in Calcutta. Do you know the place?

"Nope, I only know of Goa, Bombay and Jaipur."

We were getting out of the city. He said, as if reading my mind, "We are about to reach."

"Wish me luck for my new job."

"Oh I wish you luck for your life. Jobs will come and go..."

"Hmm...true. Life won't."

He smiled and said, "Indeed."

I smiled back, "Thanks, am sure this will help."

Up ahead I could see the port. The place was filled with action. I could see crew moving on the decks. I could see a lot of activity on the jetty too.

"One of them will be my workplace for the next seven months or so..."

He added, "And also your home."

"Correct."

We took a turn into a narrow road that led us to a huge sliding gate. The security saw the driver and waved at him. We went in and parked near the jetty.

"So long buddy," I said and extended my hand to my new friend.

We got out and went towards the rear of the vehicle to get my luggage.

"That's your ship." His words woke me up from a dream of sorts. It was real...I was here...to board a ship. I had consciously avoided looking at it though it was right there, in front of my eyes. I tried to keep a straight face as I slowly turned towards it. I was behaving like a kid on the first day of kindergarten. The ship took my breath away — not in a way a beautiful girl would but in a fearful sort of way. It stood there rock solid, looking like an unbeatable giant; it was huge and tall and magnificent. I remember going through the manual when I was going over the joining formalities. The vessel was mentioned as a mid-sized category, 188 metres in length and 28 metres wide; it kind of seemed small. But looking at it now, I found it was not at all what I had imagined it to be.

The hull was painted in black and maroon. The white accommodation structure set a perfect contrast complementing the hull. Behind the accommodation structure I could see the tall black funnel deck. On top of it there was a broad white patch, on which was painted the company's logo with COS Corp written below it.

Until now I was able to console myself that my fears were unreasonable, but looking at the formidable giant in front of me my fears seemed to be coming true.

"Hey man, you alright?"

"Uhhh...ye-yeah...am good...just a little tired." I had forgotten I had to take my luggage from the vehicle.

I picked up the two heavy suitcases and the shoulder bag. I was wondering how to take the luggage up when my friend pitched in. "Your new friends would pick that up with the provision crane..." he said as he pointed out to a crane on the ship, "Your food — meat, eggs, vegetables, etc gets lifted with that crane."

I could see movement around the crane...around 3-4 people were around it and they were wearing the same orange coloured boiler suit that I was given from the office. They were lowering a net for my luggage.

The driver looked at my face and smiled as he said, "It takes a little getting used to...it is a different life from the one you were leading a few hours ago. I was a meat cutter and back then I thought I would do that all my life. But look at how my life is now..." he said looking at the BMW "...and I love it."

I smiled at him and said, "Thanks man. You are my inspiration."

"Awww...come on." He looked at the net and said, "You need to place your luggage at the centre." The net was lying on the ground. He detached one end from the crane and the two sides of the net opened up. I placed my luggage at the centre and helped him fix the ends back to the crane. He looked towards the ship deck, lifted his right arm up and started rotating his index finger in clockwise direction – he was signalling the crane operator to start lifting. I looked up at my airborne luggage. My huge suitcases now appeared like matchboxes.

I turned around to bid farewell to my friend, "I didn't ask your name..."

"It's Bill. I know your name though." He said with a grin.

"Bill, how do you know so much about the ship?"

"Apart from being a driver I also am your company's agent in Bucksport." He said with a wink.

"Oh? Pardon my ignorance but what does an agent do?"

"I bring your provisions. I arrange for air tickets. I look at crew's transportation. It's my job to take care of you all...arrange for doctor, movie tickets...calling cards. Oh I forgot I've got these excellent calling cards for India – 30 minutes of talktime for $10."

"Amazing! I'll take two. You're some guy Bill!"

We shook hands and I moved towards the gangway – that's the huge ladder, which connects the ship with the port. I put my feet forward and the ladder shifted under my weight. I had not expected it to move but it was made from a lightweight metal and it was normal for the gangway to move to and fro as I walked on it. I was holding on to the railings as I climbed. I looked below. I could see a safety net tied underneath. I breathed easy now. When I was almost at the top, I could see that the distance between the side of the ship and jetty was around six feet. I shuddered at the thought of somebody falling from the gangway straight into the gap. Bless the person who invented the safety net! I climbed the final leg of stairs and crossed over to the ship.

I was walking on a cast iron deck. I was rudely made to realise that my days of leisure were now over; even a simple thing like walking seemed like an obstruction course in a military planning exercise. On my right side were several pipelines; if the deck is so complicated, I could only imagine what the engine room would be like! I waved at the people who had lifted my luggage. They were still around the crane. They waved back, smiling.

I looked at my watch before I bent to lift my luggage. It was 11.50 am. Bucksport time…it would be around 1.30 am the next day, back home in India. My folks and friends would be sleeping peacefully. I felt sleepy too and dead tired; my body was still on India time. Though the jet lag had gotten me, I wanted to go see what my next eight months would be like. I picked up my bags and moved towards accommodation. I climbed the stairs with difficulty. I had reached the lifeboat deck and from here I would enter the first floor of the accommodation structure. I looked at the red lifeboat — it had a seating capacity of twenty. There would be another lifeboat on the port side lifeboat deck. I opened the huge weather proof door and entered the ship. It was beautiful; the woodwork was tastefully done. I put my luggage down as I caught my breath. I closed the door and looked ahead. I could see a flight of stairs around 30 feet ahead. To my left was the officers' mess and to the right, the officers' smoke room — the designated smoking area on the tanker. Further up, towards the right, was the Cargo Control Room or CCR (this is where the Chief Officer planned the loading and discharging and operated the pumps of various tanks while discharging from the vessel). Further up, next to the CCR, was the deck office.

I peeped into the CCR and saw a tall guy in his early thirties looking at the huge electronic console in front of him. I waited at the door, not wanting to disturb him. He reached for his walkie-talkie hung carelessly by the side of his pocket, switched it to a different channel and barked into it "Param! Come in!"

I could hear another voice come in immediately, "Yes sir. Over."

The tall guy shouted back, "Where are you? Loading was complete two hours ago. You haven't reported. Over."

Param's voice said, "Sir, I was about to report. Inspected all the tanks...readings already reported to 3rd officer an hour back. Over."

"Ok."

"Sir, is there anything else that I am needed for? Over."

"Foxtrot Oscar...FO (Fuck Off)."

"Thank you sir. Over."

The crackling on the other side died out. That must have been Param, switching off his set to retire for the day. The tall guy sensed the movement behind him and he turned around with a start. I came forward, "I didn't mean to startle you. My name is Siddhartha. I am joining as 5th Engineer. I was wondering who to meet and where to go to..."

"Oh hi. No you didn't startle me. I am the Chief Officer. Which college did you go to?"

"MEII...Marine Engineering Institute of India."

"Yeah yeah I know. Which batch?"

"2003."

"Obviously, you've come here fresh from college. I know several of your seniors." He smiled as he said that. "Where are you from?"

I put my hands in my pockets as I answered, "Well, I belong to Lucknow, lived in Calcutta for four years, while doing my engineering...have done my basic schooling in Ranchi."

He noted, "That's a long answer to a small question."

I just smiled while he continued, "You are supposed to complete some joining formalities and deposit your passport. Go to the bridge."

"Ok, umm...but how do I go there?"

He looked at me as if I were a joker, "I would expect a person from MEII to know how to locate the bridge!"

I stood there not knowing how to respond.

He felt sorry for me and said, "Follow the stairs and keep climbing. You'll reach the bridge..."

"Shall I put my luggage in my cabin before I go there? Can you please tell me where that would be?" I was almost pleading with him.

"Second floor."

"Thanks" and with that I took my luggage and took the stairs. To the right of where the stairs ended was a door. It was a fireproof door, a safety mechanism to help contain fire; in case one of the floors caught fire it would help prevent the fire from spreading to the other levels. I opened the door and reached an alley. I could see cabins of the crew on this floor. I could see Bosun, Able Bodied Seaman 1, Able Bodied Seaman 2, Ordinary Seaman 1 written on the doors in front of me. I looked back at the door from where I came in. On the door was a green fluorescent sticker that said 'EXIT' in bold and a sketch indicating the way to the stairs. A similar door led me to the second floor.

My cabin was next to the rear exit which led to the funnel deck. I stood near the exit for a while breathing heavily. I looked out of the porthole, I could see the funnel. Behind the funnel deck, two deck hands were working on the aft winch. I stood there for a while, observing them. I turned around to find my cabin. It was small and cosy. The linen looked fresh and the bathroom sparkling clean. I felt like crashing on the bed but I had to complete my joining formalities.

In a few minutes, I was off to the bridge. I climbed two floors and walked in a door that opened into a brightly lit room. I had seen the bridge in countless movies and this looked pretty much like the ones I had seen on screen. At the front were huge windows through which the entire fore of the ship was visible. I could see the helm and the steering wheel, the radar equipment and other navigation controls and devices. I moved in. To my right was a door with Navigation Planning written on it. The room was partially visible; there were racks with several maps and charts stacked on it. As I moved closer to the room, I saw the back of someone thin and short. He was wearing a deck officer's uniform. He was bent over the large table at the centre of the room working on a huge map. I came to the door and said, "Hi."

He turned around with a start and almost fell to the ground as he looked at me. He managed to mumble an, "err...hi, you must be the new 5th Engineer...you scared me."

I smiled extending my hand, "My name is Siddhartha. I have come here with this," I said, as I waved my passport in the air.

"Oh yeah. You also need to sign on the joining form. Now where did I keep that?" he started lifting the chart to find the sheet. He found it after briefly rummaging for it. I looked at the chart and said, "Sorry to interrupt you, but what are you doing?"

"Oh I was charting the voyage plan. I need to feed it into the autopilot. Oh damn! I forgot where I was. I need to re-start my work. If you will excuse me..."

"Sure, nice to meet you. My passport..." I said reminding him that my passport was with him.

He looked at it for a while not understanding how it came into his hands, "Yes of course. It's in safe hands."

I was afraid he would misplace it and I would be stranded on the ship for life. I shut the scary thought out of my head, completed the form and waved at him, "Ok see you around 3rd."

$$7$$

CHAPTER

In the 'Zone'

I went back to my cabin. Though I was sleepy I wanted to go see what the Engine Room (E/R) was like and also to meet my new colleagues. I changed into my boiler suit, industrial shoes and went off looking for the room. I crossed the washing space and proceeded further down the alley towards the huge door. I could hear loud machinery from behind it so I knew it was the entrance to my new office. I had to struggle to open it. The heated air and noise got me instantly; it wasn't the kind of warm welcome I had expected. The door opened to a flight of iron stairs. The steps were small and I had to turn sideways while getting down. To fall from the iron stairs onto an iron platform was certainly not my idea of fun.

It was a sudden change, from air conditioning to heated surroundings, from silence to the hammering sounds of engines and machinery (although most of the machinery were idle since we were not enroute), from stylish wooden stairs to iron ones and from a comfort zone to an impersonal, emotionless, inhuman and unwelcoming atmosphere. I could see different types of machinery, most of which I was clueless about. I realised why the job of a marine engineer was considered the toughest in the world. No wonder then that even after the gruelling college training some of my seniors couldn't last even a month on a ship.

My daydreaming was interrupted by a voice. "You gotta wear these..." the man shouted as he pointed towards a rack on which hung several helmets and ear muffs.

I said, "Hi, I am..."

"Yea, I think I know who you are. Come in here," he said, as he pointed towards a door which said Engine Control Room (ECR). This was an A/c room and all control panels, the alarm system, manoeuvring system and electrical panels were in this room.

He was smiling real wide as he said, "Hi, people call me Sam. I am the 4th Engineer. How was your journey?"

"The journey was ok...wow, never expected the engine room to be this huge."

"Oh, you should take a round and then you'll know how big it actually is. Which college are you from?"

"MEII."

"What batch?"

"2003."

"I know many of your seniors. Great guys all of them."

I simply smiled. He continued, "Everyone will have high expectations from you. I'm sure it wouldn't be a problem for you to pick things up."

"I'll try my best." I could barely manage a confident tone.

"Sid, where you from?"

"Oh I am from several different places. Lucknow is where I am from, studied in Calcutta...and did my basic schooling in Ranchi."

"No kidding! Ranchi? It's in Bihar, right?"

"N-no...It's in Jharkhand now."

"Yeah right. I've met many people from your state. Foul mouthed, brazen and harsh but that's only from the outside...inside they are sentimental fools and very loyal friends...you know what I mean? Well, you don't seem to have that typical accent?"

"That's maybe because I hardly ever stayed there. I was travelling most of the time."

I was lying; I always did to avoid being typecast as a small town lad. I had a heavy *'Bihari'* accent as a child. I remember the trip to Bombay with my parents. We were staying with our relatives in the suburbs. The kids in the locality seemed a friendly lot. Whenever I would go out with my aunt or uncle they would smile and invite me to their game of cricket. One day I decided to join them. They were pleased to see me. But things changed when I spoke. I still remember the expression on the faces around me. The game was a torture for me and my brother; they made us field throughout the game. I took a very difficult catch and came running happily to my team just wanting to be accepted but they congratulated the bowler and went back to their positions. From that day onwards I hated my accent. The worst part was to live with it; I couldn't change it because I didn't want to become an outcast in my school or neighbourhood. But as soon as I went to Calcutta the first thing I did was quite obvious.

Though Sam seemed quite friendly, there was something about him that stopped me from being taken in. He sent for his motorman to familiarise myself with my new office. Tengalkar, Sam's motorman, was tall and well built...well he looked so but on observing closely I noticed that he was well built only around his belly. His face complemented his belly perfectly as it was swollen too. But his arms and legs were thinner and looked out of place. He was dark, had the thickest eyebrows I had ever seen and had an equally thick moustache. Sam introduced us and then told him, "Take Paanch sa'ab around the Engine Room. When any alarm goes off, show him how to take care of the problem."

"Ok chaar sa'ab," he replied gruffly. It was unbearable to stand near him as his breath stank of nicotine and caffeine.

It was five floors of machinery. When I came back to the Control Room, I was more confused than I ever was in college. Tengalkar had managed to screw my brain big time.

The watch of Sam was about to change and the 3rd Engineer was there too. He looked old enough to be the

Chief Engineer and he welcomed me with a wicked smile. His introduction was quite warm too, "I am 3rd Engineer. It would be good if you could learn fast. Till you don't learn your part we will have to do extra watchkeeping. We have been doing 6 hours on 6 hours off for God knows how long. It's a good thing you're here now."

I was at this point thinking of taking a shower and jumping into bed. He went on and on, "...I have 10 years experience. I heard you are from MEII."

I managed to nod.

"You don't need much help. Go around and learn what you can from my motorman, Gadhav."

"Sure I will try my best. Please bear with me if I take some time to learn everything...it seems so complicated," I blurted out.

3rd Engineer looked at 4th and they smiled. He turned towards me, his lopsided smile intact, "You are lucky to have helpful people like us here. When I joined, I didn't have that luxury. You MEII guys have it easy. You directly join as 5th Engineer; you don't need to do the extra one year of sailing that I had to do to qualify for the exam and viva. You get an exemption from that exam too! I put in a lot of effort for three years to reach where you are now. You guys have it real easy...that's sad. The struggle pays off."

I tried to appease him, "You must have learned a lot. I am glad to have you on board."

But I knew I was wrong when I saw him smirk. He said, "I am an Electronics Engineer, an Engineer like us all. But I had to go through a lot of humiliation by the senior engineers on my first ship. Most of them were from your college. But don't worry...I have no intention of being like them."

I was tired and wasn't expecting such a treatment from my new colleagues. I kept fidgeting in my place waiting for the discourse to be over. I was angry but I didn't want to show lest it should make things worse.

"Where are you from, Bombay or Delhi? You look like a North Indian." He said with disgust. It reminded me of that cricket match in Bombay.

"Lucknow," I said.

Sam, who had been quiet until now, pitched in, "He did his schooling in Ranchi."

3rd's eyes lit up, "Ranchi? How did you manage to get admission into MEII?"

I looked away as I spoke, "Most of the students in the IITs across India are from Jharkhand and Bihar...basic schooling there is one of the best."

3rd looked annoyed. "Oh then why do you have to go out to study?"

I smiled as I said, "Because everyone wants to get educated in the best colleges. That's why we have national level competitive exams. The better prepared secure admission...that's fair, right?"

"People from your state are everywhere...even in colleges that take donation. What kind of Engineers and Doctors would people become from these kinds of colleges...?"

I knew most of these colleges which took donation were not in my state. He was wrong but I kept quiet. This discussion was going nowhere. There was an uncomfortable silence for a while and then Sam said, "Teen sa'ab, shall I hand over the watch to you now?"

Sam started informing of routine stuff that was done around the Engine Room as 3rd yawned. I started for another round. After a while I heard the alarm ringing. Gadhav told me he was being called to the ECR; three consecutive rings was a call for the motorman. I didn't know what to do next so I took rounds trying to remember the location of different machineries within the E/R. Suddenly there was a loud noise, as if high pressure air was being released and then it was followed by the sound of heavy metal parts in motion; they were starting the main engine. We were about to move. This was my maiden voyage. It was the start of an unknown journey.

I looked at my wrist watch, "Oh my God its 5 pm and I haven't had breakfast, and now I've missed lunch as well! I think I should go to the ECR and resign for the day." One could afford to think out loud, as nobody could possibly hear in the noisy atmosphere. I wondered how in the last five hours nobody had come looking for me. Perhaps I shouldn't have been spending so much time taking rounds. Perhaps I should have been in the ECR and have met everyone there itself... but then again, I wondered if I was running away from meeting people...maybe I was afraid.

I went upto the ECR. Apart from 3rd Engineer there was a small, well built person standing in front of the main console. He was scratching his head while looking at the log book, "Why does the unit 5 of Engine always show lower temperature than other 5 units?" I was not the only one who was speaking out loud here.

3rd said, "Maybe the sensor is not working properly or maybe the fuel pump is bypassing fuel to the fuel oil waste tank. Before we came into Bucksport I observed that the fuel oil waste tank high level alarm had started to go off twice a day. I don't think twice a day is normal..."

"You have a point, let's go check it out." It was a little difficult to understand the accent of the short guy. He was the 2nd Engineer, a Filipino. I followed them to the Engine Console Platform. 3rd was right; the #5 fuel pump was bypassing fuel to the waste oil tank. Nothing much could be done about it now since the engines were running. Moreover, the leak was not too much.

2nd looked at me curiously.

"Hi 2nd, I'm 5th Engineer. I joined today," I shouted.

He shouted back, "I guessed as much. But what are you doing here at this time?"

I said grinning stupidly, "I was familiarising myself with the machinery..."

"You must be tired from the long journey. You should have gone to sleep long time back. I'm James Alibuyog. Go on, take rest," he said waving his hands as if shooing me away.

I started walking towards the E/R exit. The ship was enroute and it was rolling a little, which made it slightly difficult to move ahead, not to mention the exhaustion I was experiencing. I met Sam on the CCR floor.

He looked at me with surprise, "You were still in E/R?! You didn't sleep?"

I was tired and could just manage to say, "I didn't know...nobody told me...yeah am so tired."

"Come let's eat before you sleep."

"Ughh...I don't have the energy to...I'll just go crash."

The good person that he was, he pulled me to the galley saying, "You need to be strong for this job."

I went with him reluctantly to a door that led into a small space and then another door which led us to the galley. It was a huge room equipped with large cooking equipments quite similar to a kitchen of a 5 star hotel. Two people wearing cooks apron and headgear were doing the final preparation for the meal.

Friendly Sam immediately put on his sweet smile and wished them, "Hi Chief Cook, Hi 2nd Cook...good evening. What's for dinner?"

Neither of the cooks smiled, they instead pointed at a printout of the dinner menu. Sam went on as if everything was normal and started reading the menu. He realised he had forgotten to introduce me, "Chief cook, 2nd cook... meet our new Paanch Sa'ab. Sid you know who they are...and yes, they make yummy food."

I went up to them and shook their hands. From the galley I could see the officers' mess on my right and the crew's mess on my left...2 doors connected the galley from the officer's mess while there was only one door for the crew mess. The small space in between the officers' mess and galley had a huge refrigerator which contained the most exclusive range of ice creams, cheese, cakes and chocolates from around the world. There were eggs, butter, jams, spreads, juices, fruits and more.

The cooks had immediately forgotten about me. Sam and I were still standing there, thinking they would say something to us but they didn't, so I thought I should say something before I left, "You guys must be great cooks since Sam keeps talking about you." I felt awkward and was afraid that they would completely ignore what I had just said, but they liked it and laughed for a long time saying I was a funny guy. I obviously hadn't meant it as a joke, it was supposed to be a compliment, but since they found it funny, I wasn't complaining.

I turned around to see what was visible of the officer's mess. To eat in there I had to be in uniform, which seemed like a pain. As I stood there outside the mess, I visualised myself, going to my cabin after my engine room watch, washing, wearing my uniform to come down to eat...enter the mess and become a different person, wish everybody around, keep smiling and pull the chair gently, smile wider while sitting down, strike up conversations with people around while exhibiting excellent manners, keep smiling inspite of not being able to enjoy the food...excuse myself before leaving, getting out of the mess and start breathing again and be happy on getting back to being the same person that I had always been...and then going up to change into a dirty boiler suit before going down to the engine room so I could get sweaty and oily yet again. This painful vicious cycle would go on and on and I would have to keep doing this as a routine. One day it would stop making a difference to me and I would become like the other seasoned engineers on board: an emotionless robot-like engineer. I didn't want to end up this way. Moreover, I was quite happy not being able to socialise with the rest of the officers. I wanted to live in peace and most importantly, eat in peace.

I asked Sam, "Is dinner ready this early everyday?"

Sam replied, "Yes, for poor souls like me who have been on a 6 on--6 off forever, food has to be ready at such odd hours."

I agreed, "You can't wait till you are off at midnight. Makes sense..."

"We'll have to eat in the duty mess", said Sam pointing to my boiler suit, "Not allowed in our mess with that."

"Yea I guessed as much...I may have more meals in duty mess from now on..." I said.

Sam twisted his face and said grimly, "Actually, you lose out on good interactions by eating here. We should eat in the officer's mess. That way we build a rapport with deck officers, Captain, Bada sa'ab. Especially for you...if you don't go to people they tend to forget you. And this is one big family...your family, till you are here."

Though I didn't agree with him entirely, I nodded in

agreement. I was in no mood for an argument and not at all with Sam. "Bada sa'ab? Do we call a Chief Engineer that?"

Sam was surprised, "Uh? You didn't know?"

"How would I? They don't teach that in my college."

By the time I went to bed it was 2000 hours. I was having trouble even focusing on what lay ahead and could hardly keep my eyes open.

I woke up with a start and looked at the watch. It was 7.45 am. I didn't know what time I was expected so I panicked. I got up hurriedly, freshened up to the extent I could in 5 minutes and rushed down to the Engine Room. Sam and 3rd Engineer were waiting for me at the ECR.

"Good morning 3rd... 4th..." I was trying to speak normally but sounded sleepy nonetheless.

"Let's have a quiz today based on what you learnt yesterday," said 3rd.

"Oh?...ok." I was annoyed but I thought I would play along. I wasn't sure if I *had* learnt anything.

"Before we start, there are some rules," said the friendly Sam.

"Ok..."

"Get me that box and hammer. The box contains nails. For every wrong answer we will hammer one nail into your finger, so you have to keep your hands on this wooden table when you answer," 3rd said. I couldn't believe what was happening.

"What! Are you guys joking? At least give me some time to learn before I'm ready to loose my fingers," I shrieked.

"Well, we don't think we have a choice here...I had to pass this test. We all have to." said 4th as he lifted his hands to show his fingers. They had several marks, possibly from nail injuries.

I moved towards the rack, where the box of nails was kept but mid-way turned around and rushed out of ECR and ran down the stairs to the bottom platform. I turned to see 4th and 3rd rush after me. As I had assumed, they were much faster and I feared for my life.

I had been to the bottom platform a day before while

Tengalkar taught me how to transfer waste oil to the waste oil incinerator tank (all the waste oil collected in the E/R is burnt in the incinerator. As per MARPOL guidelines no oil can be pumped out into the sea.). The bottom platform was no different from the other E/R floors. They were made up of several iron plates that were bolted together; it could sustain the weight of heavy equipments and had sufficient strength to be able to tolerate heavy work done on it. Of course the most important use of the platform was to allow the flexibility of having numerous types of machinery, pipelines, open spaces, fittings, etc while having a floor to walk on.

I was running on the bottom platform. I looked up to see them on the floor above. I crossed the main engine and reached the 'aft'est portion of the ship. Just below the floor that I was standing on was the propeller shaft. Below it would be a good place to hide, I thought. I went down carefully, my eyes on the moving shaft. It didn't seem as huge as it did the previous day, and neither had it appeared that it would be rotating at such high speed. I shuddered at the thought of my overalls getting stuck in the moving shaft and my body getting pulled in between the moving shaft and the fixed platform. I could hear footsteps. I touched the bilge floor. The floor was oily so I had to be careful as I moved ahead. There were pipelines all around and overhead was the propeller shaft; my movement would be restricted and I would have to squat as I moved ahead. I moved slowly, carefully avoiding the sheathed pipelines; they were steam lines and even a slight touch would have been enough to burn my skin. Just behind me were the two aft bilge wells. I could see oily water in it. I was trying to work out its depth when Sam spotted me. He shouted, "He's there, give me the gun 3rd. You shot the previous 5th...it's my turn to shoot now."

I couldn't believe my eyes as he took a shotgun from the 3rd. He was aiming at me and was ready to fire. I squirmed in that position; with my movement restricted I was a sitting duck for him.

"Bang"..."bang." He fired twice and missed me by inches. I started pushing back, burnt my back as I touched a steam pipe, lost my balance and fell into the well.

It suddenly became dark...I was still shaking in bed. "Oh God...ughhh...shit!" I muttered as I realised where I was. I woke up relieved.

"Bang!" the noise startled me. I turned around to see my suitcase moving to and fro between the wooden bed and the door. It banged into the door again. The weather was rough and I had forgotten to latch it before I had crashed into my bed last night. My suitcase woke up half the people on my vessel.

Welcome to
the Machines

The weather became rougher and I couldn't sleep for the rest of the night. I was holding on to the sides of the bed while the ship continued to roll. I felt as if I was on a ride that turned on all possible axes of motion. I wondered how anybody could sleep in that kind of weather. Weather was still bad when my alarm went off. I looked at the time, it was 7.15 am. I felt sick. I had to report to Engine Room at 0800. I still had some time so decided to snooze for an extra 20 minutes. I was no better when the alarm went off again. It took me a long while to get out of bed. I lit my brand of cigarette.

I wondered why I had only got two packs from India; I had no choice but to switch to Marlboro, a brand I wasn't too fond of. I had confirmed with Tengalkar the previous day if I could smoke in my cabin enroute. I was happy to have something that reminded me of home. I forgot my worries as I inhaled the smoke but then I immediately blew the smoke out in disgust. The taste was horrible. There was nothing wrong with the cigarettes as I had opened a fresh pack. I knew what was happening. I remembered the time when I had viral fever in college and one of my batchmates had brought me a pack of cigarette as a 'Get well soon' gift. It tasted horrible and the after taste lasted for a day. I knew this about my system; if I didn't feel like smoking, there was something wrong with me. I took twice the amount of toothpaste to brush my teeth, but the horrible taste wouldn't go away. Walking out of the cabin wasn't easy. For one, I was sick and tired and exhausted, and the rolling was so bad that taking a step required great effort. Walking on the moon I was sure was a piece of cake.

I was supposed to be in the 4-8 watch hours i.e. in the 0400-0800 hours and the 1600-2000 hours watch with the 2nd engineer. In an engine room, though the 2nd was incharge of all maintenance work, the machinery and equipment, he still had to do the two watches. But then since he worked all day he didn't care too much about simple things like attending to routine alarms. So before I could assume watch, I had to pick up basic stuff about Engine Room watch-keeping. Till I didn't, the 3rd and 4th Engineers had to share the 2nd's watch apart from doing their own watches, which in turn meant they would be on a 6 on-6 off regime, having to keep watch in turn throughout the day, each doing 6 hours at a stretch. In normal conditions 4th did the watch after 2nd, i.e. 0800-1200 and 2000-0000 and 3rd did after 4th, i.e. 1200-1600 and 0000-0400 hrs.

I didn't feel like eating anything so I just had a glass of juice and a glass of milk; I was reminded of Arnold Schwarzenegger in the movie where he wakes up in the morning, pulls out everything edible from the refrigerator, mixes all in the blender and drinks the concoction. I felt as strong as him for the next 15 seconds and then I reached the E/R door. I had to pull the door open with both my hands.

I climbed down the stairs slowly, my hands firmly on the railing. My legs were so heavy, I was afraid the rolling would make me fall over from the top to the iron platform below. I saw the 4th engineer going down the stairs three steps at a time. I wished I were as strong as him. I felt like throwing up and was trying hard to divert my mind from my present state. I went into the ECR. Inside, 2nd Engineer was busy reading a manual.

I moved towards him and said, "Goodmorning 2nd." He was engrossed in his thoughts and said a gruff Good Morning back. He was a hard worker; Tengalkar and Gadhav were all praises for him. He would start off with the major repairs and go on till late evening completing his list of things to do. The ship was enroute so he was in business; major work happened when ships were in high seas. This was because loading and discharging was normally considered a crucial operation as that was where the revenues for the company were generated from. The objective of sailing was to buy and sell cargo. So watchkeeping during this period was given prime importance. That besides, in port, time was money; the more the amount of time a ship stayed on the port the more were the berthing charges. A lot of times doing a major work could involve delay and a delay in weighing anchor from a port could cause a lot of people to lose their jobs. If the weather was good, stopping the main engine for some work was not a problem. It was only in bad weather, like the one we were in right then that the engines should have been running.

2nd told me, "5th, let's go and work on the fuel pump." I still was struggling to understand him. We came out of the ECR and I was again hit by the sudden change. The noise was maddening and so was the high temperature. He went down to the Engine Main Console in a jiffy and I took forever to reach him. He had his ears on the pump and then went towards the Main Console and shut some valves on a very thin pipe. He didn't realise that I was with him.

He would not have if I had not asked him, "Did you find the problem 2nd?"

He didn't turn and spoke after a long while, "This Engine is controlled by 7 kg air; all controls on this ship are pneumatic. I've just bypassed our pump so that we can repair it."

I could barely understand him...the noise around was too much.

I asked, "2nd can we carry on with the work with the main engine running…?"

"How does that matter! Even now, hardly any fuel is going in there." With that he concentrated his efforts on his job ahead. He looked so intense that I feared asking him any further questions.

"I need 19." I couldn't understand the remainder of his sentence and felt stupid asking him what he had asked for.

The E/R store was behind me and I walked towards it. I saw a tall guy in the store. He was a good looking guy in his early thirties. He looked smart enough to solve my predicament, "Hi, 2nd is asking for something of 19."

He couldn't believe it, "What?!"

I said, "I dunno…I couldn't get what he said. The noise you know…I couldn't hear him properly."

The fitter was grinning. "He would have wanted this. It's called a spanner and the size is 19."

I felt sorry for myself as I took it from him. I was the dumbest person on this planet, I felt convinced, and I knew I didn't belong there.

I went back to give the spanner to 2nd. I looked at him engrossed in work. He was wearing an old green boiler suit, which possibly belonged to another company that he must have worked for earlier in his career. He wasn't wearing any protective gear: no helmets, no gloves and no ear muffs. I looked at myself; I was wearing an orange suit with reflective material on the arms, on my head was an oversized white helmet, over my ears were huge red ear muffs and on my hands were thick cotton creamish gloves. I looked like a person going to a fancy dress competition dressed in a cheap spacesuit.

I wanted to know how not to look like an over-dressed rooster. "2nd, don't we need to wear protective gear?" I asked.

"You can afford to wear it, I can't. If I wear the muff I will not be able to make out if my machines are behaving properly. If I wear gloves I will not be able to work. Noise and touch are most important to understand machines." He added with a wink, "…and also to understand women. But machines are much easier to deal with."

I smiled and said, "Will remember that. And as soon as I go to ECR floor I am discarding these."

He was too busy to be bothered about my clothing. He had opened the pneumatic lines to check the air pressure, which was normal, so he began opening the fuel line. Tengalkar had already kept a lot of rags and buckets nearby as he was expecting 2nd to dirty the area.

After a while he said, "The problem is with the bypass valve, it is leaking fuel constantly through the bypass line. We will have to remove the valve and see. Call the Fitter and the Motorman here."

I brought them both to 2nd and he started explaining the job at hand to them. The alarm went off; it was a loud siren and someone had to run to the ECR to attend to it. There was a switch that had to be pressed to make the noise go off. Though Tengalkar and Gadhav had shown me how to attend to different alarms, I couldn't remember where to go to or what to do in case of any particular alarm.

Since Tengalkar was busy with 2nd I had to go up to attend to it. I climbed the stairs somehow. I went into ECR and looked at the red light flashing on the control panel. It was aft bilge well high level alarm. I pressed the round red knob like button to silence the alarm. The red light of the alarm kept blinking and it would continue to do so till the problem was rectified. I knew the location of the aft bilge well; I had, after all, dreamt about it the last night. I felt like throwing up. And the best place on the ship to be on during rolling was the lowest platform of E/R, the place I was going to now.

I approached Tengalkar told him which alarm it was and went down with him. I looked at him open a few valves quickly. I was too bad a state in to remember which ones were opened. I went to one corner to sit down. He knew I was seasick but he was amused. He said as he laughed, "The sea has got to you. I have seen the bravest cry like babies on a ship…and bad weather is only one of the many reasons to break a guy here."

I puked in reply. My liquid diet came out and then for a while I kept throwing up saliva and mucous. Inspite of emptying out my stomach the feeling of nausea did not go away.

"You should always eat solid stuff in rough weather." I was in no state to register what he was telling me. "What did you have for breakfast?" he said looking at the vomit from the corner of his eyes as if he was expecting to understand my eating habits by studying it.

"One glass orange juice, one glass milk." I said somehow. I didn't feel like getting up.

"Huh?! Oh that's why I don't see any solid stuff in there," he said, pointing at my breakfast. There was something else that was apparently troubling. He kept standing there looking at me and thinking. A few minutes later he asked, "Who drinks milk and juice together?"

Sam came looking for me. He asked, "All well?"

I replied, "I am sick...the weather..."

He said strictly, "When you feel seasick, you should work harder. Work makes you forget this feeling. Now get up."

Where was the energy to work in this environment, I thought. The alarm went off 3 consecutive times. Someone was calling the motorman up in ECR. But Sam was with me, so I wondered who was calling Tengalkar?

Sam told me, "It's for you. Bada sa'ab wants to speak with you."

I held the railing to stand and somehow reached the stairs. It was not even noon, how was I going to last the day? And the next seven months! I could see the *baba*'s smiling face in front of my eyes, mocking me. I climbed up to the 4th floor, was about to faint as I entered the ECR after struggling to push the door open. I saw a tall man in his late forties; he was wearing glasses, which covered half his face, the other half was covered by his moustache and partly by his beard. He was very restless, as if everything around him was not quite right.

He roared, "Which alarm is this?"

"Its bilge high level alarm." I read it out for him.

He suddenly shouted, "The air pressure is dropping in the tank. There would be a leak somewhere! Go check."

I panicked with him, "Sir, which tank? Where do I

check?" He was the Chief Engineer after all and I assumed something would be very wrong.

He shouted, "Don't ask me! Go search for the duty engineer. Rectify this problem fast!"

It was an emergency...I ran out hunting for Mr Sam.

I saw him standing below the blower duct near the boiler. The blower's cool air coming from the duct inflated his boiler suit. He looked like an orange pumpkin.

"4th Chief is calling you. Air pressure of some tank has come down."

We came up again.

Sam rushed in the ECR and said, "Yes Sir."

Chief asked him, "Sam, why is this pressure low?"

"That's the normal pressure chief. The compressor cuts in when starting air bottle reaches 18 bar and cuts off at 25."

Chief said gruffly waving his fingers at me aggressively, "Hmmm, teach the 5th fast. He doesn't seem to be picking up stuff."

Sam responded obediently, "Yes Sir. I will make sure he learns everything."

Sam signalled me to move out with him and once we were out he said, "Sid, buddy you need to pick up stuff fast. Chief Engineer is a different kind of a guy. 2nd Engineer would forget you exist since he will keep on working on his todo list. You need to make that extra effort to learn. Ask me if you need to know anything in particular. But you will have to make that extra effort first."

I saw Chief leave the engine room. I followed Sam to the compressors. I said, "I actually wanted to know about the compressors but I get your point...I will read the manual."

He nodded and said, "3rd is here. It's 12, I need to hand over to him. I will come back again at 6 pm. Until you don't pick up, I've to do 6-12 watches. Don't look so grim. It was just a joke buddy."

3rd had the usual smirk on his face. He signalled to me to join them in the ECR. Another *gyaan* session was coming up...I quietly looked at the handing over procedure. After he was done, he looked at me "So, picked up everything?"

I replied frankly, "No, hardly anything yet 3rd."

He said, "You should already know everything, you are from MEII right? When I joined as a 5th, I wasn't given any time. You are lucky that all of us are helping you out."

All the while that he was speaking, he was wearing his socks and shoes. He should ideally have worn it at the Engine Room entrance.

"I was on duty the first hour itself. Conditions were tough back then. I used to keep working for 12 hours everyday non-stop," he continued.

I tried to look attentive as I thought, "I will not miss food today...can't afford to grow weak." He kept on for the next half hour and as soon as he started a conversation with Gadhav I sneaked out of the ECR.

I wasn't hungry but I knew I had to eat, so I scouted for 2nd and took his permission to leave for lunch. I came out of the Engine Room, went to the day mess and ate some fried rice and chicken. The sight of food was repulsive and I had a few bites somehow. I sat there for a while, looked at my watch. It was 1 pm. I got up and then decided I would sit there for 10 more minutes. I reluctantly got up after 15 mins; my legs couldn't take the weight of my body as if I were chained down in one of those rides which turn in all the directions at very high speed. My thoughts were unclear, my mind dazed as if I were drugged, except that instead of feeling ecstatic I was feeling pathetic.

I came down and decided to divert my mind by studying the engine room. I started taking rounds familiarising myself with the machines, their location, the feel and sound of them while they were running on partial and full load or while performing different operations. I saw 3rd at a floor below standing in front of the fresh water generator. I knew we were overhauling the fresh water generator the next morning. I went to ECR and started searching for the manual on fresh water generator. Main engine, compressors, purifiers, there it was — fresh water generator. Nothing on the rack was where it was supposed to be. I read in the log-book, we made 22 tons of fresh water from sea everyday. This water was utilised in the engine room as a coolant for the main engine and Boiler for making steam. This water was also utilised for us — both for sanitation and drinking; we made our own drinking water! This water was passed through a special electro ion filter which made it bacteria and virus free and also added essential minerals into it — it became as pure as any bottled mineral water. There were different tanks for water to be utilised for different purposes. Though I had studied fresh water generator in the marine auxiliary course, I couldn't recollect the basic fundamental on which it operated. It was so simple that I wondered why I couldn't understand it in college. It worked on a similar principle on which a pressure cooker works. In a pressure cooker because of pressure created inside the vessel the boiling point of water increases from a 100^0 C to 120^0 C. This fastens the cooking process because of the high temperature. In the fresh water generator the exact reverse happens; a special ejector pump creates vacuum inside the bottom portion of the equipment because of which the sea water boils at 70^0 C. The vapours are collected and cooled in the upper portion of the generator and water is collected from there by a pump and sent to different tanks for treatment.

The whole pipeline systems were designed beautifully, but an intricate balance had to be maintained. One little fault somewhere could have serious repercussions for the whole system. I realised the importance of studying all the pipeline systems. It would help me understand how the machines were running and it would help me troubleshoot in case anything went wrong. Chief Engineer wasn't there to disturb me so I set off to go under the bottom platform as that was where some of the complicated pipelines were. Most of the pumps were at the bottom of the platform so it was a good idea to start off there. I felt faint so I sat down on the platform for a while. I started feeling uneasy so got up to go beneath a duct to catch some fresh air. I hadn't even walked a few steps when I started feeling nauseous and within seconds I was throwing up in the bilges. I went to the nearest potable water connection to wash my face. I was feeling weak but better otherwise. I went down in the bilges, there were lots of steam lines. Some of them had exposed parts and I burned myself in a lot of places. There were several jagged edges around and I cut my hands at several places but continued to trace the lines for the next 6 hours. I now had my own diagrams which I could refer to; now I would know how to attend to alarms for all tanks at bottom platform. I knew where the emergency suction valve was, I knew which lines to open to start the two different purifiers. I needed a week to trace the complete pipeline. It was 9 pm and I thought of signing off for the day. I had forgotten all the lessons my mom had taught me since childhood (I had last taken a shower at home) four and a half days back.

While I was taking shower, the crew in the smoking room were discussing me. Like in our smoke room, there were several DVDs, CDs and games available for the crew's entertainment. After dinner people gather in smoking room to chit-chat or watch a movie. The engine room crew, the fitter and motormen where talking about the new 'Paanchu'.

Fitter was laughing, "He doesn't even know what a spanner is! What kind of an engineer is he?!"

Tengalkar nodded, "He runs to a different pump when alarm is for another. I have taught him so many times but he always gets confused. He was puking all over the engine room today...such a weak guy."

The Deck AB (Able Bodied Seaman) said, "He will not last long here. Look at the strong cadet we have on deck. He works with us day in and day out, braves the rough weather and still is cheerful. "

Another AB said, "I haven't seen him yet."

Bosun said, "Nobody has, he's just been here for two days. I would want to meet him too."

The cook had kept aside food for me like last night. Nobody in Engine room cared about my meals but the cook sure remembered. I was feeling much better after the shower. And the food was great. There were two different preparations of meat, and the regular Indian food: *dal*, two *subzis*, *roti* and rice. It was my first meal in the officer's mess. I washed my plate after dinner since I was having meal at hours when the galley was closed. Gone were the days when each ship had 70 people on board. On this ship there were 27 of us. Though the functions were called by the same names as before, each crew member performed beyond the written roles; competition was tough and shipping companies were under pressure to cut costs. Moreover, the infrastructure was much better than before and hence it was easier to get the job done with fewer hands.

Apart from all that, the hygiene factors were much defined and taken care of, safety was of utmost priority and a lot of importance was given to nutritious and tasty food and other hygiene factors like, entertainment facilities and gym for people on board. People had less time to go out and blow away their money in bars and on girls, people drank less as no hard liquor was allowed on board. One could drink beer but then it was allowed only if their watch was not in the next 6 hrs.

Adjoining the mess was the utensils washing area. This was the same place that led into the galley. Apart from the huge twin door fridge there were two microwave ovens and a juicer-mixer-blender. Even if you missed your meal there was enough stuff in the fridge to feast upon. After I had washed my utensils I was conscious of the silence and the fact that there was no one around me. My life had taken a complete turnaround. I was so far away from my loved ones. I wondered how my mother would be coping. And what about Anoushka? The last time I had called them was from Frankfurt airport. The vessel was reaching a small US port called Providence two days from then. I thought I'd call them from there. I ran upstairs to my cabin, hit the bed immediately and started crying like a baby. I don't remember the last time I had cried out loud, the tears kept coming for a while and I don't remember when I dozed off.

I woke up with a start and I thought, "...did I miss the

alarm?" I looked at my watch. It was 6 am, "Ohhh...I can still sleep for an hour more," I thought to myself. In the next one hour I woke up around 10 times and looked at the watch thinking it was time to get up. The alarm went off finally and this time I was in deep sleep. I got up mumbling...the last thing I wanted to do was to go to the engine room. Sam was in the ECR. For someone who didn't know him, he would come across as the friendliest guy on the planet. He was taller than I and looked stronger too. But if we were to have a fight, perhaps I would win. 'Maybe I will hit him with a 19" spanner and stick it up his ass or maybe I should just break his balls,' I smiled when I imagined how his face would twist when the cold metal went inside him.

He smiled warmly as he saw me and said, "Hi Sid! Good morning! You look very fresh today, and for a change, you are smiling!"

I was surprised by the warm welcome, "Hi Sam! Yes I feel fresh...maybe because yesterday I took a shower after five days. I smiled as I pictured something quite interesting."

He shut his eyes, twisted his face and stuck the tongue out in disgust. He said, "We make enough water buddy. You can take shower thrice a day."

"Sam, are we working on the fresh water generators today?"

"Yes we are. Be there, it would be good for you to learn."

I went down, 2nd was already there instructing the motorman and fitter on the job at hand. I had done my homework and wanted to see how it looked from the inside. It was a D-shaped machine. I helped the team open the huge nuts and the door swung open. For Tengalkar and fitter Satya it was a regular job. They must have done this several times in their 20+ years' career. The filters were corrugated titanium sheets; each sheet had gaskets attached to it which separated the water from the fresh water used to boil the sea water. I realised the importance of doing this job correctly. Any small leak meant sea water would enter the fresh water system and Main Engine breakdown was one of the several problems which could be caused because of it.

The total headcount of the engine room was 10 and the handful bunch of people managed the entire operations of this complex and critical part of the vessel. I was glad to be a part of this small team working together on running this ship in proper order. It was cool out on the deck while we were sweating down there. I had burns and bruises on my hand and oil and dirt would get in the wounds- the bruises looked like tattoos and I hoped they stayed there for a long time as I wanted people back home to see how tough I was. No doubt there was a lot of manliness in this job.

"Wooo...wooo...woo..." the alarm went off three times. I could see Chief Engineer in the ECR from down here. He was signalling me to come up.

He asked me, "What are you working on?"

I said panting, "Fresh Water Generator."

"Yes I know that. Where is the 4th?"

"No idea sir, I am working with 2nd."

"What work was happening yesterday afternoon?"

"I was below the bottom platform, tracing pipelines. I don't know what others were working on."

'The bastard thinks he can use me to spy on others,' I thought. I realised his red and puffy eyes were not because of a lack of sleep but because he drank too much. He was chewing cardamoms but inspite of that his breath stank of whisky and nicotine.

He said annoyingly, "You should know what is happening in the Engine room. That's your job. I have to rate you on these parameters."

With a nod I said, "I understand sir." Blackmail, I thought to myself.

He warned me, "You seem to be a little lost. Be smart and alert. People in my team need to be intelligent and strong. Remember that."

"Yes sir."

"We are reaching Providence day after tomorrow. There will be an audit on shore. Come to my cabin after watch. I need your help in seeing whether I have all the required paperwork. It'll be a good learning experience for you. After all you will become Chief Engineer one day."

I said softly, "Maybe..."

He shouted, "Here you go, lost again! What do you mean maybe?"

"I mean yes sir..."

He stated, "You need to improve yourself to a large extent. I need to have confidence in you before I give you any responsibility. And do you understand the meaning of responsibility here? Lives of others are dependant on your watch. It's not an easy job to take."

I promised, "I understand sir and I will give you no reason for complaint. I am giving my best shot."

Batti Sa'ab and 'Discotech'

A thin fair guy entered the ECR. I had seen him running around the Engine room.

"Batti sa'ab, all well?" roared Bada sa'ab.

"Yes sir, I am working on the generators today. Things in place," he said smiling wide, confidence overflowing from in between his teeth.

He next looked towards me, "Hi, you must be the 5th."

"Hello Batti sa'ab." He was the Electrical officer. He smiled in a very peculiar manner, his thin lips tightly pursed together while they twisted upwards and his eyes remained shut; someone could very well confuse his grin and think Batti was in extreme pain...the kind of pain one would experience after being kicked in the balls. Batti was fair, thin and five and half feet tall. He had pencil thin moustache which looked funny on his stupid thin face.

He went and stood in front of the E/R control panel as if checking the alarms. He started a switch which switched on all the tiny bulbs which were under the alarm indicators. He changed 2 bulbs which had gone bad. Chief engineer was looking at him like an owner looks at his stupid dog, and Batti was the stupid dog, who in an over-enthusiasm to please his owner brings in the newspaper all wet with saliva and torn to pieces between his teeth.

Batti noticed Bada sa'ab wasn't interested in his work so he told me, "You need to be very observant. The work that I am doing is very important. If the bulb goes off we will not know whether an alarm has gone off."

I nodded but I had a doubt so I asked, "But Batti sa'ab don't we have an audio alarm too? We will come to know even if a bulb fuses, right?"

He looked uncomfortable and angry, "Of course. I check the audio part of the alarm too every week. And today is that day." He turned the calling switch on for a good 30 sec and then looked at me and said, "You need to be very observant."

Chief engineer looked out of the ECR. He saw 2nd on the other side so he rushed out to meet him.

I responded to Batti, "I will be. I have seen you running in the E/R...attending to any emergency yesterday?"

"Oh no. I was a marathon runner in college. Old habits die hard you know." he said smiling proudly.

Batti went to the electric panel opposite the control console and started dusting it. I came out as I wanted to find out about the pipelines related to the Main Engine, the Boiler, the Control Air System, the Steering Hydraulic system... there were so many things to learn and explore. It didn't matter who the people I was working with were. I knew I would find my happiness in the machines. It was strange when I first entered the Engine room; what hit me was the whole mechanical impersonal feel because of the machines and the pipelines and the heat and noise, but today I was finding solace around these iron beings.

I took off my gloves and helmet and the ear muffs. My plan was to go to every single machine close my eyes and feel the vibrations as they moved in their natural rhythm, gauge temperature of the outer body with my bare hands and then to bring my ear to closely listen to the sound in the different scenarios 2nd mentioned. But I felt exposed like a warrior who had just given up his armour; the noise was too loud and there were high chances of permanent ear damage, there were chances of me being burned and cut on the now exposed hands or worse, something could have fallen on my head and broken my skull. According to my safety training I was not at all being safe but then I somehow believed in what the 2nd had told me. He didn't have an Engineering degree and still was a better engineer than all of us. He treated the machines like his babies while we looked at them as inanimate, hot and noisy objects. It's because he knew that engineering was way beyond the books. It's because he was a hard worker and most importantly it's because he loved what he did.

The 3rd and 4th were all gas; I had hardly seen them work with their own hands. And when they did there was this lazy 'let's get over this fast' look on their face. While when the 2nd worked, it was like a musician composing his nth symphony. It was fun to watch him give directions to people with so much pride. At the end of the day when the work was finished, he would himself try out to see if everything was in order. If all was great, his face would light up and if there was some fault, his face would become stern. Then the very next moment he would clap his hands and start working again till the job was completed to perfection.

"Wooo....wooo...woo..." the alarm was sounded again. I guessed I was being called in. I wondered whether Chief was still around. I climbed the stairs with help from my hands as my legs were not able to support me at all. Chief engineer was walking around the engine room impatiently.

He was panicking yet again. He asked nervously, "Is the fresh water generator running properly?"

"Yes sir, the checks were done long time back and everything is fine."

He commanded, "Now onwards you need to inform me about work progress going on in here."

"Sure sir."

He asked, "What is the water level in the fresh water tanks? Do we have enough water for the boilers? And what about drinking water? We all will lose our job if things go haywire here."

"Sir, I am not aware of that. But I am sure 2nd would have factored that..."

He cut me short, "Hah...the Filipino! He doesn't understand the big picture. He is a good worker, that's it. I am afraid he will screw up some big machinery and then we are doomed."

I understood the problem that this drunkard was facing; 2nd didn't report his jobs to him maybe because he had no respect for him. I went down for my rounds after wasting some time listening to the Chief's babble. I was hardly down for ten minutes when the alarm went off. Tengalkar had stopped attending to the alarms. I had a feeling he had been instructed to do so. I came up again. Chief engineer was hopping mad in the engine room when I reached.

It seemed as if he was about to have a heart attack. He was shouting at the top of his voice, "Boiler fresh water tank low level alarm! Can you see the alarm? I feared this would happen. Do you know what would happen when no water reaches the boiler? It will have to be shut down otherwise it would just buckle under, because of vacuum created inside! With boiler not running, all heavy oil lines will coagulate and the Main Engine would be screwed beyond repair."

I tried to calm him down, "Sir, the FWG is running and I know 2nd started filling one of the tanks. I will find 4th and ask him how to change over and start filling in the boiler tank."

"Do you know the change over valves to boiler tank?"

I nodded my head in negative with a sorry look on my face. He looked as if he was about to explode.

"Where is 4th?"

I sensed trouble but I said calmly, "I will go find him."

He was still shouting as I turned to go find 4th, "I am not confident about you at all. Learn something from Sam. He is so good in his job."

I listened to some more of the mental torture before I told him I better go find 4th and start filling the tank.

I located Mr. Sam chit-chatting with the fitter. I told him about the alarm and he shook his head saying, "Start tracing all the lines. Will be good for all of us."

Once we reached the place he showed the valves, "It's very simple, these two valves have to be opened and those two on the right have to be shut."

"Oh. I see the markings have been made on the pipelines." I observed.

Sam said patting his own back, "Who do you think would have made them? Hmm?"

"Oh. How long have you been here Sam?"

"Ten months."

"Oh wow! You still traced lines inspite of being a 4th!"

He liked what I said and tried not to look happy when he said, "Once you trace lines 50% of your job's done."

I nodded my approval.

"I heard fitter call you Paanchu. Don't entertain this. You are an engineer and Paanchu is demeaning. If you don't speak out, people will take you for granted."

I nodded again. That was a good suggestion.

Batti was coming running towards us.

"He doesn't work, he only runs," said Sam.

"Hi Batti sa'ab. You must be very popular in your hometown since you were an athlete?" I was teasing him.

His lips turned upwards to that silly smile again. I simply loved his smile!

"Yes I have won several medals for my school and college. Nobody knows me anymore in Bombay. But when I go to Himachal some people still recognise me. I was hot property at one time."

I agreed with him, "I am sure you were Batti sa'ab."

Sam excused himself and took off in a hurry.

Batti was really happy with me so he asked, "5th, do you want to go to a 'discotech' in Providence?"

"Discotheque? I am not too sure. It's my first port and not sure if I will get time. I will have to ask 2nd."

Batti said, "You can come with me when you are off. I will ask 2nd to let you go with me."

"But I am not too fond of discs especially in strange countries. I won't be too comfortable."

He said assuring me, "I'll be there, not to worry. I always go to discotech in every port I go out to. It's always a refreshing experience to dance away your worries. In fact I'm so fond of dancing that on the day my kids are home I turn my drawing room to a discotech and then teach my latest moves to my children."

"Oh?" that is all I could manage to say.

"You must be wondering where I learn my new moves."

I had to nod, "Of course I was just about to ask."

He smiled (oh how I loved to see him smile!) and said, "Instincts! I have it inside me. I just go with the rhythm."

I looked at him with amazement; if I dressed him suitably he would look like a waiter in a tea stall. His mental capabilities too would suit that job perfectly; I could just imagine how he would dance. I had to ask, "How do you turn your drawing room into a disc?"

"Oh I am a Batti sa'ab, I can do that in seconds."

"Oh yes, so silly of me to ask you that." I looked at him acting as if I was super-impressed with him. And he obviously loved me for that, "5th, if you need any help here you let me know. I will teach you. I'll tell you a secret, it seems complicated but it actually isn't. It took me years to realise this..."

I almost saluted him for what he had just shared with me, "Batti sa'ab, you're a life saver. Thank you!"

Everyday was different here. Some things were always the same though. I was ridiculed daily by the Chief, 3rd and 4th but then there was solace in the fact that at least I was learning something new everyday. I still had a long way to go before I familiarised myself with basic stuff.

Chief engineer had called me to arrange the filing cabinet. There was nothing to be done. He was gulping down Blue Label and making me arrange his stupid cabinet as if I were his servant. He was the only person on board who had absolutely nothing to do. And there I was to double check in his cabinet if some file was missing; his files never went out anywhere so there was no reason why anything would be misplaced. He had called me at 10 pm and it was midnight now. I had checked the cabinets thrice in this time and finally told him that all was in place, but he wouldn't let me go.

"I have three daughters. Have to marry them one-by-one." He continued as he took another gulp "Very difficult to get good guys these days."

I was trying hard to keep my cool, "So true sir."

"You can't even trust your own sons and daughter these days. The new generation of today doesn't understand the responsibilities."

"What's your plan?" he continued when I didn't react to his previous statement.

"I will continue with tracing the lines till..."

"No, no. plans for life, career, marriage, etc."

"I am seeing someone. One day I will get married to her."

His expressions changed but he kept shut. I didn't want him to think I was available to get married to his daughter. He kept mum for a long time almost sulking and then he let me go with an advice, "You pick up stuff fast and for that you'll have to keep an open mind. Be ready to listen to your seniors otherwise even I'll not be able to help you."

His sudden rudeness was uncalled for but I was happy to get away from his stinking cabin, "Goodnight sir."

I was like this ghost on the ship. I did meet some of the crew members while rushing down or coming up but I never spoke with anyone except for an occasional 'Hi'. I am sure everyone was curious to know me. After all I was the new member of the family.

Next day on my way down to the Engine room store I heard the fitter call me out "Paanchu, Paanchu..." I didn't enter the store, took a left and went towards the boiler. He came up behind me.

"Paanchu, good morning. I was calling you," he said in a friendly manner.

But I remembered what Sam had told me, "Satya, my name is Siddhartha, or you call me 5th like others do."

"Sure Siddhartha. Sid is fine?" I had taken him by surprise.

I immediately realised that I had been rude to him. He was being nice to me and maybe he didn't deserve this treatment. He went back with a wooden face as I stood there thinking what to say next.

Meanwhile in ECR, Chief and 2nd were discussing an important subject, Watch keeping.

"4th and 3rd can't go on doing 6 on-6 off forever. When do you plan to start keeping watch...you can keep 5th with you," Bada sa'ab was telling 2nd.

2nd brushed the suggestion off with his trademark movement of hands in air, "He wouldn't be ready so early. He's just been here for four days? Five days? I took a month to learn everything about the Engine room. I am sure you would have taken the same time. We'll see in a week or two. Not before that."

"But till when would this 6 on-6 off go on?" Chief was concerned about his blue eyed boy, Sam.

"Chief, I have got a lot of stuff to do. I can't do that while I am on watch. I need people with me to complete maintenance jobs. I can't call the fitter at 4 am on my watch. I will have to continue with the day job (0800-1800). One way can be to keep 5th on the 0400-0800 and 1600-2000 watch of mine. We will keep Tengalkar with him, he is our best motorman."

Chief panicked, "5th independently handling a watch?! No way! Let 3rd and 4th continue 6 on-6 off till 5th gives me the confidence."

Though I thought I was getting used to the taunts I had to listen to throughout the day, and though I thought it was ok that I had no friends on board and though I thought I would be alright, I actually wasn't. That night was the third night when I ended up crying in bed, while a Rajnikant movie was running in the Crew's smoke room. It was 2200 hours and attendance was highest at this point of time. Normally the old guys went to bed by this time but the others didn't sleep before 2300 hours.

Bosun was enjoying his South Indian superstar flick. He suddenly asked the few members of Engine room crew, "What's happening down there these days?"

Tengalkar was smoking his 555 cigarette, "Paanchu is learning very slowly. He is so confused, still can't remember what to do for a particular alarm."

Satya, the fitter, was making faces as he said, "He's got a lot of ego because he is an Engineer."

Bosun asked, his eyes on the TV screen, "Why do you say so?"

Satya replied, "He doesn't like being called Paanchu. We always call a 5th Engineer that."

Bosun looked at Satya and Tengalkar and said, "Hmmm... yes Paanchu is the name and that's what we will call him."

Able bodied seaman, Ramanna asked, "But what does he want to be called as?"

Satya replied, "Either 5th or his name."

Bosun said smiling, "He will have to prove himself to be an Engineer on this ship. We don't understand university degrees, we understand people. If he is competent enough, he can choose his name, otherwise Paanchu is fine. I have seen many paanchus in my career, they are confused throughout their tenure. Today I saw him go down to the Engine room. His body language clearly states he is a loser. His confidence level is low and he should be bothered about learning rather than what people call him," he chuckled naughtily and continued, "Even Sam was a Paanchu here. He joined this ship as a 5th; he was promoted on board to 4th 3 months back. He is flying now because he has spent this long on this ship. He has been a Paanchu in his last two ships and you would expect one to learn in 18 months. Inspite of that when he came here he was pathetic. He started picking only after two months of working here and that too only after 3rd engineer complained to 2nd and Chief. 2nd also isn't bothered about his people and this guy was having a good time initially. The bastard is having a good time again. Nobody grows fat on deck and in the Engine room, while this guy is getting fatter by the day."

On the ship Bosun was a respected guy. He had spent his life working as a deck hand and he knew how to take care of the deck and the machines and equipment on the deck. The whole exposed portion of the ship and the deck was his responsibility. The whole deck crew reported to him. Not so far back when there were no restrictions on the manpower, the able bodied seaman was only supposed to be on the bridge and would follow Deck officer's instruction on turning the wheel to a particular direction. The able bodied of today worked on deck under Bosun and he was required on bridge with Deck officer only when in high traffic routes or tricky waters or in bad weather or when maneouvering into a part. Other than that he worked on deck with Bosun and his team like a regular deck hand. There were a total of 27 people on board in Motor Tanker Limar and the headcount would become 28 the next day as a Turkish fitter was joining the Engine room in Providence.

Next day in the Engine room the only guy who was charged up was Batti; afterall he was visiting the 'discotech'. And I was going there with him. 2nd was quite cool about me going out and he told me to go have fun.

I was ready by 8.30 pm and Batti had told me that he would be ready by 9. I had purchased calling cards to call home. From the deck I could see two phone booths at the jetty. I went down and called home first. My mom picked up the phone and she sounded quite tense.

"Ma, it's me. How are you doing?"

"God! Where are you? Why didn't you call for so long? We were going crazy thinking whether you were alright!"

"Ma, I can't call from the ship, it's very expensive. I can call when I reach a US port or a European port. Not from South America. So there may be days or weeks that I may not be able to call. But don't worry, it's a good strong ship and people are nice. I am well taken care of."

She said almost sobbing, "How are you feeling? Do you miss us?"

"What kind of a question is that? Of course I miss you folks."

I spoke with her at length describing my journey, my stay, people on board and the food. Of course I didn't tell her the facts, just cooked up some good stories so as to make her comfortable.

The next call was to Anoushka. Luckily she picked up the phone.

"Anu! Baby how are you?"

"Sid! Nice to hear your voice! It's been a long time! How have you been?"

"Am good Anu. What's up at home? I miss Ranchi so much!"

"And me? You don't miss me?"

"Obviously I miss you, miss you the most actually. But am happy to have met you and feel your importance in my life today, when you are not near me. The wait to see you again is painful but it makes this journey worth taking, as I know am gonna see you soon, super soon."

"You are a sweetheart Sid. Am glad you came into my life."

I could see Batti coming down to the jetty. I tried to tell him the other phone was out of order and that I would be done in two minutes. He still went in the booth and kept on looking at the "out of order" sign for a while. On the phone, the typed instructions said "In case of emergency dial 911". A 911 can be dialled even if the phone is out of order. And I would have expected Batti to know what 911 stands for since he had been on the ship for 'Oh so long'. As I had expected he went ahead and dialled 911.

A woman picked up, "May I know your location of call sir? Sir, all well? How may I help you? Sir?"

Batti responded, "Ma'm I am trying to call India. There's a strange dial tone on this phone...I am not able to connect."

The voice on the other side said, "Sir, can you respond properly to my questions? I cannot understand your accent. You are not in India, sir I need your location?"

"Oh it's mentioned here that the phone is out of order! I am on a jetty..." and then Batti looked at me and I was signalling him to cut the crap and keep the phone down.

Batti finally knew he had fucked up big time and immediately hung the phone. The port official sitting at the exit saw Batti using the phone and came to us and asked "Who were you speaking with? The phone's out of order! I hope you didn't dial 911!"

I was trying to pay attention to Anoushka as she

described how she scolded the neighbours for throwing stones at a street dog who she fed everyday.

Within seconds four police vehicles, lights flashing and siren wailing arrived on the jetty.

I panicked, "Listen Anu I will call you in a few days. I am ok here and you take care too. Miss you badly…gotta go now."

"I love you Siddhartha. Be back soon."

7-8 armed cops came out immediately and flashed lights on us. One of them shouted "Sir, all well here?"

The jetty officer said, "Nothing to worry, they are new to this place. The phone is out of order and one of them dialled 911 by mistake."

Batti's face was ashen and so was mine. He had lost his voice completely. I came forward. "It's my mistake, sir, I dialled 911. It's my first ship and first time to the US…I didn't know it was an emergency number. I am sorry."

They looked at my face for a while. One of them asked "Which country are you from?"

"India," I said smiling sheepishly.

They asked a few routine questions and warned us not to repeat this mistake.

"Officers, we understand we have wasted your time. It will not happen again," I said as they moved to their cars.

Our cab was already there and the cabbie was witnessing the drama with interest.

Batti took lead now, "Take us to a discotech please."

He asked amused, "Do you mean Discotheque? There's one in downtown. What did you guys do? Kill someone?!"

"Oh, nothing unusual. He was just trying to call home!" I said pointing at Batti.

The cabbie was laughing while Batti was enjoying the attention.

"Ok take us to the nearest Discotech," ordered, Batti,

It was a midsized US town. It was a massive change from India: wide roads, fewer vehicles, not a human on the roads, obviously no animals either. We were moving towards the busy side of the town.

At the entrance of the disc stood a bald, burly, very tall man. He asked for our identification. I showed him my driving license from India.

He demanded, "Raanchiii, where is that place?"

I said with a smile, "Oh, it's not in the US, it's in India. We work on a ship."

"Do you have your shore pass?"

"Yes."

He let us in reluctantly giving us warning looks as if saying "You guys better not create problem here."

Inside, the mood was exciting: neon lights, great sound system and loud techno music. I could see only young guys around, mostly couples or groups. Batti and I were the odd couple here. Batti sported his usual stupid grin on his face and his grin was wider today...his expressions were as if he had just taken the party drug 'ecstasy'. I went to the bar and made myself comfortable on a stool. It was a nice place. There was a huge dance floor on the left portion of the disc. Straight ahead of me was an extended part of the dance floor which was elevated in a way that would be visible from all the corners of the disc and would have been made for special performances. This circular portion had steel rounded railings and a pole in between. Special lights were devoted to this portion as well. On the right were the seating areas for groups who wanted to quietly enjoy their drinks.

I asked Batti what he wanted to drink. He replied, "I don't drink but when I come to a discotech I normally dance with a beer bottle in hand and a cigarette dangling in between my lips."

I asked worriedly, "You smoke while dancing?"

He said, "No... I don't light my cigarette. I don't smoke either."

I couldn't make up my mind about what would look better on Batti an unlit cigarette between his lips or a lit one. I just hoped he didn't get us into trouble. He took an unlit cigarette from me and a pint of Budweiser, and headed straight to the dance floor. The dance floor was occupied with young couples enjoying their moment of togetherness.

There entered Batti with a bottle in hand and a cigarette in his mouth and he obviously was dancing like a big jerk, spilling beer on the floor. He had the silly grin on his stupid face and his face was twisted as if he were about to have multiple orgasms. I wanted to hide my face when I saw him dance. His steps were obscenely ridiculous. I sat there wondering how somebody could be so amazingly stupid. Since he was dancing with his eyes tightly shut he could not notice the repulsive glances he was getting from people around him? I felt like walking up to him and kicking him on his butt, hold his ear and pull him back to the bar. His dance steps were totally out of this world; his legs were wide open and his arms were wide open too. He was shaking his chest sideways and he moved his arms and legs out and in with every body movement. I was worried sick that he would hit someone dancing next to him. I didn't want to see him anymore. I turned my attention towards a young lady dancing on the elevated dance floor. She moved like a silk cloth in a light breeze. Her body moved effortlessly in sync with the beats of the music. She used her hands to support herself on the railings at times and sometimes the centre pole. What a contrast! We should bring Batti and this young woman together, I thought. What a couple they would make! I was smiling at the thought. I saw a guy in a black leather jacket walk by me, giving me a stare. He went up to the woman and gave a kiss her cheek. I wanted to tell the big guy, "Hey it's not like what it seems, and I am just looking. No intentions at all buddy." He kept staring at me. I turned towards the bar and asked for another Budweiser for myself. The guy sitting next to me spoke to me in a language I didn't understand.

"I didn't get you," I shouted

"Are you Greek?" he said in English this time.

I replied, "No, no...Indian. Are you Greek?"

He said smiling, "Nah, I am from here but I understand some Greek language. I travel to Greece quite often for work. You look Greek so I thought I will chat with you."

This Greek lover moved in closer, apparently so that

he could converse with me. I wanted to tell him that my mom had told me not to talk to strangers.

He asked nervously, "Are you done from here?"

"Don't know, it depends on my colleague dancing there," I said pointing to Batti doing the jungle dance. He kept studying Batti for a while and then he said, "What does he have that I don't?"

Just because I am not here with a girl doesn't mean I am not interested in them but then this guy was too drunk to see reason so I thought of playing along with him, "Can you move your ass like that? He does so in bed too. And he's got the softest pair!"

He wasn't expecting me to come out with that so soon and so brutally so he moved back a little. I felt sorry for him. I have been given a pass by men before. It used to disturb me initially but then I realised that I was as different to them as they were to me. For some liking a guy was a reality, but for me it was different.

And reality can be different for different people and that was something which Vikram taught me. It happened around two and a half years back. I was in the 2nd year and Vikram in 3rd. It was the time when Vikram was in a real bad state. He had started going heavy on pot, his friends had drifted away from him. In the loneliness of his room he would start imagining himself to be the character he was reading about as he smoked countless rounds of marijuana. He would be reading about killers, mad men, artists, etc, all geniuses in their own right. Slowly his mind started playing games with him and he went into serious depression. He began to act strangely: he would roam around the college without his slippers and sometimes he would come naked to play volleyball with his batchmates. His behaviour had become very unpredictable and hence he had become more dangerous than he had been before.

We, the second years, lived in one wing and there was one phone in the hostel. One of my batchmates was shouting for me, "Sid your phone call."

I went down. "Hello?"

"Son, this is Vikram's father."

"*Namaste.* How are you sir?"

He said, "*Beta*, Vikram is not too well. He has stopped taking our calls. We are worried about him. Will you visit him at times to make sure he is alright? It will be a great favour to us. His uncle would come next week to bring him home. Till then please take care of him."

"I will, don't worry sir."

After the night fall in (attendance used to happen four times daily and we had to report in our uniforms and fall-in for attendance; it was a paramilitary institute.) I went searching for him. I learned that he had stopped reporting to the fall-ins. I found him outside his room, in his trousers, no slippers, no shirt...

He had seen me coming and kept staring with eyes drawn narrow but he looked away when I reached him. I didn't know what to talk to him about and I feared he would react aggressively. I stayed quiet for a while, looking in the same direction as he was.

I said finally, "How you doing Vikram? It's been a while..."

"Do you have cigarettes on you? Go away if you don't."

"Ha! Yes I have cigarettes."

He turned towards me and started punching me on my body. I was surprised that he didn't hurt me at all...maybe he had grown quite weak or maybe I wasn't as weak as I thought I was. I didn't retaliate and while he was still at it I said, "Showering your love on me, are you?"

He smiled. He must have smiled for the first time in months. He realised he wasn't supposed to as he was playing a role in which his character didn't smile, so he became wooden again.

I sat next to him in the balcony. The sun had almost set and the sky had turned crimson, the birds were returning to their nests and hence there was lot of activity around the trees in front of us.

He said looking at the *Ashoka* tree in front of us, "The crow that lives in this tree comes to visit me everyday. He comes in my room, takes two circles around my bed and sits on top of the cupboard for a while and then talks with me. He then leaves."

I asked curiously, "Do you understand what he says?"

"Not yet but I will in some days. I think he was my brother in my previous birth."

He wasn't making any sense but I had to act normal with him. It was important that he felt comfortable with me around.

"When I sleep naked, the red ants in my room come all over me. Thousands of ants cover up my body completely. I know what you are thinking, none of them bite me." He continued.

I remained silent for a while digesting what he just said and then asked, "Are you taking your meals properly? The body and mind need the fuel."

"I eat when required, one meal a day is enough for me. Mind gets accustomed to anything; it can be trained to do anything. The body listens to the mind and I can go on weeks without eating."

"I understand all that Vikram. But you would become weak and your mind may not be able to function at its optimal level..."

He said angrily, "You don't want to believe what's difficult for you to grasp. Magic is all around you, open your eyes to see it. Supernatural events take place in our world. Ghosts exist amongst us. Just because somebody can see things and others cannot, doesn't mean he is schizophrenic. What a normal human mind can't understand is termed 'hallucination' and when somebody starts to see it, he's either put on medication or sent to the asylum. In our Vedas, in Mahabharata, in Ramayana, there are several instances in which a king or a warrior or a sage goes on meditating for years together to achieve enlightenment or to meet God. Those people also go without eating or drinking for years. Do you know how they survived?" he paused for a while and then continued, "They had trained their minds to reach a different dimension...a dimension where the reality that we know of, ceases to exist, a dimension where our world exists but in a way that is beyond your imagination. So the next time when you meet a mad person, there's a lot of chance that he isn't mad but that he has reached that different dimension. The reality as you see it may be different for me."

Vikram's uncle came to take him in two days. They took Vikram to a mental asylum in Ranchi. He was there for a month or so and was given electric shocks on a daily basis. He came back and joined college but he was not his usual self anymore. My meetings with him had become quite irregular and whenever I met him he remained quiet most of the times. Today, he was getting back to a normal life, maybe not back to his normal self; his old self was lost somewhere in the past. In spite of the state he was in, how could he stop the crickets from chirping?

I didn't realise I was looking at the girl again. She had amazing moves; I wished I could dance like that. She was looking at me too. Whenever she turned towards me she kept watching me as she danced. I knew her jealous friend would be somewhere in the crowd watching me. I looked away; I didn't want to get into any trouble; not now, not here. Batti was still dancing away to glory, making a big fool of himself. People around him were visibly angry and I had to bring him back or else we were getting into a lot of trouble.

I tapped on his shoulders and said strictly, "Batti sa'ab, we have to go."

"Hey come on join me for a dance. I will teach you." He was talking as if he were drunk and behaving drunk as well. The bastard hadn't even taken a sip of his beer. I held his arm and pulled him out of there. He looked surprised and angry.

I explained, "You are the only single guy dancing amongst couples. It's time to go back to the ship."

We came out. I knew the way back was simple but it was a little long; not that it wasn't walkable but I had not seen anybody walking on the highway. We had to call a cab but we didn't have the number. We stood near the road to take down the phone number displayed on the cabs passing by so that we could call and book one for us.

A crowd of young guys came out of the discotheque. They crossed us and began kicking at a beautiful sports car parked around ten feet from us. The alarm went off. Batti was unaware of what was happening near him, he was ogling at the women drivers on the road. The guy who was kicking the car returned with a few more people pointing towards us as he had an agitated conversation with them. The guy who was kicking the car was the boyfriend of the girl dancing inside. He had set off the alarm and called the owner most likely telling him that we were responsible for it.

He came near me with the group close behind. He walked towards me aggressively and shouted, "What the fuck man! What were you doing with my car?"

I raised both my hands in the air and said, "We have been standing here since we came out of the disc. I didn't touch your car but I saw your friend kicking it." I tried to remain calm. I feared he would hit me and had he done that I was sure other friends would have joined in; they were eagerly waiting for the ring leader to make the first move.

The guy in leather jacket told the owner, "Look at his nerve. He is blaming me for it. Hit him hard."

I tried to remain calm, "Look friend, I don't know you so I have no reason for messing with your car. I am a guest in your country and I was standing right here waiting for the cab to arrive. Why would I touch your car?"

The owner was livid and real angry apart from being drunk. I don't know if he saw reason, I don't know if he saw truth in my eyes, or don't know if I was plain lucky as the guy didn't hit me. He held his arm pointing to the highway. "Go back to your fucking country!"

Batti still didn't understand what was happening. I told him urgently, "Batti sa'ab lets leave!"

"Huh? And what about the taxi? What were they telling you? Did you do something wrong to them?"

I couldn't believe he was saying that. I said angrily, "They were not telling! They were threatening. Now if you want to reach the ship in one piece run away from here."

We made a quick exit in the opposite direction. The guys threw some stones our way, luckily all missing target. We decided to walk back to the ship. Midway it started raining. I was impressed with Batti; this guy goes to 'discotech' in every bloody port but he still doesn't know how to call a cab! I had come out thinking Batti would know which part of town we were in but he wasn't sure. I remembered some of the landmarks I had seen while going to the disc so knew we were on the right track. I felt stupid walking on the road as vehicles zipped by us. Everybody was giving us strange looks; it must have been quite a sight, two Indians walking on a highway in US and that too when it was pouring heavily. We reached the ship after walking for an hour. What an eventful evening it had been...

10
CHAPTER

The Case of the Left Eye

As soon as I set foot on ship, the sudden change reminded me how different our life was from that of people on shore. It was as if the gangway ladder had brought me to another world, a world where a person was of no consequence...where there was no room for errors, only logic and practicality worked.

I feared if I stayed longer I would become like them, emotionless and mechanical. The ship looked like a cold heartless dark knight. I shuddered as I felt a cold shiver go down my spine. The doubts were back. Walking on the highway in the cold rain felt better than being here.

I was standing alone on the deck. I could see Batti up ahead getting in the accommodation from the lifeboat deck.

"Hey 5th!" The noise startled me to death. I turned around and saw a tall young guy coming towards me.

"Hello?" I said extending my hand towards him.

The young man said, "Hi, we have not met yet. My name is Param. I am the Deck Cadet." He was tall, well built and good looking.

I said as we shook hands, "Hi Param. Siddhartha. You working late?"

"Yeah have to, discharging is still on. Have you met the Deck Crew?"

"No, I have hardly met anywhere here."

"You had gone out with Batti sa'ab. Enjoyed?"

"Yes thoroughly. I am glad to come back here though."

He looked confused but I didn't know what to tell him.

His walkie-talkie crackled.

"Param come in," said the voice on the other end.

"Param here Chief."

Chief Officer said, "Pump # 2 is losing power, switching over to pump # 3. Be there at the Pump Room, check and report."

"Copied that Chief."

With that Param went inside the pump room. The entrance to this room was just ahead of the accommodation. The stairs led to the four huge pumps which were used to discharge cargo from our tanks to the shore. These pumps were run by engines which were on the engine room side. These engines were actually engines cum generators. On voyages these machines ran on generator mode so as to supply power to the whole ship, while they were engaged to gear when the pumps had to be run.

One of the pumps was not building up pressure so next day I joined the 2nd and fitter to go down to repair it. We were en route at 0800 hours and planned to go to pump room once we were at full speed ahead.

The pump room is an enclosed space and since oil vapours are present here, a powerful exhaust fan keeps purging the space all throughout the discharge operation and continues to run two to three hours after the discharge is complete.

It still was hot inside the pump room and oil vapours present, so breathing was difficult and the smell was quite pungent. The pump was huge, to dismount it wasn't an easy task for three people, especially when I wasn't too much of a help. We used a lot of portable cranes to affix different parts of the pump before it was overhauled. The problem was not major, just a faulty gasket, but replacing it required a lot of expertise. We struggled for over three hours before the final nut was tightened. By this time Chief Engineer was there. He must have gone to Engine Room and Sam would have told him about the problem. It was time to test the pump; Engine Room was signalled to start the engine and engage pump. The pump started with 2nd and fitter near the portion where the shaft entered the pump; there was no leak. The Cargo Control Room confirmed the pump was working to its full capacity. I was wiping my hands with a rag. These waste clothes were the most important useless stuff in the Engine room. They are made from discarded t-shirts, shirts and tops cut into small pieces and disinfected before being sold to ships. 2nd had a habit of choosing the best one of these to tie around his head like a bandana. Today he was wearing a 'D&G' bandana.

"The pump is not working properly! Did you guys even check the pressure gauge? It is fluctuating! Tell Engine Room to stop the engine fast!" roared Bada sa'ab.

"Chief, everything is in order; the cargo room just confirmed that the pump is working on full capacity. The gauge isn't showing proper reading maybe because of air lock. It just needs purging." 2nd replied in an agitated tone.

Chief ordered, "So purge it now."

2nd tried to reason, "But Chief the pump is..."

Chief insisted, "Purge it now 2nd."

2nd thought for a while, threw his hands up in the air as if saying "Ok, what the fuck!" he then started opening the gauge. He was careful to bend himself in one direction. Chief was standing on the other end. And it happened exactly the way he had planned it...oil at full speed jetted in Chief's direction. The jet splashed all over his left eye...lucky for him, he was wearing his spectacles.

Chief screamed in pain, "Ahh....close it...close it! Fast! I am blind! Someone give me a rag!"

Since nobody offered him one he took the liberty of rushing towards 2nd and borrowing his D&G designer rag. From that day onwards his left eye shrunk in size and it kept blinking. He tried hard to keep his eye from constantly blinking and that resulted in further damage to his already ugly face; it became his habit to contort his left cheek muscles while the right side seemed relaxed. His face had begun to look like an over-sized pumpkin half of which had shrivelled because of over-ripening.

I had completed a week on board. Things hadn't changed much for me. I was working non stop throughout the day and till late night. I had no clue whether I was learning anything. I would work with 2nd on something, then 4th would 'borrow' me from him for his work. When his watch of six hours would get over, 3rd would do the same. When an alarm rang I would accompany the motorman to see how to resolve the particular issue. There were hundreds of alarms; I would still get confused between them. There were so many things going on at the same time. I had to talk to 2nd about this.

"Hi 2nd, can I talk to you for a minute." He was in the store room inspecting the high pressure tools of Main Engine.

"Yes? He said looking at the hydraulic connector."

"How do you think I should learn the basics of watch-keeping?"

"Oh, you can learn with motorman. Trace pipelines." I was beginning to understand his English inspite of the accent.

I blurted, "But 2nd there are too many things happening. I am getting part knowledge of this and part knowledge of that. This way I don't know when I will learn anything."

"Are you complaining 5th? You will have to manage the learning part with the regular work." He stared at me as if I had blamed him.

I said carefully, "2nd I didn't mean that. I am asking for your help...guidance."

"I already told you how to do it. I had a talk with Chief. Till the time you learn, 4th and 3rd are 6 on-6 off. You have to pick up fast." I looked at him confused and helpless. He didn't care anything apart from his work. He looked at me and went back to work. Satya was overhearing this. He signalled me outside. I followed him out of the store room. He was standing near the A/C compressors.

Satya said comfortingly, "Wrong timing...he is in a bad mood. Main engine repair is due and Chief Engineer wants to delay it. He thinks Chief doesn't trust him. He was saying he has worked on 50 different kinds of main engines and he has carried repairs on engines a thousand times."

"Oh...I didn't know. I needed help." I felt ashamed of myself. On top of that I was rude to Satya but he was helping me out.

Satya confided in me, "Listen I have been with this 2nd for seven months now. Sam, 4th Engineer was here too. But then he wasn't a 4th."

This was news! I exclaimed, "What was he then? No don't tell me he was promoted on board!"

"Why do you think he is having a good time? Yes he joined as a 5th here. You can learn a lot of stuff from him. He knows the pipelines in and out."

"Oh, I will ask him then..." I said though I knew he would not help.

Satya looked at me and understood, "I will tell you something else...2nd is a hard worker. He will forget you exist. Take this opportunity to learn basic stuff. Start tracing lines. The duty engineers are there for the watch. You are not responsible for any machinery...you are not responsible for any watch so basically you don't have any responsibilities. Get it?"

He was right. I had to prioritise my work; I had to make myself busy otherwise people will keep using me as an additional motorman. I had to disappear behind the pipelines and keep learning. I would have to learn about all the alarms with the help from the motormen. But I had to trace all lines first in order to stop getting confused between the alarms. I went down below the bottom platform again and continued where I left the other day. I kept tracing lines till late night. I had informed the motormen of all watches that I would be in bilges, tracing lines and that it would be difficult for me to attend to alarms. They would have informed duty engineers; 3rd and 4th were smart enough not to disturb me as they wanted me to pick up stuff ASAP. As a special favour I had asked the motormen not to disclose my location to Chief Engineer. He would not trouble them once they told him that they had no idea where I was. I knew he wouldn't come down searching for me as he always came to Engine Control Room improperly dressed for the occasion; he would be wearing 'unwashed for weeks' uniform on his stinking leather sandals.

I came up to ECR at 2130. Sam was sitting there chatting with the oiler.

He looked surprised as he said, "Oh. 5th, you were still down there?"

"Hi 4th. I was tracing lines."

Sam said coldly, "You should have completed all by now, right? It takes only two days of sincere effort to complete all the lines of Engine Room."

I said apologetically, "Sadly I haven't yet. I have completed 80% of pipelines beneath the bottom platform. I still have to trace the remaining 20% and then the ones on the other floors."

He was clearly not happy. He said, "You are going real slow buddy. At this rate you will take time to get ready. 3rd is getting impatient, you see. We have been 6 on-6 off for a long time now. "

"Yes-yes, I understand and am trying to just focus on learning these things first. That's why I remained invisible throughout the day. "

He shook his head with disgust as he said, "You are lucky. I never got to learn stuff like you. If I were you, I would be multi tasking all the time. We all are making an exception for you, you need to appreciate that. Understand that things aren't made so easy for people; you can't just trace lines and not attend the alarm. Tomorrow onwards you will have to manage both and also help me and 3rd on whatever work we are doing. I am saying as a friend, don't misunderstand me as I say this, till the time you have learnt your work nobody will respect you here."

Maybe he was right; I guess I was slow after all. And yes I couldn't afford to just do one work all through the day, I was at work and I would have to multi-task.

I asked, "Do you think I should continue tracing lines even now?"

He advised, "No, it's dangerous. Only two people on watch now. Start afresh tomorrow but finish it off as soon as possible."

I went back to my cabin dejected.

Next day I started tracing lines as soon as I hit the Engine Room. Armed with a flash light, a paper and pen I went down in the bilges again. I started from where I had left the other day. I hadn't spent ten minutes there when the alarm went off. I was in the bilges and that day I had gone into areas not very accessible. I had gone in between pipelines, carefully avoiding moving parts and steam lines, to reach where I was. There was no way I could come out from there and climb up to the bottom platform in less than five minutes. Then I would have to dry and clean my shoes so as to not dirty the floors with oil stains, and by the time I would have rushed up a good nine to ten minutes would be gone. I had no option but to attend the alarm as I knew motormen would not be attending it. I was right, the alarm kept ringing as I was doing an obstacle race in the bilges and it kept ringing when I was rushing up. I reached the ECR and saw Sam coolly sitting there chatting with Batti. I came in ignoring them and pressed the button to stop the alarm. I looked at the flickering light; it was Heavy Oil Purifier tank high level alarm. I would have to transfer oil from this tank to waste oil storage tank. I hadn't seen this alarm before so I went scouting for Tengalkar.

By the end of the day I could not even complete one percent of the bilge pipelines. I had to slime in and then slime out hundreds of time for the different alarms. And then Chief had come in and he needed an audience to see his panic stricken performance. When I heard the siren go off 3 times I knew I was being called. He started off by asking his usual questions about what was happening in the E/R and this time I looked towards the board on which 2nd writes every morning about the job to be done and the person responsible for it. He didn't catch my hint so I read the list out for him. He wasn't satisfied with that, maybe because he needed a live update on what the reactions of people were on doing their respective jobs, the amount of energy people were putting in, screw-ups if any which happened in the day, politics in the E/R, what was being talked about, who was loyal to him and the usual gossip was what he basically was interested in. So he wasted a lot of time before I could free myself and the only way I knew to do that was to disappoint him. I answered all his questions with an 'I don't know' reply. I knew I was pissing him off but then I knew it was right for me to do so. Well another day went down the drain. I had to do my work but it had to be done smartly. Nobody would give me time-off to learn here, that was for sure. I could see Sam had made markings on all the pipelines. I just needed to follow the markings and keep checking intermittently to know if I was on the right track. I had to make good of whatever time I got and to find out ways to do it quick. Day workers would work from 0800 to 1700 hrs. The duty engineers too relax after 2nd was gone. So between 8 am to 5pm I would work with others and learn whatever I could and then 5 pm onwards I would trace the lines without any disturbance.

By the end of second week, I had learnt all the pipelines. It helped me a lot to understand the procedures to be followed in a particular alarm. Knowing the layout of piping helped me understand how different systems work. In the next few weeks I just had to concentrate on the different alarms. I had learnt how to fill in the log-book and where to get the readings from to fill it in.

I would take one system at a time. I had completed studying the fuel oil, fresh water, sea water, sewage, control air, inert gas generator, boiler and purifier systems. I realised that everything was quite logical and hence simple. If I had a doubt I would search for the manual in the Control Room and read it. Information on everything was available. I was glad that I was pushed into a corner because I needed the wake up call.

We reached several ports in the US but I didn't go out after Providence. Going out the first time was a bad experience. Moreover I didn't want to go out before learning my job. People here would not like it. In the middle of the third week I had learnt more than half the systems and I knew almost half the alarms. So I thought of leaving early one day. I left Engine Room at 1900 hours, went up and took shower and wore uniform to have dinner in the officer's mess. This was the first time that I was going to dinner almost on time. The serving time was over but the food was still warm and I enjoyed it more since I felt good myself.

After dinner I thought of going to the smoke room and chat with the officers. I had hardly met anyone here. My life revolved around the engine room and the cabin. I could hear animated conversations as I came out from the mess to the corridor; it was clear people were having fun inside. I opened the door. 2nd officer, Param, Batti, 2nd Engineer and Chief Officer were having a loud discussion and laughing.

Batti the most active member spoke first, "5th! Come...come."

2nd officer said, "Hi 5th. I haven't seen you around too much. When do you come to the smoke room or you don't come here at all?"

I went upto him, shook hands with him and said, "Hi 2nd! Today is my first time in the smoke room."

2nd Engineer spoke next, "Help us decide which movie to watch, it's a tie. 2nd officer, Param and I want to watch Tigerland while they want to watch a Hindi movie."

Chief Officer said, "Our group wants to see *Baazigar*."

My vote immediately was for Tigerland. From what I could gather from the cover, it seemed like a good war movie to watch.

The movie had just started when the Chief Engineer came in. He kept fidgeting as he stood there looking at all was present. His expressions changed as he spotted me.

Param was excited to see him, "Bada sa'ab! We have just started the movie, please join us."

Chief engineer said, "Actually I was just out for a walk. 5th can you join me for a few minutes?"

"Please continue the movie, I will join you," I said and went out.

Chief's face became more twisted when he was annoyed, "I thought you would be in the Engine Room now."

I responded coolly, "I used to work late everyday. Since I completed a lot of work I came up early today. I have traced the…"

He cut me short, "You should have caught up on your sleep when you had the time. You should utilise your free time in reading manuals. I have some useful books with me in my cabin. Come with me, I will show you."

I knew he was drinking and he needed company while he got drunk. I still asked when we reached his cabin, "Where are the books, sir?"

He poured an extra large peg of scotch for himself and asked, "Did you arrange the filing cabinet last time? Can you check if the files are in place?"

It took me sometime to re-check the whole cabinet again.

I looked him into his eyes as I said, "It's in order Chief. You have not moved anything."

He avoided eye contact and said, "So you are learning ok in Engine Room?"

"Yes I am satisfied with my performance so far. I was slow in the beginning but have picked up now."

He said bluntly, "You have to put in a lot of hard work. You getting time to watch a movie is not a good sign. I have come to know you are taking it easy here."

I remained silent.

He continued, "I allowed you to go out in Providence. But I am concerned about your future."

"I understand Chief, I will try harder."

He kept talking about his career. He never asked me to sit so I continued standing for more than two hours that I was in his cabin for. When I left I was in no mood to go to the smoke room, so I went to my cabin.

I went on about my job as I had planned to and by the end of three weeks I knew all the systems in the engine room.

Monday morning I went up to 2nd and said, "Goodmorning 2nd! I know the entire pipeline diagrams and can attend to all the alarms now. I am ready to be on your watch."

2nd was working on the meat and fish room compressors. "There is a lot of ice on the gas lines and the temperature is not going down in the deep freezer..." he was thinking out loud. I assumed he had heard me and took off from there to revise my recently learnt stuff.

Provision stores were on the same deck as the entrance to the engine room. There were two separate cold storage rooms; one for meat and fish where the temperature was maintained at -12^0 C and another the vegetable room, where temperature was maintained at 8^0 C. I had not yet gone to see where these rooms were. I went down looking for where oiler Ali was. An oiler is below the rank of the motorman but does the same job as motorman. Ali was not shrewd like the likes of Tengalkar and Gadhav and that was why his work had gone unnoticed and maybe that was the reason why his promotion was long overdue. I looked at him work sincerely; he was cleaning the filters of the SW line. He was preparing the standby sea water cooling system so that he could shut the one he wanted to do maintenance on and start the standby one. I had done my homework so started helping him open the respective valves. He started the standby pump and when he confirmed the pressure was alright he shut the already running pump. We immediately started closing the inlet and outlet valves of the shut system so that the filter could be opened for cleaning. The huge filter had a heavy top and to open that we needed to open eight 36" nuts. I was eager to work and picked up a spanner to start opening the nut but couldn't.

Ali spoke, "Paanch sa'ab, they are rusted you'll need to fix this on your side." He was talking about an iron cylinder which was hollow from inside. He showed how to fix it on the other side now with the extended piece the torque applied to the nut increased. And voila! I could open the nuts with ease. Once all the nuts were open he hung the small flexible hand operated manual crane on a metal frame at top, inserted a wire sling on the top portion of the unit. After ensuring that the sling was attached to the crane he started pulling the chain. This chain moved a gear, which in turn moved another, which in turn moved another gear attached to the crane. The crane lifted the top easily...it must easily be around fifty kilograms, I thought. With one hand I pulled on the crane's chain while with the other I helped him pull the filter top away from the filter so that it could be rested on the bottom platform. He next fixed the sling on the filter and pulled the filter up. The filter was choked completely. I didn't know from where the water was getting in all these days; it must have increased the load on the pump. There were thousands of shiny particles attached to the filter. I went close to inspect, and to my surprise, they were prawns! Tiny little prawns being sucked in by the huge sea water pumps must have gotten stuck in the meshes of the sea water filter.

I asked curiously, "Ali, how on earth did so many prawns get in the filter?"

"Panama Canal. Whenever you cross the lake this happens to the filter."

"In that case as soon as we cross Panama we should call Chief Cook and 2nd cook here. Let them clean the filter and cook prawn curry for lunch."

Ali liked the joke so much that he kept laughing for a while.

He said playfully, "The fat guys can't even handle their paunches. What will become of them when they come here to work?" he started laughing again and continued, "They would flood the engine room with their sweat dripping down from their fat asses!"

I laughed with him though I didn't find it as funny. I asked when Ali was quiet, "When did you last cross the Panama?"

"That must have been a month back."

I asked again, "But don't you think the filter should have been cleaned?"

He exclaimed, "You are right! Gadhav reported he had cleaned the filters; it was *teen sa'ab's* watch immediately after we crossed the Panama. No wonder they were so dirty."

I blew out a whistle as I said, "So Gadhav never cleaned them!" I could expect something like that from Gadhav. There definitely was more beneath his friendly exterior.

After cleaning and putting the filter back we changed over the system to this filter so that the second filter could be cleaned. I went over to the pump; this motor was consuming 2/3rd of the electricity it was consuming earlier. The second filter too had lots of prawns, small fish, sea shells and aquatic plants attached to it. Cleaning the filter was fun; this part was directly connected to the sea, sucking in water 15-20 feet below the sea surface.

After we were done I asked Ali, "Can you show me the cold storage? I want to see the meat and vegetable rooms."

We went out from the other exit. This one was on the other side of the Engine Control Room. Stairs near the boiler platform led upstairs to the Inert Gas Generator Room. I looked up to see the inside of the huge funnel of the ship. I could see the silver painted boiler exhaust lines lead up to the top of the funnel. I could see the same stairs lead towards the top. But we went out the door on the inert gas generator level and exited the engine room. This door led to an alley at the end of which there were two strong silver coloured doors. A round temperature gauge above the rooms showed the temperature inside and two red bulbs could be seen on the top, the same one would see outside the Operation Theatre. When somebody went into the room one had to switch on the light, which indicated there was a person inside.

Ali said pressing the huge steel handle, "You have to release this part; if not the self locking door would close on you. Only someone outside can then open it."

"And that's why the red light has to be switched on. I can imagine someone getting stuck in the meat room. He would become frozen meat himself." I shuddered at my pathetic joke.

He pointed towards two jackets hung outside, "We gotta wear these...it will be cold inside."

We wore the jackets and went into the meat and fish room. When my eyes adjusted to the dimly lit space, I realised I was standing on wooden planks, and when I looked around, even the walls were covered with them. It was around 500 square feet in area and almost a square in shape. Wooden racks all over the place and different kinds of meat and sea food were neatly stacked on them. Fish was kept separate from the meat. I was impressed with the cleanliness with which the cooks had arranged food here.

I asked, "Any idea how long would meat and fish remain good here?"

"I guess we consume the fish within two weeks but I guess it still can last more than a month easily. Meat remains good for a while. But our provisions come in every fortnight, so we get very fresh food to eat. Don't worry," he said with a smile.

We went to vegetable room. This was much cleaner than the meat room. The racks were covered with colourful exotic vegetables. Everything looked so fresh there. The fruits were arranged neatly in different racks. Not easily to be found fruits...so very fresh and perfect in shape and colour...there were pears, bananas, plums, strawberries, mangoes, kiwis, tangerines, black and green grapes. I went further in to explore the loot. One big rack was dedicated to cheese; choicest ones of hundreds of varieties and shape. I wondered how many different countries these were brought in from. The next rack stored big packs of yogurt, milk and fruit juices.

I felt secure; we would not die of hunger if we got lost in the sea. I have never been too fond of vegetables and fruits but I simply fell in love with them there. They reminded me of land, of greenery, colourful flowers and vegetation. The sea was beautiful, but there was nothing like land...there was nothing like home.

Chief Engineer was in the ECR at the same time that I was in the vegetable room. He was having a discussion with 2nd.

2nd was telling him, "Chief, 5th is ready to operate independently."

Chief didn't agree, "I don't trust him. Are you telling me he can handle a watch independently?"

"Yes, we will have our best motorman Tengalkar with him. I will tell him to call me in case he faces a problem."

"I am still not sure he can handle it..."

2nd insisted, "Don't worry Chief. I will be a phonecall away. Moreover, we don't have an option. 4th and 3rd cannot do 6 on-6 off forever. Also I want 5th to be comfortable with watchkeeping before we cross the Panama Canal."

"Ok if that suits you 2nd. But I want you to observe him for one week before you give him the responsibility."

11

CHAPTER

Retarding the Clocks

Life for me had changed a bit as I was made in charge of the 4-8 watches. In the mornings I would work from 4 am to 1 pm, would again come back at 4 pm to continue till my watch time i.e. 8 pm. Chief Engineer continued to create problems by coming down to Engine Room in mornings. He had cultivated a habit of calling my cabin in my off time and he would find excuses to call me to his cabin. Though he would call me on pretext of work I realised there was none at anytime; he just wanted to make sure that I didn't spend my time interacting with others or watching movies or even getting rest when I was off work. It was as if the only work he had was snooping on me; he would keep searching in all the possible places to find out what I was upto. The Deck Crew had begun to think of me as a snobbish person. Thanks to Sam's idea of not letting anybody call me Paanchu.

I met Bosun on the deck one day.

"Hello Bosun. I am the 5th Engineer."

"Yes…yes the new Paanchu. How is everything with you?"

"Thank you for asking. I am good."

"First time on ship?"

"Yes."

"Were you sea sick?" he said smiling.

"Yes I was," I said while I enacted a vomiting scene in front of him.

He was smiling. "One of my AB has been sailing for fifteen years and he still becomes sea sick in every rough weather."

We were quiet for some time and then he said, "I heard you don't like being called Paanchu?"

I said frankly, "Yes, you heard right Bosun."

He asked in a cocky tone, "Why? It's a nice, cute name."

"Bosun, I agree it's my first ship but I am not a kid. And I don't like cute names. You can call me Siddhartha if you think by calling me 5th Engineer you would be giving too much respect to me."

I had taken him by surprise. He kept shut. I knew I was screwing with the wrong guy, as he could make more than 50 percent of the population on this ship against me. But it never struck me that the term 'Paanchu' may not be demeaning at all.

It was the breaking story. Paanchu doesn't like being called a Paanchu!

Everyone on the deck was talking about it because Bosun is their boss. The galley was talking about it as Bosun has a huge influence with the steward team as well. The deck officers were talking about it as Bosun had talked about it to Param and the big mouth had talked about it with his senior officers.

Doing a watch was quite different; I would be the engineer in Engine Room...for those eight hours I was the king. Chief Engineer would never disturb me then, even if he happened to be there, he would be quite respectful, for his standards. One more important difference was that my breakfast menu had changed considerably. Apart from a glass of juice and a glass of milk I started having eggs and the 'special of the day'. Since most of the crew were Indian and the captain was an Indian too we would have *dosa, poha, uttapam, upma, puri-sabzi, paav-bhaaji*, etc on fixed days of the week. I would get fifteen minutes for my breakfast which was more than enough to feed myself well; it was drastic change from the earlier fifteen-second breakfast.

One morning after my watch I reached ER after having my breakfast. ECR was charged up. Sam, Batti, Fitter and Tengalkar were excitedly discussing something. I got a 'hi' from Sam and they continued their discussion.

Sam spoke excitedly, "We were there a month back. I am going to the beach again!"

Satya asked, "Oh is there a beach? We only go to bars every time; beach should be good for a change"

"But Jack's place is good. It's got a good discotech!" said animated Batti.

"Oh God! Hasn't he had enough?" I thought.

"Batti sa'ab, we'll take you there too," Sam said making Batti a happy man.

"Umm...where are we going?" I asked finally.

Sam spoke, "We are going to heaven. It's called Esmeraldas. We are crossing Panama and moving South to South America."

Fitter added, "Have you crossed Panama Canal before? We will be crossing that in two and a half days."

"I have heard a lot about the Panama Canal. It's a man-made canal which has been built to connect the Pacific Ocean with the Atlantic."

"This is very important for you Sid. The clock would be retarded by an hour tonight and two more times in the next four-five days till we reach Esmeraldas," said Sam.

I asked, "The ship clocks? Retarded by an hour? Wait a minute, because we are crossing the time zones and so that we can be on Esmeraldas' time when we reach there..."

"Yes Sid, right. But the important thing is to know the impact it would have on our watch," Sam replied.

I was curious to know, "Oh...and?"

Sam stretched himself in the chair and raised his arms to support his neck as he rested his back on the chair. When he was comfortable he said, "This means we get an extra one hour which will be distributed among all three duty engineers, starting from the evening watches."

"Ok. That means I would do the watch till 8:20 right. No, but when will the 3rd do his extra 20 minutes, in the noon or night?"

He shook his head and reacted in a way a strict teacher would do on getting a wrong answer from his student, "You are only slightly correct. 3rd starts with doing the extra 20 minutes from his afternoon watch. He works from 12 noon to 1620 hours. You come down at 1620 and work till 2040 hours. I will come down at 2040 and work till 0100 hours. So when I leave at 0100 of now it would be midnight at ship's watch."

I was impressed. "That's a smart way of doing this," I said.

What Sam didn't tell me and I didn't realise was that retarding the ship's clock was a good thing. I had to do twenty minutes extra watchkeeping, but since we were gaining an hour, I got a net of forty extra minutes at night! Actually it was the best for the day workers; they signed off at their usual time, 5 pm, and then they freshened up, would eat, watch a movie and at midnight an officer at watch on the bridge would retard the ship's clock to 11pm.

What I also did not think about then was what goes up, comes down eventually. Usually the cargo which is loaded in South America has to be discharged in US and mostly on the eastern coast so when we were going back this route the ship's clocks would have to be advanced to the same timings. Then I would be doing twenty minutes less on my watch but sleeping forty minutes less too.

I had learnt the best way to avoid Chief after watch; the plan was to not be in the cabin for a while but also remain untraceable, as he would first call the cabin and if I didn't pick up the phone, he would run down to smoke room to check whether I was watching a movie. To watch the movie in crew smoke room wasn't a good idea. For one, I was not supposed to be there and other, I had generated enough bad blood with crew members. So, I would go on to the life boat deck; this part is on both the port and starboard side, usually on floor above the main deck.

Like other days, I was standing near the railing on the

deck looking at the sea. That day, I had come straight from the engine room to the main deck and for a change I didn't go to the lifeboat deck, which was just above me. Moreover, the view of the sea was much better from here. The sea was a wee bit rough, sky was overcast and the sun would come out at times. This was the best part of my day, standing and watching the sea and the waves, imagining the world beneath the surface. This world is more than two times our world and there is only so much that we know about the life underneath, I thought to myself. The breeze was invigorating as it had the freshness and the coolness of the sea. Like always, I felt relaxed, losing my tiredness, anger, anxiety and fears when I was there. The winds were stronger than usual, but I could smell the sea better.

As it always happened with me, the happy thoughts would normally be replaced with strange cold ones. In the midst of this happy moment I began thinking of what would happen if I fell off the ship. There was nobody out on the deck at that hour, as it was lunch time. Nobody would know that I was missing till the time of my watch i.e. at 4 pm. That would mean being in the sea for a good three hours! By the time the ship turned around to come for me I would be resting at the bottom of the sea. I always would end up imagining myself in the sea bobbing up and down with the waves. Someone once told me not to look directly into the sea at night, especially on a clear moonlit night, as the sea attracts you towards it. And there have been several instances when people have jumped overboard while doing so. I will try to see what happens one of these nights, I thought. The sea was attracting me towards it. It felt as if down there it would be cool and relaxing, that my pain and suffering would be taken away. Maybe the way to heaven was through the sea. Maybe...but I was scaring myself.

I was trying to block the unpleasant thoughts in my head and so I looked away towards the horizon. When I looked far ahead I thought I saw a movement right below...I looked down; something was moving beneath the sea's surface, quite close to the ship...it sent shivers down my spine. At one point you are thinking of how inviting the water looks and then you suddenly realise that there are sharks and octopuses and whales and eels beneath. I could see two pairs of eyes beneath the surface, moving fast and swimming perfectly in tandem with each other. It couldn't be a shark, as I couldn't see the trademark fins out of the water. I looked harder, and I realised they were dolphins. They must have seen me standing and hence came close. I tapped with my knuckles at the side of the ship's body. They responded by making themselves partially visible. I had learnt to whistle a year back. I wasn't too good at it and hoped to still remember how to do it. I put my fingers in my mouth pressing my folded tongue. I blew out air anticipating the loud noise that would come out, but instead there was only a flat 'pphhh' sound; nothing but the noise of air coming out my mouth. I tried again -- 'pphhh' -- nothing again. I tried again and this time there was a slight sound of a whistle. I put my fingers in, closed my eyes and blew out, and this time it was a success! It was a nice and loud whistle.

It was indeed my best one as the dolphins responded by jumping up and doing a single tailspin. There were three of them and they did it in unison. Not a bit of imperfection in their synchronisation, it was hard to believe they were untrained wild creatures. I whistled again, this time louder. They jumped again and this time they performed two tailspins. I lay down on the deck and extended my hands outside the railings. The surface was still a good ten feet below my hands but when the ship would roll to this side, the distance would reduce to five feet or so.

The ship rolled towards the dolphins, at the same time instance one of the dolphins jumped up and kissed my hand. I couldn't believe I had made contact with the wild, I wished somebody with camera would have captured this moment. I looked around there was no soul visible. No testimonials either. The dolphins had had their share of fun with me so they moved ahead of the ship as if racing with the huge giant. They reached the hull and after they beat the ship they performed their final act, three jumps with 1, 2 and 3 tailspins, all with flawless perfection.

I started feeling lonely again. I didn't know how long I could go on like that, without anybody to share my sorrow with. I was all alone fighting for a cause that seemed trivial until now because I'd always stayed in a protected environment. The cause was survival. Now, survival wasn't only about not dying. I was losing my self esteem, my confidence levels were at an all time low, I wasn't sure I could gain respect, and I wasn't sure whether people found me an interesting, friendly person anymore; I was losing the essence of me, and I wasn't sure anymore whether I actually was the way I had always assumed I was!

Regarding death, well, there were several ways that I could have died on that ship. Tumbling down from the stairs in engine room and breaking my neck. A two-ton piston falling off the crane when engine routine maintenance was being done, boiler explosion, fire in engine room, falling into rotating parts of machinery...the list was long. Existence, it seemed, had a greater meaning than life itself. I was struggling to make a point here. I was trying to prove to this handful bunch of people that I was someone and in-turn, make a place for myself in this world. It was important for me that people at least acknowledged my existence.

"Siddhartha!" came a familiar voice from behind.

I was not expecting somebody to acknowledge my existence this soon! I said, "Gosh! You scared me to death! Don't ever sneak on me ever again Param."

He smiled slyly and asked, "So what's up? Taking the pressure well?"

I replied looking at the sea, "So far so good. Surviving somehow."

He laughed as if he understood what I meant.

I asked, "How long have you been here?"

He said proudly, "Four months. Six more to go. But I like this place. I have good friends here. Plus, I have picked up things fast so it's going great with me. You seem a little lost. All well with you?"

"Yes, I am a little lost. It's my first time on ship. Thanks for asking."

"I felt like that on my first ship. But you should be able to spring back in a few days...I did so in a matter of a week or two. If you are good in your job and are strong, nothing can stop you. It helps if you can build a strong rapport with people around. Take these tips from me. I won't charge you," he continued to chuckle.

I looked at his boiler suit; not a spot of oil stain on it. I looked at mine; it was all sweaty and had black stains all over.

He noticed the difference too, "What do you do down there in the engine room? Play *Holi* with oil?"

I replied, "No choice buddy, it is a part of my job."

"Don't you have assistants? Motormen would help you right?"

"Yes they do. But I like working on the machinery myself. I like to change the gaskets. I even do the cleaning of the parts myself. I am in learning mode you see, and it feels good to do it myself."

"Oh?! That's surprising. It doesn't seem you would do all that stuff."

I was thinking about this conversation long after it was over; his words kept ringing in my head...' I did so in a matter of a week or two'. I had been there for more than a month and still did not know so many things down there. The doubts were back. I thought, "Are 4th and 3rd right about me? Am I taking too much time to learn?"

In cabin I suddenly felt very lonely. I wondered what Anoushka would be doing? It was 1.30 am in Ranchi. She must be asleep. I wanted to be near her, cuddled close, watching her as she slept peacefully. I realised I hadn't been sleeping properly for a long time. I didn't cry that night; the tears had begun to dry up. The humiliation in the E/R continued so did the cold treatment from the deck crew. Though I didn't like Param too much initially, he was the only person who talked to me. He was haughty to the core but then he was a fun guy to be with...I had started considering him a friend. My best friends, however, were the cast iron machines down there in the E/R.

We had lifeboat or a fire drill every alternate Saturdays. But when the Captain would come to know that we had scheduled an important job on a Saturday he would make an exception and cook up a drill in the evening even though a drill had happened last Saturday. And the drills were a total farce. All of us except the Captain were divided into different teams that were supposed to act according to the emergency. The team leaders would keep reporting to the Bridge over walkie-talkie. The duty officer would make entries and the Captain, who would also be at the bridge, would be having fun seeing our performance. In case there was a mistake from someone from the E/R he would be quick to point that out over the loudspeaker so that everybody could hear it. I was sure that in case an actual emergency were to happen, everybody would forget their respective roles.

Life here had become too mechanical. I remembered how I would get bored easily when I was home. I would complain about movies on HBO and Star Movies, I would whinge about the food and I would sulk about the club being closed on Mondays. I realised now how precious those moments were, which I had wasted complaining about irrelevant things. I realised now that I would perhaps never get a chance to laze around in front of the TV with all the time in the world to surf channels and watch programs other than news. I realised that no matter how tasty the food on board was, it could never be as good as home cooked food.

I wasn't performing too well here but I just hoped that I could survive the trip; I didn't want to fail. I wondered how Vikram was doing on his ship. He had joined the ship the same time as I had; he had lost a year because he had to spend few months in the mental asylum and he took a few months to recuperate. He wanted a hassle free first ship so he chose to go on board an Indian vessel; work was quite less, there are no constraints on manpower and major repair work wasn't done by the engineers but was done on shore. Vikram was getting back to his normal self. That day in the stadium, he had managed to silence those crickets after all. I was sure he would be doing great on the ship as well. There would be people reporting to him and he would be wearing a boiler suit as clean as Param's. Param was a friend now and he reminded me of Sachin, my school friend who was in the army now...actually reminded me of him in not a good way.

I knew Sachin since I was in class IX. I was a short thin weak guy. Sachin on the other hand was tall and well built, he had a strong jaw line and he shaved everyday. He had learnt taekwondo and would show off his moves especially when girls were around. He would bully me quite often. I was quite used to being bullied by now; as a kid, juniors in school would threaten me and I would shy away from fighting with them. One day Sachin kicked me on my face in front of girls from the junior class. I then decided that I would start working out; so I woke up at five next morning and started jogging. Jogging became a habit and soon, I was also doing push-ups. In a couple of months I had enrolled myself in once a week karate classes in school.

I would eagerly wait for my Karate classes but then I never took that extra effort to compete and pass the exams for higher belts. I was OK with just learning the kicks and punches. I knew I wouldn't be able to pass the tests as I was too timid to fight. Nevertheless I did succeed to acquire some muscles and had started looking fitter. I could notice that the change in me had its effect on people around me; in came attention from girls and out went Sachin's bully sessions. And he became my friend and I considered him one but then he surprised me with the choice he made one winter evening; he too chose not to fight!

It was my first break from my college and my winter holidays coincided with that of Sachin's break from the NDA. Garu obviously was in Ranchi doing nothing except his occasional trips to the market to bring in grocery and vegetables for his mother. One evening after tennis we decided to stroll down to my locality and see if there was anything interesting to do.

Though we played tennis in the same court and Anoushka lived in the same house, I hadn't noticed her then. It was a year before I made my acquaintance with Anoushka.

It was a cold winter evening, the sun was about to set and the sky was bright orange. I breathed in the fresh air; as far back as I could remember the air smelled the same during this time of season; the fragrance was a mix of dry eucalyptus wood and roses. I looked up at the tall trees and it gave me a warm feeling to see the numerous birds come home to their little ones. We crossed a bunch of girls who looked at us and giggled. I smiled back. There was something special about that evening. We reached the stadium and stopped.

Sachin said first, "So what do we do guys?"

Garu, the greedy one, said immediately, "Let's go eat."

Sachin said, "I know just the place. The food is good and young girls visit the place at this time."

We reached the place listening to Sachin's stories about the NDA. I was interested and so was Garu. They had a very tough life and somehow I felt I wouldn't have been able to cope with the hardcore physical training. The joint was small and nice. They had an open kitchen and the aroma of food being cooked was enough to make us all hungry. The best thing about winters is that one can hog on junk food and the system still digests it all within no time. And hog we did on hakka noodles, chicken manchurian, *moghlai parathas, paneer* chilli. We ordered coffee next. Every time Sachin took a sip, the cream of coffee would stick to his newly grown moustache.

I asked him, "Why did you grow this moustache?"

He replied, "It adds to my stud looks. Don't you think so?"

I said, "Not like that...generally asking."

He looked relieved. "Oh I look like an army officer now. I'm moulding myself into the role. Now look at my aviators...," he wore them and continued, "You see...it all complements my charming personality. Someone told me I look like Hrithik Roshan."

Garu, who was enjoying his coffee, nodded vehemently in agreement. I looked at the jokers in disbelief. Yes, he looked like the actor in a way; if Hrithik's face was made round and fat, his body fatter, his nose small and hair sparse and receding then there would be a remote similarity between the two. I turned my head away not wanting to see them two for a few moments. The same time I looked towards the entrance, a girl entered the joint. For some reason I couldn't take my eyes off her. She was tall, had a thin frame yet a curvy body. She was wearing a turtle neck sweater with jeans, both of which clung to her athletic physique. She wasn't very fair; the complexion accentuated her sharp features and intelligent eyes. She looked at me with an expressionless face; it was as if a model on a ramp was facing the camera. She waited for few minutes as she waited for her takeaway and all this while she avoided turning towards me. On her way out she turned and looked at me for a good 5 seconds. My dear friends were unaware of what had just transpired...they didn't even notice that I was suddenly in a blissful state.

They were still discussing army life when I asked them, "Can we come back again tomorrow?"

"Sure," said Garu.

"See I told you the food's good," Sachin was pleased that we liked the place he had brought us to.

The next evening I made sure we all reached the place on time. She came in at the same time. She glanced in my direction more than she had yesterday, but she still had that distant expression on her face as she looked at me. I was totally clueless about what was going on in her head. But then Sachin noticed there was something cooking so he whispered in my ear, "Hey, do you know that girl?"

I whispered, "No, I don't...but I would want to."

Sachin said ogling at her, "Even I would want to. She's beautiful."

Garu looked at us with disgust, "You guys! Can you not think beyond girls for a while?"

Sachin said, "I think she's interested in you. Look she's looking in your direction again! Congrats Sid, how did you manage to...?"

I was blushing when Garu mimicked Sachin, "Congrats Sid!" and then added, "Grow up guys!"

The looking game continued for the next few days. By this time I had drawn up enough courage to smile at her. But only this day she wasn't even looking at me. I obviously was all eyes and was waiting for her to turn towards me so that I could smile at her. I noticed a guy standing all alone in the eatery staring at me. I forgot about him as I looked at her leave. She went up to the guy. They had some discussion during which the guy kept looking towards me. I smelled trouble. She went out without looking at me.

This guy approached us and while looking at me asked, "What's your name?"

I was surprised by his question. I didn't know why he would be interested in my name but I was stupid enough to respond, "Siddhartha...why do you ask?"

He chose not to reply to my question rather asked, "Where do you live?"

I said, "Satellite...but why are you asking? What's your name?"

"Oh generally. My name is Arvind."

Sachin acted as if he hadn't heard the conversation.

Garu on the other hand was almost jumping, "Baba, you shouldn't have told him your name. But good that you didn't tell him you live in this locality itself. That guy could well be the jealous boyfriend. I always tell you guys to avoid girls...that would save us all from a lot of trouble!"

Next evening Garu called his tone high, "*Baba* don't go to the eatery today. They are waiting for you."

I didn't understand the reason for this commotion but I was afraid, "How do you know? Did you go...?"

"Yes I went to get some stuff packed but I turned around as soon as they spotted me."

I said angrily, "But you should have stayed there to see what they want!"

"Hello!? What for? Most likely they wanted to beat me up. This is all because of you and your girls!"

He made sense. I asked, "Hmmm...how many were they?"

"Oh around 7-8. Let's not even play tennis today. You

had told them Satellite! What if they come here? Now I can't even go out to get my dinner packed."

"*Arre baba*, wait for me. I'll be there in sometime."

"Are you nuts? Don't come here. If they see me with you I'm gonna tell them I don't know you. They looked bloody dangerous!"

I hung up the phone and looked at Sonu who was lazing around in the room.

"*Bhaiya* I think you're going to get beaten up," he said nonchalantly.

"What makes you think so?" I said apprehensively.

He said coolly, "Why would a stranger ask your name and location? If I were you I wouldn't go out for the next few days."

I retorted, "Well I am going out now. And now onwards don't listen in to my calls."

"Don't give yourself so much importance. You are so loud that I can't help but hear."

I got ready and kicked Sonu on his butt before going out.

He shouted, "Why don't you beat up those people who are searching for you!"

When I closed the door I heard him complaining to mom about what I had just done to him.

I passed by the court, reached Garu's building, parked my bike and doubled up the stairs.

When Garu saw me his eyes almost popped out, "You are totally crazy *baba*! I told you to stay in!"

"Come on, I reached here right? What's the big deal?"

He said nervously, "These people are looking for you. I saw an open jeep...around ten of them inside. This is serious stuff."

Now this was disturbing. It seemed those people wouldn't rest till they had found me. I stayed at Garu's place and left for home only when it was a little dark. Sachin had gone underground. Three days after the incident, and those guys were still looking for me. Garu had seen them, they looked like *goondas*. I had gotten us involved with the wrong guys! But we couldn't go on like this. I had a short leave and didn't want to spend my time sitting at home fearing what would happen next. Moreover, they would have been enquiring about me and would one day know where I lived, only to harass my parents and Sonu. "Garu, I'm going to meet them."

He couldn't believe it but somehow knew I would do something like that, "Sure, why not! That's what's called the height of idiocy."

"But I can't live in this constant fear. Are you in?"

"I knew one day I'd be screwed because of you and your girls! Do I have a choice? Yes I'm in," he said unhappily.

I called Sachin next.

I asked, "Where have you disappeared?"

"Oh Sid. Some relatives turned up at my place. How're things?"

"Not so good...they're still searching for me."

He advised, "Oh then stay indoors."

"No I'm going to discuss this with them and try to sort out the differences."

"I think you should avoid them. They don't seem to be the type who would understand your point of view. Lie low for a while..."

I said impatiently, "You are getting trained in the NDA. You will be fighting wars soon. This is but only a small time scuffle...are you coming, or not?"

"Of course...of course," said Sachin promptly.

Sonu as usual was listening to the conversation lying in bed. He sat up as I kept the phone and said, "You'll need my help."

I knew he could, "I think I will."

He quickly made some calls and in half an hour we had twenty kids to help me. Out of these guys there was one guy called Imran who knew the right kind of people. He told Sonu, "No point taking the whole crowd to the café. It'll make matters worst."

Sachin fretted, "But we will need people to fight if they attack."

I saw sense in what Imran was saying. "Sachin, Garu, you stay here with them. Sonu, Imran and I will go there."

Sonu said next, "If we don't return in half an hour you all come see us."

We started on my bike. My heart was beating so fast that I could hardly drive. We reached the café in two minutes. The place looked like a war zone. There were around thirty of them waiting for us and I could sense the rise in tension as we approached.

I parked the bike forgot the keys in the ignition as I moved ahead. Imran took the keys out and handed them over to Sonu. A short heavily built guy in his late twenties came forward as he shouted, "Look, look the hero's here. You like passing comments at girls! Only this time you teased my friend's girlfriend!"

I replied calmly, "I've never ever passed comments at any girl my entire life, and I've not said anything to this girl either."

"We have a smart person here," he shouted to his gang as he moved in as if to beat me up.

Imran came in between us with his hands raised, "We can resolve this peacefully! I don't want any problems in my area."

The short guy slowed down. He looked at me and pointed towards a tall guy, "Why don't you discuss this with the boyfriend?"

I approached the tall guy, "Look there's some confusion. Like I said, I don't behave that way with any girl. Why don't you ask your girl?"

"Oh I've asked her. Moreover, my friend told me he has seen you staring at her." He said this as he looked towards the guy who has asked my name. So this guy was the one who has created this entire ruckus. He kept staring at me from a distance.

I said as calmly as I could, "Yes I did look at her but I didn't know she had a boyfriend. Now that I know, I respect that. Where's the point for a fight over this?"

The short guy started approaching us looking for a reason to thrash me.

Imran pitched in, "Guys this discussion is between these two. Let them clear the misunderstanding. Why do we need the crowd here? It's a residential area...people have started noticing."

The short guy was near us now and so were his goons.

"Are you satisfied with his explanation?" he asked the boyfriend.

The tall guy looked sensible, "I think he's telling the truth."

I sighed in relief. I shook hands with the boyfriend, "I didn't mean to disrespect her. My apology to her if she thought my behaviour was inappropriate."

He smiled, "Don't bother, it's alright."

I started moving to Imran and Sonu when the short guy shouted, "I'm not done with you yet!"

He wanted me to react. I knew he would create trouble. I turned towards him and looked at him in the eyes.

He came closer, roaring, "Don't move till I tell you to." His gang surrounded me and he started circling around me as a ringmaster does around a chained lion...except that I felt more like a sheep. I stood still as I noticed something very disturbing; the bulge in his jacket was most likely a gun. He knew what was going on in my mind and he opened his jacket a bit. He was indeed carrying a country made pistol. He kept shouting at me while I maintained my peace and kept shut. From the corner of my eyes I looked at Sonu who was standing ready for action in case things became ugly. I signalled him to relax; it wasn't the right time to be a hero. The class went on for what seemed like a long time. Finally Imran held my hand and pulled me away from the scene.

The short guy was still shouting, "I should not see you again. There won't be anybody to save you next time."

We rode back to the place where our gang was waiting for us. By now most of Sonu's friends had left. Garu looked concerned. He immediately stood up and came running to us.

He said, "What happened?"

I was still thinking of ways things could have gone wrong, "Garu come I'll tell you over a smoke."

Sonu said, "Ya I too need to smoke! Imran, *chal raha hai kya?*"

Imran said, "I'm expected at the shop. Am already late...some other day."

I went up to Imran and shook his hand, "It would have been very ugly without you. Thanks man."

He looked at Sonu as he smiled, "Awww it's nothing. Sonu is a good friend of mine. You are his brother...anything for you guys."

I realised Sachin wasn't there, "Garu where's Sachin?"

Garu looked angry, "Oh that slimy bastard! He ran away as soon as you three went to meet those goons. I tried stopping him but he said he had to buy some grocery."

Sonu was surprised too, "Why has he joined the army? To run away from war?"

This incident ended peacefully but it wasn't over still. These goons kept a tab on my activities and though I was aware of their presence I ignored them. I went on with my life as if nothing had happened, and in a few days I was back in college. This incident was an ugly reminder of how weak I actually was. Had Vikram been in my place he would have handled the situation like a man. Though my relation with Sachin didn't suffer I often wondered how he felt about chickening out when I needed him most.

12

CHAPTER

The Déjà Vu

I wasn't sleeping too well since the night I had boarded the flight from Bombay. I wanted to shut out all thoughts, give my mind a rest and for once go on to sleep like I used to not so long ago. I looked at the watch; it was midnight yet again. And I had to get up for the 4 am watch. I was still thinking about the incident that happened in that cold winter evening. My thoughts drifted to my childhood.

It would be celebration time when our parents would go out for work. Sonu and I would either prepare eggs at home or one of us would go outside the colony gate and buy boiled eggs from a guy with a mobile *thela*. This guy came there every evening and he prepared the best boiled eggs in town. He would cut the egg in the middle, add chopped onions, green chilli and coriander and sprinkle spices on top. Four eggs would cost us eight rupees but price alone wasn't what made the experience worthwhile. It was the fact that it was exciting for us to complete the activity without getting caught. Also we both were huge egg fans and mommy would ration our daily diet. "Eggs are warm. You shouldn't have more than one a day or it would bring in ugly boils on your face," she would always say.

"It's your turn today. I brought the eggs last time mom and dad were out," said Sonu.

So I went off on the bicycle. Strangely, the locality looked too quiet and lonely at this time of the evening.

"Must be some strange coincidence...everyone's disappeared at the same time," I thought. I crossed the small hospital. I looked in the parking. It was totally deserted. I could see no activity inside the hospital either! I reached the intersection in front of the school. Not a single person was there. I slowed down and looked into the windows of the houses by the side of the road. Normally, you would find someone standing in the balcony. That day there was nobody to be seen; neither could I see any movement inside the windows. An eerie thought crossed my mind, "What if I go back home and even Sonu's not there! What if my parents never come back?" I quickly took a U-turn. There was no one up ahead. I felt some activity behind me so I looked over my shoulders. I could see some people in black flowing clothes running behind me. They were approaching fast. I increased my speed but inspite of that they were closing in. After cycling for a distance I turned around again. They had country made pistols in their hands. There was no one ahead so I figured they were chasing me. I was wondering what they wanted with me when one of them shot. Others began shooting too. I bent forward to escape the bullets as I pedalled harder. I was about to take the left towards home when a shot hit my cycle's rear tyre and I fell away from the turn. I didn't have the time to come back towards the turn so I ran ahead, away from home. I could hear the bullets whiz by most of them almost hitting me. I had reached the other end of my locality, the cemented boundary was a few feet ahead. There was no place to hide and no option but to jump over to the other side. I jumped up to hold the edge of the wall but couldn't hold onto it as my palms got cut by the glass pieces which were cemented on top of the wall. I could hear their footsteps very close by. I was cornered. I didn't run...there was nowhere to go. I couldn't make myself turn around...I kept facing the white wall waiting for the bullets to hit me. I wanted to shout to cry for help so I opened my mouth and shouted with all force but I couldn't find my voice!

I woke up with a start...the alarm had been ringing for sometime now. The dream was so real...my heartbeat was loud and my pillow was wet with my sweat. I took a little while to realise where I was. I 'snoozed' the alarm for 5 minutes. It was 3.45... I could sleep for 5 more minutes. The next 5 minutes' sleep was the best sleep I had had in months...unfortunately it was over in what seemed like 5 seconds.

I got up reluctantly, went to the loo, thought for a few seconds and decided against brushing my teeth now. I could brush before breakfast, I decided. I wore my overalls and ran down to the E/R. I took out my industrial shoes from the rack, left my floaters at the rack and ran down to the ECR.

3rd was waiting impatiently, "Here you are! You're late by fifteen minutes!"

I looked at the watch, "But am on time 3rd...it's exactly 4 am," I said slowly.

He said sarcastically, "Ha! You need to be here 15 minutes before your watch starts so that you can take a round before I hand over. That's proper watchkeeping and since you've just started doing this everyone would expect a proper job from you."

"I will keep that in mind 3rd."

"I need sleep...but before I go, there's a leakage from the outline pipe of the auxiliary sea water pump. I've done temporary arrangements by clamping it with rubber. Inform 2nd that this pipe needs immediate repairing."

I said, "Sure 3rd I will inform 2nd." I looked at him as he slowly rose from his seat and thought, "He needs sleep?" He looked like he had been sleeping all his watch. I was damn sure he never went down for rounds. I went to the alarm panel; all the four bilge well high level alarms were on.

I turned towards Tengalkar who was busy making tea for himself. "Goodmorning Tengalkar."

"Good morning paanch sa'ab."

"I am going down for rounds..."

Tengalkar suggested, "But have tea first..."

I said worriedly, "Not now. All the bilge well alarms are red..."

Tengalkar said smiling, "Don't worry paanch sa'ab. That's the most common alarm on a ship and the least dangerous one. Sometimes, even when the ship's rolling, the alarms come and go. I'll pump out the water when I go down for my round."

"Tengalkar, you relax. Finish your tea. Teen sa'ab told me there's a leak in the sea water line. I'll go down and see how it is. And maybe you need to speak with his motorman Gadhav. He should hand over the watch to you with no alarms, right?"

"Oh yes, he told me the alarm came right when the watch was to finish so he left it for me to handle. But he did mention that to me paanch sa'ab. But yes, he should have seen that the water levels in the bilges were up when he handed over the watch to me and ideally he should not wait for alarms to come but take the water out much before that. He's a lazy bum."

Or it meant that there was a sudden leak in the bilges. The leak! What if 3rd's makeshift arrangement had given way and the E/R was flooded! I rushed out from there even as Tengalkar was saying something. I peeped from above. A portion of bottom platform was visible from top...I could see the platform...no flooding! I could breathe now.

There was still a possibility of flooding; beneath the platform there was sufficient capacity to store hundreds of tons of water. I increased my speed, peeped down from the second floor but couldn't see beneath the bottom platform from there. I was relieved to see there was no flooding beneath the platform. I reached the part from where I could see the aft bilge wells; since a ship is inclined towards the aft so water leaking trickles down mostly to the aft bilges. I stood at the platform over the propeller shaft...water was about to spill out from the wells. I started the bilge pump to pump water out of the ship through the oily water separator.

This time of watch was the best time on ship. There was nobody to disturb me so I could learn without disturbances, and since there was no one to give me 'gyaan' I was free to take the decisions pertaining to the E/R...no one to mess with my mind, no one to demean me and no one to evaluate my actions...I was the king of the bilges! I went to the leaking seawater line. Water was still leaking out the makeshift arrangement made by 3rd. I was sure the clamp would give away if somebody were to start the pump by mistake. The line was one of the widest pipelines in the E/R. The water from this system was supplied to the deck and the accommodation to be used for fire fighting in the event of an emergency. The deck hands mostly used this water to wash the deck or the cargo oil tanks.

The thinnest pipelines on the ship are the control air lines. Air at 7 bar pressure is used to control various points in the Main Engine system; it's the most complex system on the ship wherein the air controls everything from starting and stopping of engines to when to inject fuel into the cylinders, operation of fuel pumps and fuel cams, various interlocks are there as safety features...all of these controlled and operated by air. We had studied the system in college, I didn't remember the lectures as I was either sleeping or doing the daily crossword. But I did remember the good students discussing about how complex the system was. I had gone through the diagrams the previous day and I could understand everything else except the operating mechanism of the fuel cams. So I went to the emergency manoeuvering platform which was between the bottom and the second floor; when the various main engine commands Start, Stop, Full Speed Ahead/ Astern, etc failed to respond from the E/R console, which is when the commands were given locally from that console. There was a telegraph lever and a phone to keep in touch with Bridge. Tengalkar who was at the bottom platform came up after sometime.

He asked smiling, "What you doing here paanch sa'ab?"

I couldn't understand it then since the engines were not running. I said aloud, "It'd be interesting to be here when we are manoeuvering in Panama. Got to see how these valves operate when a particular command is given."

He was laughing as he said, "Everybody tries to understand this system when they are new on the ship. Chaar sa'ab used to spend a lot of time understanding this but couldn't, so he asked teen sa'ab to help him out one day...and you know what teen sa'ab told him?"

I guessed, "That he himself doesn't understand the system?"

"Yes! Teen sa'ab said, 'Why waste time on this...when there'll be a problem 2nd will see. Main engine is his responsibility not ours.' After that chaar sa'ab never came here. You too will stop coming." He continued laughing.

I said flatly, "It's not that complex."

He looked surprised. He asked, "Do you know something about the system?"

I said pointing to the camshaft, "There's this cam part remaining... I need to see it running and then... I'll just need to refer the manual again."

His smile had completely vanished by then and he stammered as he spoke, "You mean to say apart from that you know everything else!? It is a complex system...I doubt anybody on this ship knows it...you know people would be happy to learn about this."

I knew it was difficult for him to grasp how a person who doesn't remember which valves to open to line up a simple system can understand hundreds of complex valves of the most complicated system. Actually it was difficult for me too to understand.

I confided in him, "I had it in my course during engineering...but I don't remember anything that was taught. Actually I learnt it here."

His already big eyes were bigger. He asked curiously, "Here? How could you? You are joking right?"

I pointed out to him, "After these interlocks are cleared the control air knows that the engine is ready for the starting air. This air also makes some very critical decisions...it checks which piston has reached which position and when should starting air be released into a particular cylinder out of the 6 we have in the main engine, it decides in which cylinder fuel pumps should be activated to inject the fuel in..." I feared he would go into coma so I ended the conversation, "...it's a beautiful system. Ask me if you need to find something about it."

Before going to breakfast I informed 2nd about the leak. 2nd instructed the fitter, "Make temporary arrangement...and not like this. Who's done this pathetic job? You, 5th?"

I shook my head.

2nd looked up as if praying to God, "What a great team I have. Help me please!" After his act was over, he started laughing. Satya laughed and I couldn't control myself either.

Satya had done a good job of clamping it, not a drop of water was leaking out anymore. The clamping was just a stop gap arrangement which couldn't sustain the pressure in the line in the event of the pump running. Instruction that this system was not to be used was written on the board in the ECR and a red tape was stuck over the remote start button on the console in the ECR. I went with Tengalkar to see him line up the stand by pump; I was not confused about the valves he was opening anymore since now I knew the pipelines.

Next day I was working with Sam on the compressors. I looked at the watch, it was 1045. An engineer does 2 hours of over-time apart from his 8 hours of watch-keeping. I wondered when that day would come when I would not be required to do my over-over-time. The answer to this was quite short, 'LONG'! In fact it would take a good few months till I knew sufficient stuff to start to feel like an engineer.

Since Tengalkar had come in with me for 2nd's watch, Sam had to manage with Ali, the oiler. Ali was new on the ship, hence he wasn't too confident, but then he was very sincere and a hard worker. Sam wasn't too happy about this decision for obvious reasons; his easy watch-keeping life had gone for a toss and on top of that he had to put in extra efforts to train the oiler.

Since we were crossing Panama shortly and since manoeuvering required a lot of starting air, the compressors kept running most of the time and it was important for them to work efficiently on full load. Sam had replaced the special inlet and outlet valves of both the compressors. I looked at the valves which had been taken out. They were packed with carbon deposition.

Sam, as if he had read my thoughts, said "No matter what you do oil does come in the air and this deposition is caused by that. And if you are entering an area like Panama, you should put in fresh valves so that the compressors work like a cake. Now we need to try #2 compressor and we are done!"

He switched the compressor on and took a step back as if expecting something to go seriously wrong. He had acted the same way while trying out the first one. He started breathing when it ran fine. I later heard the story of Sam putting in one of the outlet valves in the opposite direction, after he had done a regular maintenance, because of which when he started the compressor a mini explosion had happened in the crank case. Fearless Sam then did something totally unexpected; instead of turning the switch off he ran for his life from there. 2nd who was in the ECR heard the noise came running out and switched it off. Because of the delay in switching it off, the valve seat, the crankshaft and the piston rod were damaged beyond repair.

The compressors were on the same floor as the ECR. We were standing behind the two huge air bottles which the compressors filled. We were almost hidden from everyone in E/R but I could see the activity going on the floor. Ali was cleaning the ECR. Batti came out from the ECR lazily, reached the basin near the exit and started washing his hands as he looked into the mirror and whistled. He suddenly became quite active, shut the tap and ran inside ECR. He quickly came out with his voltmeter and started running towards the electric panel for the meat and vegetable room a/c compressors. I wondered why he would act like this...there was no alarm. And then the reason appeared, it went in the ECR and almost immediately sounded the siren three times. Ali was already in ECR so apparently the call was for me.

2nd had given me a list of jobs to be done and I could have chosen to ignore the call. But I knew if I didn't go Chief would tear Ali to pieces. He was actually doing that when I reached ECR.

Chief was shouting, "Ali your evaluation is due. 2nd told me you are pushing for your promotion. But you need to prove your calibre."

"Yes-s sir," said Ali meekly.

Chief turned his attention towards me, his favourite punching bag. "So what you upto?" he roared.

"I was assisting 4th on the compressor maintenance."

He panicked yet again, "What happened to the compressors? We have serious manoeuvering in Panama tomorrow!"

I replied, "Sam told me this work has to be done before crossing Panama."

He ignored what I said and continued, "Why do work now? What if something goes wrong? You people do not plan work properly!"

I signalled Ali to leave and he ran out as quickly as possible. Chief looked around when the door opened; whenever the door opened the noise from the E/R reached in and so did a blast of hot air. "Where did Ali go to? I wasn't finished with him. Call him immediately!"

I lied, "Sir 2nd had called him."

He asked, "What do you do in your off time these days? Still movies or do you sleep on time?"

"In the limited off that I get, I sleep mostly…you would be happy to know that I've stopped watching movies these days."

"When I was a 5th if I got 4 hours off in a day I would consider myself lucky."

I knew he was lying. He didn't look like a person who had worked hard in his life. He worked in the same company that Vikram had joined. On their ships they even had a person to make tea. When there was the slightest of technical problems they called in engineers/ technicians from port to do their jobs for them. I was sure this guy would roam around the E/R in his uniform instructing people to do nonsensical work. He could never understand the high level of work which was being done here by this small team.

He went on and on and I was looking at his rotten cabbage like face twist and turn as he spoke. His damaged left eye suited his personality. He should have auditioned for the Pirates of the Carribean.

That night I hit the bed early and slept soundly for a good six hours. Next morning I reached for my watch 10 minutes early. I felt fresh and somehow felt good about everything around. I entered ECR. 3rd was sitting on a chair, his legs spread out in front and his body slumped towards left...he was snoring. I cleared my throat but that didn't wake him up so I shook him gently.

"Hi 3rd I am here..." I said looking at all the 4 bilge well high level alarms. It felt like déjà vu. I somehow knew I would be running down yet again and hopefully there'd be no flooding either.

"Anything happening 3rd?" I wished that he went away soon... I wanted to rush down to check if all was well. But he sat there lazing around.

I felt he hadn't heard me so I repeated my question, "3rd..."

He yawned lazily before replying, "Deck called for water to wash the decks half an hour back. We need to be spic and span before reaching Panama." He said that and left.

I looked at the console panel to find out which pump was running. I looked at the green light S.W. Pump #2 running. It was the same pump which is supposed to be out of order. I looked at the board, on it was written in 2nd's handwriting, 'S.W. P/P #2 out of order'. I wondered whether they had repaired the pipeline yesterday. I didn't want to take any chances so I pressed the red button next to the green one to stop the pump. I ran out sweating. I peeped down from the top praying to God that the déjà vu comes true! But what I saw killed me. There was water all over the bottom platform. For a moment my brain went into a tizzy, everything went blank before my eyes and I felt my knees would give way...I wished it was some bad dream. But then I somehow took control of my mind. My analysis of the situation was that we were truly, deeply and madly fucked!

I shouted for Tengalkar as I rushed down…there was no time to think, I had to act. There was knee deep water on the bottom platform which meant that E/R was flooded with 5-6 feet of water; enough water to fill an Olympic size swimming pool! If I were late by a few minutes sea water would have gone into electrical circuits, motors and the generators, which meant that we would have lost main source of electricity, the ship would be running on emergency generators, this generator would have powered the emergency bilge pump but with the motor of this pump spoilt we would have to bring in air driven portable pumps to pump out water…it would have cost us a lot of time. I went in the water as I had to reach the faulty line to close the valves.

Though the pump was not running there was enough pressurized water in the line to continue flooding for a long time. The water was freezing cold. I started moving towards the pipeline carefully keeping my steps ahead. I didn't want to fall of the platform into the bilges; could easily bump my head on anything down there and drown. I could see the top of the railings which meant there would be stairs here. I knew there were three steps, which I counted as I reached nearer to the pump. Water was rising fast and I was down till my waist. I prayed Tengalkar would have heard me. The inlet valve was submerged and it took me a while to close it. Water was still oozing out with considerable force. I would have to climb up to the raised platform above to close the outlet valve which was not accessible from where I was standing. I would have lost time reaching the stairs to this platform so I held onto the motor of the pump with one hand, kept one foot on the pipeline and with the other hand I pulled myself up.

With the outlet valve shut the leak was contained and now I had to pump out the water. I looked towards the emergency bilge pump and the suction valve; both of them were above the water. I saw Tengalkar coming towards me.

I shouted, "This is done. Now start opening the bilge suction valve, we need to pump out the water now!"

He looked totally lost but he moved faster than me...he had been on this ship long enough to be able to run blindfolded all over the E/R. He reached in front of the valve in no time but he couldn't open the valve with his hands. The valve was stuck! 4th Engineer was supposed to try it out and grease it every week.

"Tengalkar what happened to the red coloured valve opener which is supposed to be near the emergency valve?" I shouted.

"I can't find it! I saw it here on our last watch! Someone must have used it and forgotten to keep it back!"

This valve opener is an iron rod which has two extended parallel portion on one end which are to be put in the wheel of the valve.

I shouted, "Do you know this valve opens in the opposite direction to other normal valves?"

"Yes paanch sa'ab I am turning in clockwise direction. It is stuck."

I looked around and found an opener hanging near the outlet valve of the faulty line. I took it and retraced my steps back to the short flight of stairs. I was much faster now. I gave the valve opener to Tengalkar and as he put force on the valve I applied pressure with my hands. The valve creaked open after a little struggle.

Tengalkar started the pump. It started but I was tensed whether it would take suction. Since 4th hadn't been maintaining it, there was a chance that a cloth piece was stuck in the suction pipe.

Tengalkar was looking at the suction line exclaimed, "It is taking suction!"

I looked down and could see the water around the pipe moving and I shook his hands. In 10 minutes the platform above the short stairs was visible. In the next 5 even that platform was visible. It was a powerful pump. Tengalkar had started the bilge pump as well. Though it was a small pump it helped us get the work done faster.

We reached the ECR drenched and dead tired. It was 7.30 already.

"Tengalkar do you have cigarettes?" I looked at our drenched overalls and said, "Oh forget it..."

He opened his chest pocket and took out a packet which was carefully wrapped in plastic.

He looked at my raised eyebrows and the mischievous smile and raised his hands as if to stop me from making any comments, "I wrap in plastic to save it from my sweat. Don't think I come prepared for flooding in E/R. That would be the last thing on any seaman's mind!"

I didn't mind that I was not smoking my usuals. In fact I hadn't ever enjoyed smoking as much as I did that day!

Satya was the first one to arrive, "Goodmorning! What happened to you guys? Went swimming?"

"You'll know in sometime. Let others come in," said Tengalkar.

4th came in next fake smile firmly in place, "Goodmorni..." he stood still when he set sight on us, "...what? You guys cleaning the bilges today?"

I said, "Yeah Sam sort of."

2nd came in after a few minutes, "Whoaaa, all well?" he asked me.

"All well now. Lot of action today on the watch..." and I narrated the whole story. I could see jaws drop all around me.

"You should have called me 5th! Next time any emergency I want all engineers and motormen down here." said 2nd visibly angry.

Sam added, "Yes you should have raised the alarm..."

I replied, "I know it was a mistake but then we hardly had any time. I needed Tengalkar around...water was filling fast...we had to act."

Sam looked angry too, "There are protocols to be followed in an emergency. What if you couldn't have handled it? Calling others after damage is done wouldn't have solved any problem, right?"

2nd looked hard at Sam and said, "5th is right. He took a risk by not informing us and utilised the time to solve the problem. In an emergency following a protocol is the dumbest thing you can do." He looked at me and said, "Good work."

I smiled, "Couldn't have managed without Tengalkar."

2nd nodded and then his face was stern again as he looked around and asked, "Who started the goddamn Pump #2?"

I replied, "Call for water on deck had come in 3rd's watch."

Tengalkar replied, "Gadhav started it..."

2nd was angry, "Was 3rd sleeping? 4th did you inform him that it has been put out of order?"

Sam replied, "Y-yes 2nd. Of course I told him. Moreover it's written in bold over here." He pointed at the board.

2nd said, "I'm sure everybody here knows that we could have been screwed in a big way...if sea water had even touched the coils of the generator all of us would be shitting blood by now to make them operational. If the motors were drowned we would need 100 battis here working for us. And we are to reach Panama today afternoon. The entry fee is huge and the company has already paid for our ticket to cross Panama. We can't communicate to H.O. with a mail reading, 'Sorry we can't cross the Panama because we were sleeping in our watch and the engine room got flooded and we have managed to fuck all the machines. So we request for a dry dock so that repair work can be carried out. Regards, the efficient hard working engineers of M.T. Limar.' What a sham!"

I had never heard 2nd speak so much and that day he not only spoke, but was good at it. In terms of expressions and dialogue delivery he had suddenly transformed from Arnold Schwarzenegger to Al Pacino.

13

CHAPTER

The Spirit of the Panama

When I reached ECR for the afternoon watch, the ship wasn't moving.

3rd said, "We are anchored in the Carribean sea. Engines are on Standby...on half an hour notice. It means bridge would call half an hour before they need engines. Call Chief, 2nd and Batti when a call from bridge comes."

He didn't make fun of me. 2nd would have given him a good session, I thought. I went for my round. I reached the compressors, they were running fine. Tengalkar reached there...in his hands was a flexible cylindrical object which looked like lots of rings were put together to make it. When he opened the contraption the material in between the rings came up to form a flexi cylindrical duct; it was folded like a spring. He took one end and inserted it into an opening, which was around 7 feet from the compressors, in the air duct running above and brought the other end near the compressors.

He looked at me smiling, "Now they'll get all the fresh air and will not overheat due to continuous running."

I signalled thumbs up to him. No wonder Sam wanted him in his watch. I looked at the two huge air bottles. They held air at 30 bar. To start the engines a minimum of 17 bars should be there in the bottle. The air compressor cuts in when the pressure in either bottle drops to 20. They definitely would be doing overtime during the long maneuvering which requires a lot of stopping and then starting of the engines.

Bridge called ECR at 1800.

I picked the phone, "Hello, 5th Engineer, Engine Room."

"Hi 5th, 3rd officer. Engines required in half an hour."

Everyone required for manoeuvering were down in the next 10 minutes. I went down to see how Tengalkar prepared the engines. We both came up in the next 10 mins. ECR was abuzz with excitement. Crossing the Panama must be fun, I thought.

Batti asked me, "5th have you crossed the Panama before?"

"No Batti sa'ab this is my first ship...and I never took a boating trip with my father."

Everybody except Batti laughed. He continued, "You should go up and see the sight. It's beautiful."

I nodded, "I've heard so much already. I will try to see as much as possible."

Chief was listening to this conversation quietly. I knew he did not like the fact that I would be enjoying the view after my watch. The phone rang and I picked up.

"Hello 5th. Captain here...I'm giving the Dead Slow Ahead command." And with that the Telegraph lever on Bridge was moved to DS Ahead. The school bell kind of ringing stopped only when 2nd matched the Bridge order by moving the ECR Telegraph lever to DS Ahead. He also moved the speed setting regulator so that starting air was let in the engines. The noise of air going in and moving the heavy parts of the engine could be distinctly heard even inside the ECR and then I could make out as first combustion happened within the cylinders. We stopped again at Limon Bay and anchored. We were in a queue to enter the lock gates of the Panama Canal.

Bridge informed at 1930 that the pilot who would navigate us through was on board. I called the manoeuvering team down again. By the time the ship started moving, I had handed over to 3rd. I came up and headed for the port side lifeboat deck. I could get a good view of the forward, aft and the port side from here. We were slowly moving ahead in this natural bay. It was quite narrow as land on both the sides was visible. Up ahead around 300 metres from us was the first lock gate. We stopped in front of the massive lock gate of Gatun Lake. It looked like the iron door of a fortress. There are two parallel sets of locks. The lock gate in front of us was closed and I could see a ship inside, it was around 8 metres above us. A huge ship 8 metres above sounds and looks as improbable as a ship on an escalator. There were 3 lock gates, which would raise our ship around 26 metres above the Atlantic; escalator for the ships! As the ship ahead and on top of us moved into the second lock gate and the gate closed, the lock gate in front of us opened and with that water from it drained into Limon Bay. We moved in and the gate closed behind us. Water started filling in our gate. I was amazed to see the speed with which we were rising; we were up in less than 10 minutes. The ship ahead was still around 8 meters above us and when it moved into the third lock gate, the second lock gate opened and water from it drained into the first one. When the water level in gate 1 and gate 2 had become equal we moved into gate 2. The door of gate 2 closed and water was filled in again and we rose similarly. After the third gate we entered Gatun lake. We would be travelling 37 kms in the lake. No wonder this was the largest man made lake in the world; it spanned an area of 425 km2.

The view was splendid and the journey long, I couldn't stand there all that while. So I thought of spending the remaining time from the deck outside my accommodation floor towards the aft. This part of deck also connected all the floors of accommodation and the Bridge with the deck. 2 exits to this part were given on all the accommodation floors. These exits were also emergency exits; in the event of fire in the accommodation the stairs were to be used, the wooden stairs, which I used to go down to E/R everyday, would be on fire anyway. Though I would not have been able to see the forward part, there would have been nobody to disturb me. I took 4 cans of Budweiser from my cabin on my way out. My beer stock was about to get over...I would have to place a requisition at the provisions store. A case of 12 cans of Buds would cost me around $11 while a case of Coke would be a dollar costlier. Who wanted a Coke anyway?

I walked to the aft, opened the door and came out on the stairway. I walked towards the starboard side railing as there was enough space to sit down with legs spread wide. Somebody on my floor was a health freak...I thought looking at the punching bag hung in the way. I breathed in and punched a few into the bag. I stopped mid-way as I saw someone standing near the staircase which led to the upper decks. I approached to see who it was and was surprised to see a tall man standing and smoking a cigar! He wasn't from our ship.

I said, "Sir, you can't smoke out here. This is an oil tanker."

He smiled, extended his hand to shake mine and said, "The ship is on ballast...we are safe. Moreover, the winds in Panama are strong. Do not worry I wouldn't have been smoking if there was any threat."

He spoke with authority and conviction; I couldn't help but believe in him. He looked like he had served as a high ranking army officer most of his life.

I thought, "If this guy works with Panama he should have been either on the Bridge or Cargo Control Room...outsiders do not belong on the accommodation deck.

I asked, "Are you lost, sir? This is the accommodation deck..."

"No son I am not. The view is beautiful from here. Do you know what those are?" he said pointing towards green islands in the lake.

I said, "They look like islands."

"Those are hill tops."

I exclaimed, "Hills?"

"This whole area was a forest before the canal was built. The islands all around actually are submerged hills which remained uncut when this lake was being dug up."

"Very interesting! I also was amazed with the way we

were lifted in the locks...pure brilliance. Imagine someone thinking of it way back then!"

I could see the pride in his eyes. He looked towards the hills for a moment and then said, "It was John F Stevens who first suggested that to Roosevelt."

I was surprised, "Roosevelt, President of US." And then in the same breath asked, "John Stevens?"

"I am not surprised you don't know John. He was the man behind the Panama Canal."

I said sheepishly, "Oh? I am not aware of Panama's history."

"It has a rich history. Way back in 1524 Charles V, the king of Spain, Germany, Austria and Burgundy thought of getting a canal built which would considerably shorten the trip of his ships which were bringing in gold plundered from Peru, Ecquador and Asia."

I said, "Sounds interesting!"

He continued, "Then came the French in the 1800s. The man in charge was Count Ferdinand. He was the same person under whose command the Suez Canal was built. He was eager to build an inter-oceanic canal. This was his dream project..."

I blurted, "Oh, but I thought Americans built the canal."

He looked at me quizzically and then he laughed. I shuddered and wondered how powerful his punch would be when his laugh itself was that powerful.

"You thought right. Ferdinand had underestimated the project. He wanted to make a sea level canal and for that a lot of land has to be excavated. The French engineers arrived in 1881 and they dug for 8 years but they succumbed to the torrential rains and disease infested land. When people were hired for the job they were kept in the dark about difficult working conditions. The firm was already in financial problems plus they fetched a lot of bad publicity with this project."

I said thoughtfully, "It would have killed Ferdinand. After building the Suez he must have thought he will be able to succeed in Panama too."

"Suez was a piece of cake. Panama was a real tough one."

"Oh I had forgotten. Would you like to have beer?" I said, taking out the cans from my pocket.

"Why yes." He looked at the can as if he had seen nothing like it before. "Beer in it?"

I showed him how to open it. He took a swig immediately, "Hmmm...this isn't like the raw beer I am used to but it's good."

I wanted to continue our discussion. I probed, "So Panama wasn't easy, eh?"

"22,000 French lives were lost here. But their efforts didn't go in vain; they left their machinery here and they had done a lot of digging which was a lot of help for Americans. But the most important lessons were to be learnt from the mistakes Ferdinand committed."

I asked with interest, "And what were those?"

"Stevens was quick to realise that improving the living standards of his team was of the utmost importance. He brought with him his team of doctors, who had a lot on their plates when they came here. Do you know that these doctors found out for the world that mosquitoes were the disease vectors for malaria and yellow fever?"

I was amazed, "Wow! I didn't know that!"

"The poor French didn't know their very hospitals were the breeding grounds for the killer disease bearing mosquitoes. Stevens knew this so the first thing he did on arriving was build a good infrastructure. He made proper housing arrangements; good sanitation was ensured with efficient mosquito control and he also built railways for transporting soil and rocks."

"Panama Railways? Stevens built that!"

He smiled and went on, "The best is yet to come. Roosevelt was convinced about sea level canal while Stevens researched and found out building that was a waste of time. He argued against it and proposed the lock gate concept that we see today. He lobbied in government, presented data including the one that showed sea level at Caribbean side was lower than that of Pacific level."

"It seems Stevens was the man responsible for the way

Panama is today. I guess history doesn't speak of him much..."

He said lamentably, "Maybe. But the fact is that he was the chief architect of the canal. Without infrastructure built by him Americans would have met the same fate that the French met. And they would have run back one day. Without the lock gate concept the canal could never have been built. Maybe because he stood by his plan he would have created enemies. Maybe he wasn't happy with the treatment given to him and that is why he resigned suddenly."

I asked, "Did the world know the real reason for his resignation?"

"He never told anyone. He was a great guy...a visionary and a great leader. When he arrived he saw people were ready to leave on the same ship he had arrived upon. The chief engineer he was replacing too was running away. He famously addressed the team, 'There are three diseases on the Isthmus- Yellow Fever, Malaria and cold feet. The worst is cold feet. That's what is ailing you!' His presence gave them the confidence to stay back."

"It's sad that he had to resign. So he couldn't complete the project."

He said with a smile, "Yes son it's sad. But he came back to US and led a long happy life. He knew he had delivered his promise and that he had created a platform for work to go on. Colonel George Washington replaced him and completed building the canal. But he knew who the actual hero was. In one letter to his son he wrote, "Mr Stevens has perfected such an organisation that there's nothing left for us to do but just have the organisation continue the good work it has been doing. Mr Stevens has done an amount of work for which he will never get any credit or if he gets any will not be enough."

We quietly sipped beer for a while enjoying the scenery. He said looking at the lights on the sides of the lake, "It's unfortunate that hardly anyone knows the kind of sacrifice people have made to build this haloed place. A total of 30,000 people lost their lives here!"

I blew out a whistle.

I remembered Sam had told me about booster pumps in the lock gates. I asked, "How did they create such powerful booster pumps in those days?"

"What booster pumps?"

"The ones to pump in and out water from the locks."

He started laughing again, "There are no pumps son."

I exclaimed, "Gravity?"

"Correct!"

"But wouldn't they be losing a lot of water since it would get drained into the sea?"

"With passage of a single ship around 197 million litres of water gets drained into the sea!"

I shook my head in disbelief, "Oh God!"

"In a year on an average it turns out to be around 2,517 trillion."

"God! How on earth does this amount of water get replenished?"

"We need to thank Stevens yet again for this. He built the dams which retain the rain water. As of now the rains comfortably replenish the loss. Also all electricity requirements are met by dams' hydroelectric power generation."

"An environment friendly canal!"

He asked me, "What are you doing here?"

"We're going to Esmeraldes to load fuel oil..."

He said pointing his huge fingers at me, "No-no I'm asking about you."

"I'm not sure actually...maybe drifting like that log of wood there...searching for answers."

"I guess most of us are searching for answers...Stevens was too. Maybe he didn't resign because he was unhappy...maybe he resigned because he got the answers."

"I can't compare myself with Stevens. He was a man who knew! He did a great job and so many people are proud of him."

He said abruptly, "Where are those people? He never got credit and appreciation for what he accomplished. But I don't think he needed that. He did something which he felt was correct and he did it with all his heart and look at the result!"

I asked, "What do you believe in?"

"That mind is very powerful and that my potential to do things is limitless."

"Can you do anything possible?" I asked, amused.

"And anything that most people think impossible," he said with conviction.

"Then that makes you a Superman. Who are you?"

He laughed again as he found the term funny, "Superman?"

"What's your name and what do you do?"

"Name's Frank and I travel mostly."

I persisted, "But who are you?"

"We were discussing you Siddhartha. How do you solve your problems?"

I replied, "I keep thinking about how to find solutions."

"What if you don't find any...what do you do then?"

"I get worried..."

"Ok but what do you do to forget the worries?"

"I sleep."

"What happens when you sleep?"

"I feel relaxed...maybe it helps me think better...maybe it lessens the load of the problem."

"How does it happen when you sleep?"

"Frank, I'm clueless about this."

He said with a knowing smile, "Because when you sleep your mind is finding the answers. Your past experiences, your strengths, weaknesses, learning, essentially everything about you is stored in the subconscious and it tries to find the solution for you. That's why a dream maybe is a way in which the subconscious is giving you a hint."

I said smiling, "Is that why the term 'sleep over it' came into being?"

"Ok let's come to a different point now. What is troubling you?"

"Actually, so many things are. My colleagues don't think much of me. I don't know whether I belong here. I don't know what I should be doing..."

"Forget the little issues...if I were to ask you one problem which were to be removed from your life and your life would change for good, what would that be?"

I thought for a while and then said, "It's actually not a problem...it's something that I want to do. I want to be successful and happy in life but I don't know how to reach there. I like seeing the look on a tennis player who lifts the Wimbledon trophy after winning against the favourite champion, I like it when a struggling actor wins the best actor award...basically I like it when the underdogs win...you know, the best part is the way their faces glow...it's genuine happiness, not a practiced expression of conceit. I want to feel that way."

He was smiling, nodding, "I understand what you are feeling...but it's more because you're unclear of the direction you want to take. But don't stop living till then. Are you living in the moment? Don't dwell too much on the time gone by or the time to come, live in the now. Slow down, look up in the sky, breathe in the fresh air, smell the flowers...it's perfect."

"One day...that perfect day will come and then you see...it'll all seem as you are saying."

"No point waiting for that perfect day son."

"Why? There are days you feel on top of the world and that perfect day you would be unbeatable and happy and powerful...and rich!"

"Because a perfect day never comes, any normal day becomes one."

"Yes Frank but when will mine come?"

"You still aren't getting it. You make the day perfect yourself. You start feeling on top of the world now and you've got your perfect day. If you want everyday would be that perfect day you've been waiting for."

I asked, "What about the broader picture?"

He didn't get my question. He looked at me quizzically and asked, "What about it?"

I said, "Do I not need to prepare for the perfect day? How do I know when the day arrives?"

"Listen son, planning is good but don't forget to enjoy the ride. You would have heard this before but the journey is more important than the destination. Your life is a journey; don't waste even a single moment pursuing materialistic bliss."

"But isn't success important?"

"Success too is like life itself. I mean, success too should be taken as a journey not the end result. Do you think you being successful once in life is enough? Do you think Stevens' journey was over after he achieved success at Panama?"

"Hmmm...of course Stevens would have been successful in everything he would have done in life."

"Exactly, successes would come and so would failures, but then all of them give you an important wealth called experience. Neither should failure make you stop neither should success go into your head and make you complacent...you need to keep moving. After all you've got only one life to do it all!"

"I see the point Frank."

"Remember to listen to your inner voice, you won't be disappointed."

"I will...Frank? Who are you?"

He smiled again. "Like I said, it's not important who I am. I can be any of those 80,000 people who toiled to make this place. I can be Ferdinand or Stevens...my life revolves around this canal and its magnificent history. I am...the spirit of the Panama Canal."

"You are a tough one...but really, thank you."

"Well my job here is done. I've another appointment to keep."

"It was a pleasure sir."

"So long Siddhartha."

He glided down the iron stairs quite fast yet he didn't make any noise. I could see the cigar smoke for a while and then only darkness. What a guy! There was something which I had forgotten to ask him but I couldn't remember what that was. I remained in the breeze for a while not thinking anything at all...just enjoying the view like Frank had told me to do. When I got in bed I realised what I had forgotten to ask him. I hadn't mentioned my name to him...how on earth did he know it? I thought I would ask Param about it the nest day. He would know who all had come on board.

14

Mrs. Kavita

Next morning I found 3rd sleeping again when I came to take over my watch.

I shouted, "Hi 3rd. Oh sorry did I disturb you?"

He almost fell off the chair, "Huh...what makes you think that? I wasn't sleeping..." He could barely speak.

I said sarcastically, "Oh no, you were not. You look so fresh 3rd."

He looked at me in disbelief and went away after informing me of what was happening.

No alarms on the control panel today. Tengalkar came in, "Goodmorning paanch sa'ab."

"Good morning...Tengalkar paanch sa'ab sounds as ridiculous as paanchu. Call me Siddhartha if possible?"

"Ok. Do you know we have a party tonight?"

"Party what for?" I asked interestedly.

"We have one every month. Only this time it's been around 2 months and no party."

"Hmmm...batti sa'ab would be so happy!"

We looked at each other and laughed.

Around 10 I came up to the ECR. Chief Engineer came in a few minutes later. Like always, he stank of alcohol. And like always he was chewing *elaichi* thinking he would be able to hide the foul smell.

He wasn't too happy to see me there. He asked disapprovingly, "What? No work today?"

I retorted, "I just came up bada sa'ab. As it is, you would have called me up."

He was studying me but I maintained a wooden face.

He asked strictly, "How's your progress in learning?"

"It's good. Still a lot to learn though."

"You don't pick calls at your cabin."

"Then I must not be there...otherwise I would pick up." I said smiling innocently.

"How will you learn if you don't interact with your seniors? Not everything can be learned in the E/R."

"Chief what will I learn in your cabin? The last few times I've been there we discuss family."

He said threateningly, "Now-now you shouldn't be disrespecting your seniors! It's for your good that I'm telling you. Upto you whether you want to move ahead in life."

I said firmly, "Chief I am old enough to understand what's good for me. Please do not patronise me. I've come here to learn and learn I will in the E/R. Filing your cabinet is not something which will help me move ahead in life anyway!"

For the next few seconds his left eye stopped blinking, his mouth though remained open for a little longer. I felt he wanted to say a lot of things at once but he couldn't. It also looked as if he was about to cry. I was already having regular nightmares, seeing tears fall down from his cabbage face would have added one more to my list.

Right then like a knight in shining armour, Sam came in the ECR and rescued me.

"Good morning bada sa'ab. How are you today?" he said pleasantly.

Chief complained, "4th I'm not too happy. Your *guru dakshina* from last port is about to get over...only one small peg remaining."

"I'll get one more from Esmeraldes sir...no worries."

I left the love birds in the nest and came down to what I had come here for, to work.

The party as I came to know during the day was to

start at 1900 and would go on till the time people wanted it to. I was studying the cam operation when the phone rang so I picked it up from the emergency manoeuvering platform itself.

"Hello, 5th Engineer, Engine Room."

The voice on the other end said, "Captain here. It's your first party. I'm sending 4th down early so that you can come up."

I said politely, "Thanks Captain. My watch gets over in fifty minutes so will join the party then itself."

Captain insisted, "4th is willing to come down. I already spoke with him..."

"Captain please...I'll be more comfortable if I finish my watch and then come up."

Captain suggested, "Ok 5th. But don't lose out on this opportunity to meet your new family."

"Sure Captain. Appreciate you calling me up."

Parties were always held in the Crew's Smoke Room but this time they had made an exception and it was arranged in open air...on the Bridge Deck. It was an ideal night...a perfect moonlit sky...and cool breeze from the sea.

The galley was working all day long to prepare food for the party. A large table was placed in the centre. I could see different kinds of salads, cheese, fries and other starters placed neatly all over the table. The party was in full swing and I could see the excitement all around. I was received warmly. Bosun came up to me and I was taken aback by his warmth.

He said, "5th what do you want to drink?" and he led me to another table where the drinks were placed.

I said smiling, "You can call me Paanchu if you want. I have begun to like cute names." He laughed with me. I took a can of beer. Somebody hit me hard from behind.

I turned around, "Param! I should have guessed."

He was his usual self, "You're having beer. You can have that everyday! Real men have scotch!" he said pointing to his glass.

I shook my head, "It's ok buddy. Beer's good. Cheers!"

Param said, "Come Sid let me introduce you to

everyone." With that we went to the circle where the senior engineers and officers were standing. I had met all the officers once or twice during meals but not the Captain. He was a tall good looking guy in his late 40s. He seemed well-read and looked like a gentleman...the exact opposite of Chief Engineer.

I extended my hand as I said warmly, "Hello Captain."

The captain shook hands and said, "How's your first voyage turning out to be?"

I replied, "I think I'll not run away!"

He smiled and Bada sa'ab looked away, "Which batch of MEII are you from? A close friend of mine is your senior."

"I am 2003 batch. Your friend...where does he live...is he in our company?"

"He lives in Bombay. He doesn't sail anymore. He's planning to make a movie."

I said jokingly, "Captain, can you please put in a word for me...I'll act for free!"

Captain laughed while Bada sa'ab looked at me with disgust.

I shook hands with the Chief Officer. He was the first person I had spoken to on ship. He was the tallest guy and the one with the longest face. He didn't like alcohol...he didn't like food either; he survived on Pringles and Coke. The shape of his face had a stark similarity to the chips he was so fond of. He always had a smirk on his face as if he found everything wrong with the world. 2nd and 3rd officer were funny, happy people.

3rd officer was teasing 2nd officer, "Now most of the people go shore to get drunk...some go spend money on girls. Our 2nd too goes spends money on both. But you know what 5th?"

I was wondering why 3rd would speak of 2nd's conquests in front of so many people, "Ummm I don't want to hear this 3rd."

3rd shook his head saying, "You got to hear this. He doesn't drink himself, neither does he sleep with the girl! He offers free sex to one of the crew."

2nd officer looked at 3rd officer and said, "Maybe

you should drink something. Maybe you'll make sense then!"

3rd corrected himself, "Hey come on you know I didn't mean that! I meant 2nd pays for one of the crew's expenses to go with a girl."

3rd engineer who was quietly looking at the proceedings till now spoke, "Now 2nd why do you always do that?"

2nd replied quite coldly, "It's my money...I spend the way I want to. Next time you tell me first and I'll pay for you too teen sa'ab."

We all laughed madly and 3rd engineer obviously didn't like it...especially that I was laughing too. He then went to 2nd officer and wrapped his arms around his shoulders as if they were the best of friends. 2nd didn't look too comfortable. It was getting too uncomfortable, so I moved out on the pretext of getting a beer. Param came along saying, "*Sheesh* this 3rd is a shady guy man! How do you bear him?"

I said, "Do I have a choice? Anyway, Param I met Frank yesterday."

"Who?"

"Come on man. Quit playing games..."

"You alright Sid?"

I looked at him. He actually had no idea what I was talking about. "Were you on watch when the pilot came on board?"

"I was on the watch throughout the Panama. Like always I went to receive the pilot."

"Who was accompanying the pilot?"

"Are you nuts? Nobody accompanies the pilot! What's wrong with you?"

I said playfully, "Param, see I got you!" I had to fake it or else I would have got into trouble. Afterall I was having beer with a stranger who was smoking on the deck!

Param wasn't convinced. He asked again, "What about Frank? Who's he?"

"Come on Param, I was joking. He's a Ghhhoosssssttt..." I said spookily.

We joined the group after we took our drinks.

I brought the discussion back to 2nd's 'cupid'ly behaviour. "So who's benefited the maximum times because of 2nd's philanthropy?"

3rd officer's face lit up immediately, "AB Senthil gets the prize almost everytime. In fact he goes out only if 2nd is around."

I couldn't resist this opportunity, "That makes our Senthil the numero uno user of the 'Seamen's Welfare Free Fuck Fund'...we can call it SWF3 and the name sounds like a new strain of virus which has been recently found in the ports of South America!"

Everybody around me laughed...3rd officer almost fell on the deck...even 2nd officer couldn't stop himself.

I went on, "And Mr Senthil may be known as 'Fokat Cho**' (Free Fucker)...FC." FC noticed us looking at him and laughing so he came to us. He was a tall well built guy in his early thirties. But his voice was contrary to his appearance. It was very shrill...almost feminine. I closed my eyes as he spoke and I pictured the face behind the voice. The face frightened me; it was that of an old witch who had still not recovered from a lifetime of laryngitis.

Though I was apprehensive of getting cold shouldered, I went around and introduced myself to everyone. And I could see that they accepted me as their family. The change towards me I guessed would have been because of Tengalkar or Satya.

I looked around, Batti had started dancing and he was excitedly showing his 'moves' to the crew. I saw the new fitter Osman sitting in one corner having beer. He was like the genie; after getting the worklist from 2nd in the morning he would disappear from everyone's sight and would go on ruthlessly about his work. Throughout the day he took a break only for tea and lunch. Other than that he would work non-stop; no chit chat, no bullshit... nothing except pure dedicated work.

I approached him and said, "Hello Osman. You enjoying?"

As we shook hands I noticed his wrist was as wide as my calf. He appeared short because of his heavy built while actually he was as tall as me. He had a pair of light blue eyes which reminded me of the colour of the sky. They looked perfect on his fair round face.

He said his eyes twinkling, "Osman enjoying. Food good. Indian music good."

I said, "Osman I have heard people in your country have big families."

He struggled to explain, "Oh no. Osman country brother, father, mother, uncles live in one house."

"Ok joint family. How big is your family?"

"Osman family small. Osman Mother, Osman, Osman wife, Osman 7 children, Osman 4 brother, Osman all brothers' wife, Osman brothers' 14 children."

I counted, "Oh! 32 members and that's a small family?"

He nodded earnestly his eyes open wide.

"Osman may I ask a personal question?"

"Osman no problem."

"Ok...your father had 5 children, your 4 brothers 14 children, but you alone 7 children. Why do you have more?"

He laughed but I could see he was blushing, "Osman brothers work in village, come back to their wife everyday. Osman on ship, 3 months home. Osman too much love for wife. Osman no do anything...love come out!" he said as he shrugged.

I looked at him and smiled. He really believed what he was saying. I looked around me. The crew was dancing. Captain, Chief Engineer, 2nd Engineer, Chief Officer and 3rd Engineer had left. Each and every person around me was different but everyone here was real. They loved their families passionately, believed in God, they meant what they said and their smiles reached their eyes. Being away from family, they understood the true meaning of love and working in tough conditions they realised the importance of life. Almost everyone of the crew had quit school when they were quite young; the sea had taught them several important lessons in life, most of which could not possibly be learnt from textbooks. I joined them in the dance and they surrounded me happily. After a long time I felt happiness. I must have been happier than this before...but what I felt now was different, for the first time in my life I was enjoying being under my skin...for the first time in my life I felt I was celebrating myself.

My happiness evaporated when I looked at Batti dance. I froze as he started coming towards me. As soon as I came to my senses I rushed out of the group. Osman was still around sitting at the same place I had left him. He pointed at Batti and asked, "Is that Indian dance?"

"No, that is 'out of this world' dance. Batti is an alien. You understand alien?"

"Osman know. Osman saw Arnold movie 'Predator'. Now Osman take Arnold role and kill Batti!" he said it trying to imitate Arnold's wooden face. I started imagining how Osman's round body would look in leather tights...even the famous line "I'll be back!" would have to be changed to "Osman be back!". I fell down on the deck laughing. I lay there for a while saying, "Osman you're very funny." I looked up at the full moon. I had never seen it like that before. It looked amazingly beautiful and sort of eerie.

Bosun took a break from dancing, came near and asked me, "Do you believe ghosts exist?"

"Huh! Perfect question for this night," I said.

"You didn't answer my question."

"I don't know Bosun...have you seen any?"

He said, "Yes..."

So I went up to the dancing group and shouted, "Do you want to keep dancing or you want to listen to a ghost story?"

Param came running and others immediately followed suit. In five minutes everybody was seated on the deck forming a circle. There was only one guy who wasn't interested in the story...Batti. He was dancing with a can of beer in his hand and in another was his imaginary cigarette. The music volume had been reduced but it had no effect on him and he continued his monkey act. He was doing his version of Tango with an imaginary partner. The song playing was 'Aye kya bolti tu...' from the popular movie Ghulam. Batti had discovered a new dance form and he passionately continued with his running and jumping around not caring that the beats of the song demanded slow moves.

Bosun cleared his throat to attract attention, "It was a regular spring morning. The sun had not risen yet and the breeze was cool and refreshing. It was perfect weather for my father and his men. The waves gently touched my feet as I watched them prepare the boats. All the 8 boats belonged to my father. My father had started going to fish with his father since he was my age. He had inherited a boat from him and had grown his fleet in the due course of time. I went closer to the boat. I folded my cream coloured school pants to my knees. 'When will you be back Papa?' I would always ask this question before he left and I always accompanied him there. After seeing him off I would go to school. It was a ritual.

He said smiling warmly, "I'll be back before sun sets today. I will get you a cake before coming home. Happy birthday Govi."

I had turned 14. I stood there till the boats became tiny specs on the horizon. This is what I wanted to do. I loved the sea and I loved my father's job. One day I'll have 14 boats for fishing, I thought as I stood at the beach that morning.

I turned back towards where I had left my shoes. I hated this part of the day. I hated school and especially the History classes. Mrs Kavita the teacher slapped me almost everyday. 'You are a good for nothing fellow. I will make a better person out of you. I want 100 percent attendance from you Govi. Dare not fall ill on days I've classes,' she would shout at me."

Bosun looked around. He took a swig from his glass and continued, "She didn't look like a cruel person at all. She was in her late forties but looked older than that though she had a thin frame. She walked peculiarly¾she took short and fast steps. But that wasn't the only reason why I could recognise her steps from long distance; it was mainly because I was afraid of her. Listening to her steps fear would grip me and my mind and body would become paralysed. But seeing her walk was like seeing death itself; though she would be walking at a low speed it would seem that she is running to me and would kill me as soon as she catches up.

"I was sitting in the class cursing my luck. I didn't want to see her that day…I didn't want to get beaten up on my birthday! I could hear her climbing down the stairs…she would be here in a minute. This sound has been tormenting me for six years. I picked up my stuff and ran outside. I didn't have the guts to see how far she was but when she shouted I could feel her breath on the back of my neck.

"Goviii! You can't run away from me! Never! Goviii, come back here you scoundrel!' I kept running for a long time and then fell on the ground trying to catch my breath as I whined. I looked around…she wasn't there. I cried for sometime and then thought of what I should tell my father when he comes back in the evening."

"Well, I told my father that I won't be going back to school again. I told him that I had always dreamt of owning 14 boats. He never asked me any reason for quitting studies so I let it at that. Though I never went anywhere near the school I feared she would come home, convince my parents and take me back to school. Two months later my friends told me she had stopped coming to school so some teachers from school went up to her place. Her house wasn't locked so they went in. She wasn't around and strangely her house was in perfect order. Police were informed and according to them nothing looked wrong at her place. For the next few days I would hear different stories about her; some say they had seen a mad woman run towards the sea on the same night she had disappeared, some said the bus she was going in met with an accident… for me the worst had just begun. She would return every night in my dreams and I would wake up in cold sweat. I joined my father on his fishing trips to take my mind off the nightmares. I would come back home tired but when I slept I would dream about her chasing me or killing me. With time the nightmares became fewer, but they never went away. There was still no news of her and that made things complicated. I wouldn't go out alone even during the day, as I feared she would come out from behind the trees. I had to get out of this place and one day my uncle told me about this job on the ship. In those days life on ship was much tougher but I was happy that my nightmares had stopped. I did well in my career and with that my confidence grew. When I returned home from my first ship I was glad to be there and there were no sleepless nights anymore."

Param was livid, "Wow such a long story but where's the horror in this?"

Bosun looked at us all and said, "The horror started before I joined this ship! She's back!"

I felt cold. I could see fear in everyone's eyes; they had huddled closer. The moonlight falling on our faces made the setting eerier. The music was still playing and ironically the romantic number appeared devilish to me: '...killing me softly with his...my face with his fingers, singing my life with his...killing me softly...' and Batti was still at it. His moves I guess were the same but they didn't appear hilarious, his face looked pale and white. It was as if a corpse was dancing in front of me.

Bosun continued with the story, "I have a son, who is 16 years old. I've sent him to the best school in town. I knew he has always been intrigued by my sailing stories and everytime I saw that look on his face I would tell him that without a good education, I had limited options. One day he came to me and blurted, 'Pa, I don't want to continue with school...'"

"I was too shocked to react for sometime, "Wha...? Why beta? Are they not treating you properly in school? Tell me what's wrong? I'm sure I can hel...""

"My son said, "But Pa nothing's wrong with school. I just don't want to study.""

""Don't repeat the mistakes I did in my life. You've been going to the best school because I want that you grow up to have a good life.""

""Pa, I've been going to school because you were paying such hefty fees. I like working hard but I feel study is a waste of time. I don't see how science would improve my life... I've tried to do well at school but I've always been amongst the bottom 5 percent of the class.""

"I didn't want to force him. I gave up studies and I am doing well and there's not a thing I want to change in my life. But it was different for my son...what worked for me may not work for him. Moreover, he isn't old enough to take his life decisions. But then maybe I should let him decide...the same way my father had done for me. I was occupied with the same thoughts even after dinner so I went out for a stroll. Inadvertently I reached the place where my father's fishing boats were berthed. There was only one boat here now, the oldest one. My father had quit fishing and given all the new boats to people working under him. He had retained the boat, which my grandfather had bought for him. My father would come here once a week with my son and would tell him stories of our fishing expeditions."

"I stood there on the beach thinking about my fishing trips...they were the best days of my life. I would have been still doing that had I not run away from home. I started thinking of events which led to that. I shuddered on remembering her. It was strange that I was thinking of her after twenty-five years but then it was stranger that she still had that effect on me; I was still afraid of her. I started walking back. I reached the *kuchcha* road which went through the palm trees in five minutes. This road stretched for around two kilometres and joined the main road which led to Cochin. Another two kilometres on this road would take me home. Walking through this mini forest reminded me of childhood...I would be holding me father's fingers as we walked through this road. My father's stories, the noise of birds, the sound of the sea waves...it all felt so magical. I breathed in the air, the smell was still the same. I was feeling cold, which, isn't unusual in this stretch. But this feeling of coldness was causing discomfort. As I moved ahead I realised my mouth was dry, body shivered from within and the hair at the back of my neck was standing. I developed goose bumps in a few seconds. The trees started looking and smelling strange. It was as if I was in a different world which looked the same as mine but it didn't feel the same, and it didn't feel real. I tried hard not to quicken my pace assuring myself that I was over-reacting. My conversation with my son must have disturbed me."

"I thought I heard footsteps so I stopped for a while. I heard nothing except the rustling of the leaves. I cursed myself as I walked but this time I didn't control my pace...I wanted to reach the lights fast. I had almost reached the main road when I heard the footsteps again. This time it was unmistakable. I turned around quickly...could see no one behind me. I walked faster and in sometime I was on the main road. I thought to myself, 'If I hear footsteps again, it would be easier to spot him now...there was no cover here, just open road.' I had not realised until now that the road wasn't lit. But the lights of my village ahead were comforting. I heard the footsteps again and I turned around. I couldn't see anything beyond twenty feet; visibility was poor on this cloudy night. I was walking fast but I tried not to make any noise myself. I heard the footsteps again and this time fear gripped me. I couldn't forget those steps; without a doubt it was Mrs. Kavita! As I started running I knew I was being illogical; how could she return after twenty-five years...she would have turned seventy by now, if she was still alive. If she was alive! I began running faster. I saw a four-wheeler approaching me so I started walking again. The headlights would illuminate the road and I could see who is behind! I turned around and looked hard but could not see a soul. If there was someone I would have seen him...her. I was convincing myself that my mind was playing games. I still ran the remaining part of my journey."

Bosun took a pause and asked, "Hope nobody's getting late. This is a slightly long story..."

Everyone wanted to stay and listen. Even Satya, the impatient guy was in a different mood, "Take your time Bosun."

The music was still playing but Batti wasn't dancing. I noted, "Hey did anyone see Batti sa'ab leave? Hope he didn't fell overboard dancing!"

Senthil aka FC said, "I saw him leave. He wished goodnight to all of us."

After we all took a loo break, Bosun continued with his story, "It took me a long while to sleep that night. A noise woke me up. I looked at the electronic clock above my bed; it was 1.24 am. My wife was sound asleep. She had forgotten to latch the window and it was banging on the side wall. I extended my hands out of the narrow railing to catch the inner handle of the window. It was quite windy so it slipped out from my fingers twice. I pressed my face against the grill and extended it as far as possible. I caught hold of the window and was pulling it in when something cold and greasy touched my arm. I immediately left the window and pulled my hand in thinking a lizard had fallen on it. "Bloody hell!" I was wide awake now. There was nothing on my hands. I looked down from my window of my room which was on the first floor. There was no movement below. I stayed there for a moment catching my breath. When my breathing came back to normal I pulled my hand out slowly. This time my hand got stuck into something. I looked out in horror to see two white hands holding my right hand in vice like grip. They were cold, lifeless and looked horrific; bloodless hands with black coloured veins visible under the clammy skin. I couldn't find my voice to shout. So I started to shake myself vigorously so as to be able to free myself. I was trying to shout but I was hardly audible...a feeble cry came out. There was no way my wife could hear it. I could feel hands on my shoulders...they were shaking me up. I finally found my voice and shouted."

"It was my wife, 'What happened Govi? You had a bad dream?'"

"I looked around. I was on my bed. 'Ohhh...thank Goddd...' I murmured."

"'You scared me Govi. You were moving in bed making strange noise,' my wife said."

"I looked towards the window. It was open just the way I had seen it. I requested my wife, 'Can you please close it?' and I looked at her close it praying that nothing bad happens to her. She closed it and came back to me."

"Next morning I told my son that he will have to at least complete his graduation before thinking of anything else. He started going to school though reluctantly but I knew one day he would thank me for this. Somehow my nightmares disappeared and so did the sound of footsteps following me."

"Then one day I got the call. 'Hello?' I said as I picked the phone."

"'Mr Vadivel, this is Mr Nair, principal of KV school.'"

"I said uneasily, 'Hello sir. How are you? Hope all is well.'"

"The principal said, 'All isn't well. Your son isn't attending most of the classes. Sometimes he doesn't even come to school.'"

"I was feeling weak. I said feebly, 'Oh! I didn't know about it...how long has this been happening?'"

"He said, 'It started around 3 months back but then he would miss certain classes. But for the last one month, things have become worse. He's setting a bad example for other students.'"

"I assured him, 'Sir, I'll look into this...'"

"He warned, 'Mr Vadivel I want you to find a solution. Otherwise I'll have to take the harsh step myself.'"

"As soon as my son arrived I confronted him, 'Where were you?'"

"'In school Pa! Why do you ask?' he said."

"'Mr Nair called.'"

"He remained silent for a while and then said slowly, 'I told you Pa...I don't want to study.'"

"'What'll you do in today's world without studies? It was different when I was young. My friends entered engineering college on the basis of XII grade marksheet. But today everything is highly competitive.'"

"He remained quiet, but I knew he didn't agree with what I was saying."

"You will complete your education. We will have this discussion after you show me graduation degree."

"He started walking away. I shouted as he left, 'I'm not finished yet! Don't you dare walk on me!'"

"But he walked on. I looked at my wife with anger. She tried pacifying me saying, 'You should handle him carefully. He's grown up now. On top of that you haven't been around all these years.'"

"My father, who was listening to everything, quietly said, 'Your son knows you through the stories I've told him. Be reasonable...you too ran away from school.'"

"I complained, 'But Papa I didn't do the right thing by running away. I may have been successful if I had completed my education.'"

"He said with a loving smile, 'In my eyes you are successful...'"

"I was in a better mood. I said ruefully, 'On top of that my son doesn't even grow a moustache!'"

"We all laughed heartily. We had an early dinner. I was feeling a li'l uneasy. I had over-eaten so I went out for a stroll. It was only 9 and I wouldn't be sleeping until 11. I looked around feeling a sense of comfort; there were changes around me though everything more or less looked pretty much as it was when I was a child. Most of the houses still looked the same. As I walked I closed my eyes and breathed in...I could smell the sea even from there. The road looked better though and it was because a few buses had begun to take this route to get to the other side of the highway. Till now I had been thinking that my village had not progressed financially but then I hadn't noticed certain details. Many houses had four wheelers parked inside, some even had two. Cable TV was in almost every house. Some had internet at home and the remaining would go to the numerous cyber cafes which had sprung up in the village. Fishing wasn't the only means of livelihood anymore. Former fishermen had become internet providers, cyber café owners, grocery shop owners, two wheeler dealers, repair shop owners, pharmacy owner and branded cloth owners. Youth wanted branded stuff."

"As I neared the bend I wondered how Naeem *chacha*'s shop would be doing in today's scenario. While others had converted their shops to cemented ones his shop still looked the way it always was... same 8'x8' wood and tin one and located just after the bend and on the side of the road, below the oldest eucalyptus tree. How could I have forgotten Naeem *chacha*! I cursed myself for not meeting him for all these years. As a child I was fascinated both

with him and his shop. Everything associated with him
was magical to me. He looked like a wizard; his partly
grey beard flowing in the air, his thick eyebrows and the
kind soft eyes hidden beneath them and his thin long
fingers and his long round nails. In the shop there were
several glass jars and each had colourful toffees in it. I
would keep looking at the different colours and get lost
and he would smile, take one toffee out and give it to me. I
don't remember him ever charging me for one. During
summer vacations I would play with my friends in the
morning and after they went home I would rush to *chacha*'s
shop and would sit there for hours...till my mother came
searching for me. This small space was my second home.
In fact the thought of the shop reminds me of the feeling
of security and happiness. One day while sitting in the
shop I raised my finger to the small toy hanging above. It
was a plastic eagle which was hung in the front portion of
the shop with a black coloured thread."

"I asked, '*Chacha* where did you bring this from?'"

"He smiled and answered in hushed tone with his eyes
wide, 'I brought it from the jungle.'"

"I asked doubtfully, 'Jungle? But it is not real! Jungles
have real birds.'"

"He answered in hushed tone, 'Eagle...it's an eagle.
A saint gave it to me. This has to be a secret between us.
Don't tell this to anyone...ok?'"

"I asked curiously, 'Ok, but tell me the whole story.'"

"*Chacha* said, 'I was very ill. I went to the jungle to
meet the saint. He gave the eagle to me. He said it would
ward off the evil spirits. So I hung it here.'"

"I asked, 'But your illness...did it help?'"

"He replied abruptly, 'Yes...yes. But there were no
evil spirits then. But one thing is for sure, no evil spirit
can come in this village.'"

"I asked innocently, 'Why? Because of the bird?'"

"He said smiling, 'No, because good people like Govi
live here. When evil comes goodness would rise in the
air...' he said, as he raised his long hands in the air and
continued, '...and it would come near the evil like this...'
and with that his hands came to my stomach and he said,

'...and it would make the evil disappear like this...' and he started tickling me."

"I fell down laughing as I implored, '*Chacha bas bas!*'"

"He asked, 'Did the evil go away or shall I tickle more?'"

"And I said, 'No *chacha* enough...all evil gone away...'"

"But I would always look at the eagle with amazement. It moved in air as if it had life in it."

"I said confidently, '*Chacha* I think the eagle is protecting our village.'"

"'Yes Govi, it is.'"

"I stood near the shop for a while remembering the good old days. I wondered why the shop was closed this early. I hoped *chacha* was ok. I decided to pay him a visit again tomorrow morning. With that I turned around and started walking back. I looked at my watch. It was 11! How on earth was that possible! I was out for two hours and I didn't realise it. My wife would be worried, I thought. I had even forgotten my cell phone home."

"That night it was quieter than usual...not even a dog was visible on the streets. I quickened my pace. I crossed the bend, no one was in sight and it was very silent. It was as if I was the only person in the village...I shuddered at the thought. This place would be eerie without the villagers. I heard a noise. It was the noise of cloth flapping in the wind. I next heard footsteps, someone was behind me. I just hoped it wasn't Mrs Kavita! My nerves began tingling beneath the skin. I stopped for a while to hear. I couldn't possibly make a mistake... it was Mrs Kavita behind me! I increased my speed but her footsteps became louder and louder. How could she be back? She would have been dead long time back. From the corner of my eyes I could see her silhouette. She was very near now. I started running and she shouted, 'Govi!'"

"I froze. It wasn't a dream...she was there; I could see and hear her. My legs froze with my mind. I could only manage a timid groan the way it happened when I was seeing that bad dream...but this was real, it was happening.

"She came in front of me. She hardly looked the way she used to; her eyes had sunk in deeper and her skin looked bloodless...black veins were visible all over her body. Her hair neatly folded into a bun like she always tied it. Her simple face looked horrifying now. She wore a *sari* which was flowing in the air though there was no wind.

"She spoke, 'I told you. You cannot escape me! I still have to complete making a better person out of you. You will have to come with me.'"

"I was completely paralysed with fear. She held my hands to pull me away from there. I looked at her fingers; they were the same hands I had seen in my nightmare. Her grips tightened on my wrist. I was in immense pain but I couldn't shout. She started pulling me towards the trees when I heard a creaky bicycle approaching. On the handles were plastic bag filled with containers and the person riding the cycle wore the whitest *kurta* and *pyjama*. His long beard moustaches and thick eyebrow too were silky white. I recognised him."

"I shouted, 'Naeem *chacha*!'. Somehow, I had found my voice back. And with that the grip on my wrist loosened and by the time *chacha* was near she had disappeared. Yet again Naeem *chacha* had done his magic!

"He looked at me and said, 'Who is it? Govi! You took long to come back.'"

"I said apologetically, 'No *chacha* I had come before but I didn't meet anyone. You're right, I have been running away. I'm so glad to see you. I came to the shop; it was closed so I thought I'll visit tomorrow morning. How are you?'"

"He said softly, 'I've grown old...things have changed now.'"

"'How's the shop?'"

"'My son takes care of it now. Why are you running away from this place? It belongs to you Govi.'"

"'Some memories haunt me *chacha*.'"

"He smiled kindly, 'Govi this place is yours you just need to open your arms to it. You will be fine here.'"

"He opened the bag and took out a multi-coloured

toffee and gave it to me. I took it eagerly. It was delicious. I said, 'Thank you *chacha*.'"

"'Go home now, it's late.'"

"I promised him, 'I'll come to meet you tomorrow.'"

"He said smiling, 'Drop in at the shop. I have something for you...but I may not be there. Of course, if you need me I'll be around...'"

"I ran back home thinking she would pop in from a dark corner. My wife was waiting anxiously, 'Where have you been? You normally go for a fifteen minute walk...today you are two hours late. What happened?'"

"I said, 'Nothing...I was chatting with Naeem *chacha*.'"

"She asked curiously, 'Who is Naeem *chacha*?'"

"I was surprised. I said, 'He owns the *paan* shop around the corner.'"

"She looked at me in disbelief. She said, 'He's as old as you...why do you call him *chacha*?'"

"I shook my head and said, 'Oh he is the son. I was talking about his father, Naeem *chacha*.'"

"She said as she left the room, 'You must have been chatting with the wrong person. The owner's father died around three years back.'"

"That night I had temperature which went as high as 1050F. My wife sat next to me placing cold towel on my forehead. I was in a delirious state and would shout in my sleep but she held my hands and ran her fingers through my hair consoling me and reminding me that she was around. The following morning my son came to me and said, 'Pa I'm going back to school and I would be regular. I will not let you down.'"

"The storm was over and I felt peaceful inside. From that day on my nightmares ended and I never saw Kavita's ghost again."

We're all quite for a while absorbing Bosun's story. Param was the first to react, "Now that was a scary story Bosun!"

Bosun quipped, "It isn't a story...it happened!"

Param said, "Yes Bosun, I never doubted that. Logically too everything falls in place. Her ghost came back when she saw your son too was quitting school. And when he resumed his education she stopped troubling you."

Param was right, we all nodded in agreement. As I sat there nodding my head for a fraction of second a thought crossed my mind...I felt there was something not quite right with the way the story turned out to be...and in a few seconds forgot all about it. I knew an unpleasant thought had crossed my mind but couldn't remember what it was about!

The story was good but we realised it was quite late and tiredness suddenly crept in all of us. Within a few minutes the deck was empty. Bosun was walking lazily and I joined him.

I said sympathetically, "Quite a lot has happened...you must have been through a lot Bosun."

He just looked at me and smiled.

I added, "The other day when we chatted on the main deck...I didn't mean to be rude. My apologies..."

"You are as old as my son. I didn't mind at all. You are young blood after all!"

I said carefully, "What you shared was quite personal...why would you want to share it with us? I am almost a stranger, most of others were your subordinates...won't it affect your working relation with them?"

"Your doubts are right Paanchu. But I've always been like this and it works for me. I've learnt there's no set formula for leadership. Everything that works for you is allowed...in parties I always talk about my home and family. It's important that they understand me as much as I want to understand them. I have to be like their father...even to the grown ups working under me. I've scolded people having more experience than me and they take it in the right spirit because they know that when they would be right I would be on their side and protect them. When I was young I would take my juniors out, we would drink all night with girls. We would come back in the morning, have breakfast and work all day long. During work there would be no jokes, no talks and no nonsense."

I said admirably, "You're right. You are a good leader. And I will remember what you just said."

15

The Esmeraldes Chapter

I reached my cabin and switched on the lights. My eyes went to the table. Somebody had kept a bunch of letters there for me. I had forgotten all about them! How could I; I had been waiting so desperately for my first bunch of letters from home! The pilot at Panama would have brought them with him. At noon Param called E/R to inform that letters were kept in the CCR. I had picked the phone. He also told me "You've got a dozen letters, all same handwriting on the envelope."

I was quite happy, "Thanks buddy that's good news!"

He said, "But I am sad. I just got 17...last time there were 32. My girl misses me a lot!"

"I am sure she does Param. Thanks for informing about the letters."

I rushed to the letters. Below the letters was a booklet on Panama. Maybe it was a gift to all from the Panama authorities. I flipped the pages. It had trivia about the canal. There was a photo section which had photos of lock being built, excavation in progress, equipments used, etc. I reached a section which had write-up on people linked with Panama. I kept flipping the page till I reached the portion on John F Stevens. I kept looking at his photo for a while. It was a black and white pixelled photograph, a close up of the face of Stevens. It took me few seconds to realise that the photo bore a striking resemblance to Frank! I started reading the article on him, "John Frank Stevens was born in..." I went back and re-read the lines, John Frank Stevens...Frank! Was I talking to the ghost of Stevens in Panama that day? If I went by what he said-nothing's impossible.

But then it actually didn't actually matter who I was talking to that day...what mattered was the invaluable insights he had given me on life. It was best to remember him as the 'Spirit of Panama Canal'.

I broke my chain of thought when I remembered I still hadn't read the letters! Her letters were as sweet as she was. It must be frustrating for her to keep writing and then wait. I had written only thrice and called two times in all this while. I noticed the last letter she wrote was a month back. I had to call her now. It would be expensive, but then I wanted to speak with her desperately.

I ran up to bridge. It was 2nd officer's watch.

I barged in and said apologetically, "Did I scare you 2nd?"

He bent down to pick the walkie-talkie, which he had dropped on seeing me. He said, "You sure did. Wasn't expecting anyone...not after such a long party!"

"Wanted to call home."

He asked, "All well?"

"Yea, just that it's been a while since I called my friend."

"Sure! Hope you know it'd be expensive...would be around $12/min."

I said with a smile, "I know."

2nd connected the number for me. The phone was ringing and I was hoping she would answer.

"Hello?"

"Noush, Thank God you picked up!" I whispered.

"Sid! God, where have you been! I was so worried! I miss you so badly!"

I saw 2nd officer enter the voyage charting room. I said, "I'm sorry baby. It's difficult to call. I don't get to go out everytime. Calling from ship now."

"I love you Sid."

"I love you too Noush."

"Did you get my letters?"

"Yes I did today. Did you get mine?"

She said sadly, "Yea only three! Long time back...must be real hectic for you. Are you ok? When will you be back?"

"I'm ok. Will be back in a few months. Before you realise I'll be there...with you...loving you, kissing you...sigh... I miss you so much Noush. You are the most beautiful woman I've ever met!"

"Come back soon! There's so much I want to talk to you about!"

"I'd love to listen. Ok, I gotta go now. Will call you in ten days."

She complained, "Why so long?"

"Reaching US in ten days...will call from there. We are going to Esmeraldes...don't know if I can call from there."

"Esmeraldes?"

"It's in South America...a small port. Listen, I miss you and love you like crazy."

"Sid, don't forget me. Ok?"

"No-no, you don't forget me girl."

I hung up and went looking for 2nd.

I shouted, "I'm done with the call 2nd."

He came out of the room and said smiling widely, "How's your girlfriend doing?"

I asked in bewilderment, "You were listening?"

He replied awkwardly, "Ofcourse not! Couldn't help but overhear some portion..." and then he added with a wink, "...come on I can keep a secret!"

I smiled and said, "She's good."

"Ya it looks so. Your face is beaming."

I admitted, "I guess so...I am in love!"

One morning I was doing some minor repairs on a small pump when Ali came searching for me. "Paanch sa'ab they're calling your in ECR."

I went up, wiping my hands with the rag that was in my pocket. Being called to ECR was never a pleasant experience so I was preparing myself for another depressing session as I went up. Chief, 2nd and 4th Engineers were discussing something as I walked in.

Chief looked at me with a wicked smile and said, "We were discussing as to how to plan your training. You are under-utilized and need to stretch yourself much more to bring up your competence level."

My head had begun to spin already. Being subjected to ridicule had become a routine but I still was not able to handle these unpleasant situations. I knew they were trying to break me but I struggled to ignore what they were saying about me; the words would keep ringing in my head and would affect me terribly. And though I thought I was making progress, listening to Chief's comments I realised I was going down even in my own eyes. 4th was nodding his head in agreement while 2nd was looking away. Chief went on and on about how he used to work for twenty-two hours daily and how I too should do the same.

I looked at 2nd helplessly. I needed help.

2nd looked at me and then at Chief. I was standing against the wall while Chief was pacing up and down in ECR aggressively.

2nd said finally, "According to me 5th is doing a good job. He has learnt all the pipeline diagrams...he also knows the complex control air lines...which even I do not know! When I had joined as 5th I had hardly learnt anything for 6 months. He has achieved more than that in one and half months. I know 4th wasn't fast at all..." he stared at 4th briefly. "Moreover, I don't think we need to have a meeting for unimportant thing like 5th's training. His training is my job and I'll do it." He then turned his attention to 4th and asked, "Have you completed your purifier and compressor monthly maintenance?"

With that 2nd started taking Sam's work status report. I walked out of ECR feeling happy. Everything was not as bad as it appeared.

I came out of E/R at 1300 hours and as part of my routine came out to the deck to catch some fresh air before lunch. Bosun and his men were coming back from the forward portion of the ship.

"Hi Bosun...hi guys!" I shouted. Deck people were my friends now. They were happy to see me too.

Bosun asked, "*Aur* Paanchu what's happening down there?"

"Nothing special, the usual oil and grease." I said pointing to my dirty overalls.

Bosun motioned others to carry on and he came by my side, bent over his body, resting his arms on the railing.

"Bosun I forgot to ask something."

"What?"

"In your story, your son used to bunk classes...but where did he go? Do you know?"

He said after thinking over it for a while, "Ok, I can tell you. But don't share this with anyone. He used to go learn *kathak*! Can you believe it, my son learning to dance like women! There are so many good professions...but he had to choose this. He wanted to perform at national level and open a dance school which promotes Indian classical dance forms. I was so ashamed when I heard. Good that he's back to school...that would give him time to think. Hopefully by the time he has graduated he'll choose a better career."

I voiced my disagreement, "But Bosun, in today's world there's no such thing as man's profession or a woman's profession. At least he knows what he wants to do and at such a young age!"

"You don't understand Paanchu. He can't earn his livelihood by dancing...and where's the respect in that profession?"

"Listen Bosun you are right in thinking like that. But what I am saying is that your son too is right. You are his father...you're the best judge. Come let's eat. Can I join you guys?"

He said seriously, "No not with this dirty boiler suit! You will dirty the chairs."

"Ok. I'll carry on to the day mess then. See you..."

He said laughing, "*Arrey* come with me. I was joking *baba*."

There was a lot of excitement in the crew's mess. FC

asked me animatedly, "We're reaching Esmeraldes tomorrow! You going out?"

I said, "Don't know...I'll try to."

Bosun said, "Try? Go out, you're young. It's a beautiful place...beautiful girls too."

"Aw...come on Bosun."

Bosun said mischievously, "So who's telling you to do anything? Dance with the girls!"

"Bosun, I have a girlfriend back home."

Bosun quipped, "Ok in that case just dance with one!"

"You're funny. I'll just get drunk with you all."

Bosun said, "It's a deal!" and then he announced, "Who all are going out?" Around ten crew members raised their hands.

He said, "Ok we leave at 2015. Paanchu too would be free by then."

We reached Esmeraldes the next evening. Since this was a small port and since they didn't have room to accommodate our ship we were anchored in the sea and the oil transfer would happen through underwater pipelines. Scuba divers from the port would go down and connect the ship's hoses with the lines underwater.

Though my last shore trip wasn't a pleasant one, the one with Batti, but I still was excited about this trip. Moreover, I was going out with my new friends...and I hadn't gone out for a month...and I was sick of seeing the same E/R faces... and above all I desperately wanted to get drunk! So here I was in my watch waiting for it to get over. The underwater hoses were being connected and the oil transfer would begin well after my watch.

I had taken more than required rounds of the E/R, had filled in the log-book, helped Tengalkar with his routine work and was sitting in the ECR with Tengalkar trying not to feel guilty. Chief, 3rd and Sam were collectively responsible for this feeling; according to them sitting in ECR was criminal, but it was another thing that they themselves would always be found in there. I was telling myself that as the duty engineer I was supposed to spend time in there as I could see all the equipments' status on the control panel. Moreover, just running around in the E/R without purpose didn't make sense.

We were smoking as we had tea. It was one of those rare days when we both were getting bored on the job.

"So have you gone out in Esmeraldes before?" I asked him.

"Yes this ship does come here quite a few times. It's a nice place...like a village in India except that people look modern and girls are more beautiful than movie stars."

"Oh? Yes I've heard South American girls are beautiful..."

The phone rang.

I answered, "Hello, 5th Engineer..."

"Oye Sid, Param here. You coming out with us right?"

"Yes I am and Tengalkar too. Wait for us."

"We will. Bosun told me to call you. We have called the boat at 2030. Be ready by then."

"Boat? Oh yes...yes I will be ready." I had forgotten that we were not on shore and hence would need a boat to reach Esmeraldes.

4th came in to release me on time. I handed him the watch, "We should start loading in a while. Everything from our end is ready. Pumps were lined up for emergency...inert gas generator is ready in case we need it. Batti sa'ab is going out but he's informed 2nd so you can call 2nd if any electrical related help is required. I'm going out too. Will you join us after your watch?"

He said with a wink, "Yes I plan to come there with 3rd officer. You enjoy your first night in South America!"

I looked at him quizzically...everyone had this thing about South America. I had to find out what the excitement about this place was all about.

Tengalkar and I rushed upstairs. I had a quick shower, grabbed a bite and came out on deck. I was wearing a cotton T-shirt and jeans which was ok for the warm weather. The breeze was not cold but it still was refreshing...I guessed it was the smell of the sea. I could see Bosun and gang standing near the manifold. The boat hadn't come yet so I thought of enjoying the scenery alone. I put my hands on the railing looking at the city lights far away. It felt strange, looking at civilization ahead…as if I was all alone in the sea and looking at the shore. I had forgotten that I too once belonged there…for now I was a part of a rare breed. I looked towards my ship mates…they were joking and laughing. They and me…we belonged to this rare breed who have been forgotten by the world. In olden days sailors were called the poor souls and the churches built seaman's welfare societies around the ports which provided food and library and recreational activities for sailors who had come to shore. The seamen's clubs are still around for the same purpose though the mariner of today has gone through a process of evolution. Based on past tragedies new safety features were built in the ships, machineries and equipments were made better in terms of performance and safety, new tools like the electronic control systems had made life easier, ergonomic factors were given high importance and the food was great.

Looking at the distant lights I realised that I had accepted this new change in my life sooner than I had expected. But I did remember it was good to be there amongst the lights, with family and friends all around. I realised the importance of all the small little things that I had always taken for granted. I realised the importance of being alive.

I could see a speck of light approaching us. After a couple of minutes I realised it was our ride. The team at the manifold must have realised the same as I saw them lower the pilot ladder. The ladder was made up of rope which had wooden planks as the steps. Using this in the darkness to climb down the ship onto a boat which would be moving with the sea waves would be like a stunt, I thought. I ran down to the team. There was Bosun, 2nd officer, Batti, Param, FC, Tengalkar, two OS, Chief Cook, 2nd cook, Satya and Osman. Osman had the widest grin, "Osman going to shore Osman happy." He said with a wink.

The boat reached the side of our ship and turned sideways parallel to us. I looked down; though the weather was calm the waves were strong enough to move the boat up and down like a cork and occasionally the boat would move away from the ship and the pilot of boat would engage engines to come nearer. I wasn't sure I could do it. I have to observe others very closely, I thought.

Bosun went first. He turned towards us, back to the sea, held on to the ropes with both his hands, took one leg over the railing and onto the first wooden plank while one leg remained on the walkway from which one end of the pilot ladder was attached. He then brought his second leg out and he lowered one hand as he lowered the opposite leg to reach for the plank lower than the one he was currently on. The method was quite similar to what 'Spiderman' did while climbing a wall. The trickiest part was to climb the boat. One had to stop at the point which should neither be so low that the legs get crushed as the boat comes near and neither should one be so high that jumping onto the boat becomes a death defying stunt. I was scared. I saw Bosun jump onto the boat as it came near. He then stood there to help people who were jumping over. FC almost lost his balance and was about to fall in between the boat and ship. If Bosun wouldn't have caught him he would have been squeezed to death. Everyone else went down quite smoothly. I had a sudden 'performance anxiety' attack so I began considering going back to my cabin. Chief cook and 2nd cook understood my predicament.

They offered their expertise. Chief said, "It's easier than it looks."

2nd cook added, "Yes I was afraid the first time too but nothing happened. Though I have heard it's the unsafest thing on ship and it would soon be banned as serious accidents have happened due to this ladder...but you would be happy to know that I've never seen any accidents happen on the pilot ladder!"

Today you may see one buddy, I thought. I looked at them and said, "I'm so relieved to hear that guys!"

I had no option but to try it as these two jokers kept staring at me with a stupid smile on their faces. I knew if I had a grip on the ropes with both my hands I could easily take my body weight for a while. I faced difficulty in placing my leg on the first plank but it was still safe as I was holding the side ropes of the ladder firmly. Getting down was easy and now came the trickiest part. Bosun and others were shouting for me to jump when the boat was coming near. But I missed it so as to judge the speed of boat and hence the time I had to jump in.

"Guys let me be comfy with this! Please don't prompt!" I shouted.

The boat was coming in again and this time I was ready with my right leg and arm extended towards the boat. Before the boat hit the ship, I jumped and made perfect touchdown. I was sweating. I exclaimed, "Phewww! That was something!"

The pilot of the boat welcomed us. He was standing near the small cabin which housed the steering wheel and other navigation controls of the boat. He was a tall fat man in his early forties. He was wearing a crumpled T-shirt and trousers which were unevenly folded to his knees. He wore his sneakers, the laces of which were all over the place. His face was round and swollen, possibly from drinking too much.

We were talking to him when we saw her coming out of the cabin. All eyes went on her...she looked like an international lingerie model. She was wearing a lot of make-up; she actually would have looked much better without it.

The pilot looked at us staring at her and said apologetically, "Sorry, I forgot to introduce her. She's my daughter Lucia." Everyone immediately stopped staring. He went into the cabin while she remained outside trying to chat with us. The cabin was a part wooden part glass cubicle, top half of all the 4 walls were made of glass.

2nd officer was chatting up the girl in Spanish. Midway 2nd turned towards us and said, "Who wants to make out with this girl?"

I thought I hadn't heard him properly. I looked at the others' faces; nobody looked surprised except FC who looked like a greedy dog, eyes wide, and tongue out...saliva dripping.

FC said with his hands raised high, "I will 2nd!"

I turned towards Param and asked, "Did I hear right or my ears are playing a trick with me?"

Param said nonchalantly, "You heard right. Welcome to South America!"

2nd went to the pilot and told him of the plan, "When we reach shore my friend here will accompany her. You know a place where they can go to?"

The pilot said "Ya, sure. It's a clean place, not too expensive...and safe too."

FC looked at 2nd and stated shamelessly, "I am not carrying any money with me. How do I pay for the room?"

The bastard not only wanted to screw for free, but also wanted a room free! He was not carrying any money, which meant he expected others to pay for his food and drinks too!

The pilot understood the dilemma our FC was facing, "I can stop the boat now, and they can do it in my cabin. After it's done we can move ahead."

The scene was so emotional that it was almost heart-breaking...the father being so considerate for his daughter. Pilot stopped the boat and came out the cabin so that Mr FC could go in with Lucia. I still couldn't believe what was happening.

I was sitting on the port side of the boat. I bent over to the side to touch the sea. I was so close to it...I shuddered as I looked at the dark coloured sea imagining how deep it would be. The feeling was exhilarating and very frightening. I didn't know how to swim, had learnt to float a month before joining ship. As far back as I could remember water had always intrigued me. As a kid I remembered the small red plastic tub I used to bathe in. I would fill it and then go inside it; it was my swimming pool. I would immerse my head in and would not open my eyes fearing I would see a shark inside. I would immerse my feet and fingers in and look at them change shape and colour. To me the water had magical powers. I thought about it and I realised I still felt the same.

I looked behind...our ship was immovable. The powerful sea too couldn't move it. It stood there head held high like a warrior standing guard on hallowed grounds.

On the boat, however, things were still pretty nasty. Batti was peeping into the cabin to catch the action going on inside. FC took ten minutes to flush 2nd officer's $100 down the drain! Batti was still ogling as Lucia dressed up. Lucia turned the lights on and was about to open the door when she saw that FC had left the used condom by the side. Lucia began swearing at FC as she bent to pick it up. Batti, the curious person that he was, wanted to know what went wrong so he moved towards the glass door to get a better view. Lucia picked up the condom, opened the door and threw it out. It happened quite fast and was timed so perfectly that one could say it was destined to happen that way. We all heard the splat sound followed by a long pitched shriek from Batti. We all saw his ugly face smeared with FC's semen. He ran to the side of the boat, bent over and started splashing sea water on his face.

FC came out after a while grinning sheepishly. He wasn't aware of the incident. He looked at us and asked in his girly voice, "What happened? Why are you all so quiet?" he looked around and then asked again, "Batti sa'ab, you alright? It seems you're not too well and see you're sweating so much! And what is this white thing stuck to your moustache?"

Batti resumed his cleaning operation and it alarmed FC so much that he held onto Batti's legs, afraid that he would fall into the sea. I felt like puking. We started again in five minutes and in another fifteen we had reached the wharf. Rusted iron ladders led us to the cemented platform above. There were no railings and there were several portions all around which looked incomplete. We walked to the security gate. The well-dressed guard looked at our shore pass and let us through.

16
CHAPTER

Veronica

Our guide was waiting for us in an old Chevrolet pick up truck. He had the most forgettable face I'd ever seen; every 5 minutes I had to throw a glance at him to remember what he looked like. He was perfect for the role of extras who were placed around the hero...he would make any hero look good. But he was a nice guy and very concerned about how we could make the most of our time in his country.

He spoke English with a heavy Spanish accent¾male version of Penelope Cruz, "Hi everyone, my name is Juan. Welcome to Esmeraldes! Where would you like to go? Bar, beach...?"

While others thought of where to go, one person who had recently been through a tragedy spoke instantly, "Discotech!"

We decided to go to the beach and most of us voted for it mostly because we didn't want to see Batti's sick dance. Batti was heart broken...

Off we went to the beach amidst grumbling from one corner of the Chevy. The road was like a village road in India. The houses were individual row houses as you would find in a small town back home. And the people, their clothes and the culture as could be found in metros.

Most of the houses were painted from outside in vibrant colours; most of them were multi-coloured. Wall paintings were quite common: political messages, caricatures related to singing and dancing was a common sight. Even at this hour the main doors were open and we could hear music playing in each and every house. Families sat outside their houses chatting, laughing and dancing. It looked like a big carnival. People around looked genuinely happy and the whole atmosphere was playful and jovial. After a while I could smell the sea again...we were closer to the beach. It was so well lit that it looked like day time. The beach was crowded with families and youngsters. Groups were playing football and beach volleyball all around us.

Our guide Juan asked, "What would you like to drink?"

Everybody voted for Bacardi. I gave him a $10 bill and he came back with two large bottles and returned some change. Back home it was twice as expensive. We made ourselves comfortable around one bench fixed at the sidewalk. We poured our drink in plastic glasses, mixed cold water and said 'Salud' to each other. All of us except Param took a sip. He kept looking in one direction. We followed his gaze to a group of girls standing a few feet from us. It was quite obvious as to which one amongst the three that Param was staring at. She was the most beautiful woman I had ever seen. She had long thick curly golden hair which looked perfect on her fair skin. Her large eyes sparkled as she chatted with her friends. She looked so innocent and naughty in a childlike way. She was wearing a sleeveless blue cotton floral dress with large white flowers with yellowish centre. The dress was short and fitted. She had an amazing figure but she didn't look sexy...she just looked very pretty. It was a pleasure to watch her have conversation with her friends... she was so unconscious of her beauty and the attention she was attracting all around her.

Param saw us looking at her and warned us, "Guys...she's mine. I saw her first...I think I'm in love. I desperately want to speak with her. Juan please help."

I couldn't blame Param for how he felt. Juan too

sympathised with him so went upto the ladies to offer them a drink. I could see her refuse the offer quite politely. Param folded his hands and gestured Juan to try again. Juan took a deep breath and requested again. Juan came running, "She would come over for a round of introduction. She may stay if she thinks the company is nice."

She came over. She knew Param was the one dying to meet her so she shook his hand first; a film star meeting a die-hard fan! Param kissed her hand and she smiled. By now Batti had forgotten all about his 'discotech'. There was a round of introduction and she politely came forward and shook hands with each one of us.

"My name is Veronica," she said in Spanish. Param and I understood some Spanish, enough to understand what was being said.

Juan spoke to Veronica in Spanish, "My friend here has lost it completely for you and would like to spend time if you could please take some time out for him!"

She said something in his ear and he listened carefully nodding his head. He then turned towards us and said, "She's expected home now but she'll call her parents and see if she can be excused for one more hour." He then turned towards Param and whispered in his ears, "She's a student of Psychology...she's not the kind of girl you would find in a bar...you understand? Please do not get me wrong!"

Param replied, "Of course...ofcourse! We will treat her with respect."

I looked at her as she took out her cell to call home. She obviously was far too sophisticated to be a bar girl. She appeared sensible but I failed to understand what made her accept our offer. Maybe she was a romantic...maybe she liked Param too. Or maybe she was plain bored and wanted to try something adventurous.

She completed her call and motioned Juan to approach her. Juan came back and told us, "She would be joining us but she wants to go to 'La Libertad' bar! The one frequented by sailors like you! No locals are allowed there and definitely not a girl, as the bar has its own girls.

Moreover, it's risky for her. I tried to tell her but she doesn't listen."

So that's why she was spending time with us! Because she wanted to see the place which she knew existed but was out of bounds for her and all others in the city.

I remained quiet as I saw heated discussions within the group.

2nd officer said, "I think we can get into big trouble here. Param you'll find more beautiful women in the bar..."

"2nd please. I'll take care of her!" pleaded Param with folded hands.

Bosun too gave his point of view, "I too think it's not a wise decision."

Batti came to Param's rescue, "She'll be OK. She herself wants to visit the bar and she looks mature enough." He said looking at her body. I immediately looked at Veronica; she didn't like the way Batti sized her up. I felt sorry for her.

FC spoke next, "2nd sa'ab, it'll be alright. We all will take care of her."

2nd officer said after thinking for sometime, "I'm out of this. If something goes wrong I wasn't with you guys."

"Sure 2nd. Thanks." Said Param and he went to Veronica to say she can join us.

She chose to drive to the bar with her friends. We reached the entrance and waited for her to come out of the vehicle. She opened the door and looked around, not too sure of her decision now. Param went close to her smiling and offered his hand to help her out. She was smiling but the smile didn't reach her eyes. I wanted to tell her to run away from us but I did nothing. I stood there looking at Param put his best foot forward; his manners impeccable. He looked like the sweetest, most caring and sensible man on earth.

We moved to the bar. I looked at the six and half feet burly guard who wore black army overalls and carried a semi-automatic gun. He stood at the entrance, his shrewd eyes sizing us up. As we approached the door he raised his right tattooed and 'as thick as my thigh' arm in front of us motioning us to stop. He then raised his finger towards Veronica saying a stern "No". Param looked helplessly towards Juan. Juan sighed and started explaining to the guard in Spanish. I don't know what came over me. I interrupted their discussion, held Veronica's hand and took her in inspite of repeated warnings from the guard. He could have hit me and that would have been enough to turn me into a vegetable for the rest of my life. Thankfully he didn't and we all were in.

I was trying to get accustomed to the loud music and the flashy disco lights inside. I looked by my side and was surprised to see Veronica standing next to me. She was smiling at me, I smiled back and we looked at each other for that brief moment. I felt something; the feeling wasn't comfortable; my mouth went dry, my heartbeat was way too fast and my body was sweating profusely. I wanted to run away from her but when I turned in the other direction and started moving ahead I realised I was still holding her hand!

I left her hand immediately, looked at her with a stupid grin on my face and I shouted so that she could hear me in the loud music, "I'm sorry...I didn't realise I was holding your hand!" When I finished shouting I realised the music track had changed so there was this brief silence before the next track started. Everyone around was smiling, some were showing me a thumbs-up sign. Only I could perform two back to back dumb acts. I wished I could disappear from there. I turned to Veronica, she was laughing. I looked at my ship mates, everybody except Param and Batti were laughing too. I had blown my cover! Now everybody on the ship would know that I was just another run-of-the-mill fool.

I saw Param come towards us and I needed an excuse to run away so I told him, "All yours." Veronica and I looked at each other briefly. I smiled at her, excused myself from there and went to the group. They were cheering Batti who was on the dance floor showing his latest moves. I looked around, the bar girls were giggling as they looked at Batti dance. I hid myself behind the pillar but Batti spotted me and came running. He said, "You didn't dance with me in America. Now you should dance in South America! Come on let's dance!"

Such a solid argument, how possibly could I have refused? But then I had had only four pegs of Bacardi...not enough to make me dance. I requested, "Please continue Batti sa'ab. I'm studying your complicated moves now, let me learn them and then I'll join you."

The silly smile was back on his face, "It's difficult to learn but you can catch some part of it. But I am sure you can be a good student."

I said sarcastically, "Oh, wow, I would love to learn from you!"

With that he went on to do his complicated stuff. The dance floor was a huge square colourful glass platform with lights beneath it. Colourful dancing lights were all around on the ceiling. The two adjacent walls of the dance floor were made of huge mirrors. Batti was looking at himself dance...for him there were two of him but for me there were three Battis dancing in front. I wanted to puke so bad that I located the direction for the loo just in case I had to rush in an emergency. I wanted to go get drunk. I turned around to see the love birds. They were talking but her eyes would occasionally be on me. I left from there to go to the table next to the love birds; some of my ship mates were sitting there. Mid-way a pair of soft hands held me from behind. I turned around to find a young petite girl smiling at me mischievously. I smiled back and she took my hand and led me to the dance floor amidst protests from me that I didn't know how to dance. She was saying something in Spanish which I couldn't understand in the commotion. She was pretty and danced well but I just wanted to go back and get drunk. I made a few attempts to go back to my table but she wouldn't let go of me. I helplessly looked towards the tables where my friends were sitting. I saw Veronica get up and Param looked confused as to why she had gotten up suddenly. I could see glances from all around the bar as she walked towards us. There definitely was something special about her. She tapped on my partners shoulder requesting her to leave.

The dancing girl complained, "But I saw him first!"

Veronica replied, "No I came here with him."

The dancing girl complained again, "But you are sitting with someone else! How many guys do you want?"

Veronica looked at me and winked, "Oh the more the merrier!"

I blushed and she became conscious realising she may have gone overboard. The girl went away and Veronica held my hand and pulled me back to the table. Param looked really confused. He was asking her, "What is happening?"

She looked at me and said in perfect English, "Now that I have rescued you too, we are even."

I saluted her mockingly at which she gently hit me on my arm. Param was livid, "Veronica, you speak such good English! Why were we talking in Spanish till now?"

She looked at him and smiled innocently.

It was enough drama for one day so I said aloud, "I wanna get drunk!"

"I want to drink too", said she.

Param moaned again, "But I offered too. You didn't drink with me!?" He kept looking at her and when she didn't reply he stood up, threw his chair back and stormed towards the bar stool. Now, it was only she and me on this table and between us we had a bottle of Bacardi to finish. I was ordering coke but she cancelled it and said, "I'll teach you how to have this drink." She then poured the clear rum in our glasses and added a few ice cubes. She raised her glass and said, "Now when I say 'Salud' we do bottoms up."

"Are you crazy?" I almost screamed.

"Do as I say. You'll be alright."

I sighed and then nodded.

We raised our glass with a 'Salud' and then gulped the drink. My throat was on fire...my eyes were shut tight, mouth open and tongue out as I could just manage an "Arggghhhh....!"

We repeated the act and this time the noise from within was different, "Woooooo..."

We kept doing this till we had consumed the entire bottle. I searched my pocket for cigarettes but couldn't find it. She took out a pack of camel from her purse lit one and gave it to me. I struggled to take it from her fingers. She was far more composed than I was.

I shared my observation with her, "You don't look drunk. You're such a pretty young girl...and still not drunk...I mean you don't look like you have so much capacity to drink and then not get drunk. Am I making sense? I think I'm drunk."

She waited patiently for me to complete my statement and then smiled and said, "Are you giving me a compliment?"

"I didn't mean to...not that you are not a pretty girl. Yes you are beautiful but I wasn't giving you a compliment. But if I did I think I'll not take it back because you deserve it."

She was blushing, "Do you like me?"

I stammered, "No. Can't say. Not that you are not beautiful...you are very beautiful actually. But very difficult to say whether I like you."

"Why are you in doubt? Are you married? Or is it because your friend is interested in me?"

"Do I look married?! And it's not about that guy liking you. I know you are not interested in him. My point is...it is sweet of you to give me your attention but you needn't do so because I brought you in. You would be surprised to know that I am far from the hero you think I am. Do you know the kind of impression my colleagues carry of me?" I said with thumbs down.

She smiled again and said, "You are cute."

"You women! When you are out of words you go into mono syllables. And by the way I am not cute! I am a stud!"

"You are very cute."

"And you are drunk too."

"What's your name?"

"Oh didn't I tell you? Sorry, I mean how could I not have! My name is Siddhartha..." but the music was too loud and my name too complicated, "Sid...my name is Sid."

She was looking at me and I did something stupid yet again, "What's your..."

"You already know my name, remember?"

I was stunned for a moment, "Of course, it's the drink." I looked at her, she was smiling mischievously. I looked into her eyes for a moment longer this time, "Maybe it's you..." I felt something burn deep down in my chest.

"It's me what?" she asked.

"Ummm...it's you who is making me do stupid things."

I noticed she had no make-up on; her lips were a natural pink, her eyelashes very dense and her skin radiant and fresh. I shared my observation, "I was thinking, you had applied make-up...you look so good without it."

She blushed. I looked at her and added, "Don't get me wrong...maybe you are right, I am giving you a compliment."

She said smiling cutely, "You think too much...come with me and let's dance."

I was surprised I didn't refuse. We were on the dance floor, I was sure I was dancing like a fool and in this inebriated state I could still tell that she was a good dancer. Soon, other dancers had left the floor and it was only us. I was running around her in circles and then I started dancing real fast. While I continued my buffoonery she remained composed. I noticed that everyone around was cheering us. We were entertaining them; I like a circus clown and she like a diva performing in front of thousands of fans. The track changed to a slow romantic one. She came close to me and I held her...the jumping around had made me more intoxicated. I could hear applause from across the bar as we moved slowly looking into each other's eyes...only that my eyes were so skewed by now that they were looking at each other. The track changed to an Enrique number and with that I started removing my T-shirt. After my partial strip tease was over I started waving the T-shirt in the air. She stood there shocked at first and then smiling shyly. She wasn't ashamed of my antics, instead she came near still smiling and looking at me adoringly and then took the T-shirt from my hand and made me wear it.

She whispered in my ear, "I want to go to the loo. It's a common one for ladies and gents. Please accompany me, will you?"

I faintly remember walking towards the toilet sign. She was holding my hand as we went in. There was nobody in.

I found myself saying, "You go in...I'll stand guard outside..." before I could finish, she kissed me and then looked at me with that expression again. I was too drunk to be romantic. I kissed her passionately and my hands started moving all around her. She held onto them and brought them to her waist and told me, "Behave properly!" and then she started kissing me again. We must have been inside kissing each other for a long time because when we came out, our bills were being settled. I contributed my share by throwing a $100 bill on the table. Veronica picked it up, put it back in my wallet, looked at the bill, took out some currency from her purse and settled our share. I had begun to lose my senses by then...there were partial blackouts which had begun to happen. I next remember standing out near the taxi and she was standing next to me.

She asked, "How long would your ship be here?"

I said as I tried to balance myself, "We are leaving tomorrow evening."

She implored, "Can you come back tomorrow?"

"I'm not sure..." I looked at her sad face and then I lied, "I think I can. Ok I can come in for a few hours."

She said excitedly, "That would be great. I wanted to discuss something with you...and I want that discussion when we are not drunk." She was so happy that she was almost jumping with joy. I couldn't believe it was happening.

My colleagues were looking at their watch trying to tell me that we are late but I was not in the state to notice subtle hints. They finally came over and made me sit in the cab. They almost formed a queue so that they could bid her goodbye. She was a rockstar!

I didn't know how long I was in the cab but finally I realised I was all alone for sometime now and the car wasn't moving. I asked the driver where my colleagues were to which he replied in Spanish with a "*Non comprender*".

I climbed out of the car and saw the group standing at the pavement. I tried to focus my eyes on what was happening. In front of the group stood Veronica and Param. Param stood still, his head hung low, his shirt open while Veronica was shaking him up and slapping him at times. She was crying as she kept shouting words in Spanish which I didn't understand. As I came close I looked at Param; he was in a bad shape, his buttons lay on the ground and his cheeks were red because of the slaps. Instinctively I came in to rescue my friend and did something which I had never done in my life; I misbehaved with a girl; I pushed her away shouting, "How dare you treat my friend like this?"

Her expressions changed on seeing me. Her anger disappeared and she came to me as a helpless girl who was asking me to protect her. "Do you know what your friend has done?"

I immediately realised I had committed a big mistake. Instead of being with her I had misbehaved. Since her attention was on me, my shipmates took Param from there. She kept crying inconsolably and I took her in my arms saying, "Veronica I'm sorry. Please forgive me. I didn't intend to be rude. I didn't realise...I'm so sorry. Don't cry, I'm with you."

Some colleagues came to me and pulled me away from her. I couldn't finish my conversation with her again. I looked at her as I sat in the car and as we sped away. She stood on the street looking in my direction, tears still rolling down her eyes. I don't remember my journey to the wharf but I came to my senses as soon as I came out of the vehicle. I was moving with others towards the jetty when I heard horns blaring behind. I turned around to see a vehicle approaching us. It screeched to a halt just by my side. The security guard at the gate looked alarmed. Veronica got out of the car and rushed into my arms. Seeing her, Param fled from there thinking she may decide to beat him some more.

She said crying, "Sid, promise me you'll come tomorrow."

"I promise!" I lied again. I couldn't add to her misery.

Her eyes lit up as she asked, "Can you come with me to my home now? Meet my family and spend the night with us. Go back to ship in morning."

I said softly, "That's not possible Veronica. I have a watch in a few hours..."

"Sid..."

"Yes Veronica..." I said and then looked towards my colleagues who were on the other side of the gate by now. They were gesturing that the boat was waiting and that it would leave soon.

"Sid...I am in love with you. I know it's crazy but it's true."

I was taken aback for a few seconds and then I said, "Veronica I'll try to come again tomorrow. We'll talk about it. I have to rush now or I'll be in trouble...why were you beating my colleague?"

"When I was saying goodbye to everyone the bastard kissed me on my lips. You saved him else I would have killed him today. What does he think?" I looked at her feminine figure and soft hands; power was internal and didn't depend on things like muscle mass...hence proved.

I assayed her saying, "He is a bastard. I didn't know this...and I'm so sorry for my behaviour. I regret doing that..." and with that I looked at her fondly as I held her face in my hands.

She said, "No matter what you do, I can never be angry with you."

I couldn't believe that she had fallen in love with me. An educated girl like her had fallen in love with a stranger who got drunk with her in a shady joint! I wanted to tell her that I had a girlfriend but I couldn't make myself do it. I knew I wasn't coming back again but I couldn't tell her that either. Maybe what they say is true...maybe time heals and one day she would forget this night.

She came close and kissed me; I held her hands, looked into her eyes, turned around and ran towards the other side of the gate. I knew she would be standing at the same place I left her, but I forced myself not to turn around.

17
CHAPTER

The Hangover

As I took the rusted iron stairs to get into the boat the memory blackout came in again. I couldn't remember the boat ride at all. I didn't remember how I climbed the pilot ladder. I remember getting back to senses as soon as I climbed onto the ship. The AB who pulled me in was shaking his head and scolding me, "Are you mad? Is this how you climb? Do you know if you had fallen you would have lost your life? You are so drunk you would not even have managed to swim and actually most people who fall fracture their skull and drown immediately."

I said, "I would have drowned anyway...don't know how to swim..." and staggered towards the accommodation as the AB looked at me in disbelief.

The next thing I remember was the sound of the alarm. It was ringing for a good ten minutes before I woke up. I couldn't open my eyes...I somehow reached the bathroom and started splashing cold water on my face. I wasn't in my senses but the cold water had done the trick...I had begun to see. My legs were still not able to hold me and I had to support myself to walk. It was 0400 hrs already. I was changing into my overalls when the phone rang.

I could barely speak. I muttered, "Hello? 3rd I'm sorry am late...on my way out."

I ran down fearing I would fall off the stairs and break my neck. I struggled to wear my shoes...by the time I entered the ECR it was 4.08 a.m.

"I'm sorry 3rd." I apologised as soon as I entered.

He asked, "What happened to you? Were you run over by a Redline bus?"

"I drank too much..." I said with a groan.

He said with a knowing smile, "Oh, then you had fun. Met any girl?"

I knew what his next question could be and I wanted to cut this discussion short. I replied, "Yes...but we just danced."

I went for a round. Though not many machines were running, the noise level still was unbearable for me. The headache had turned so bad that I started having trouble focusing. I came up to ECR to have black coffee. Tengalkar was having tea and smoking. I didn't even feel like smoking. I quietly made my coffee and sat down sipping it.

Tengalkar asked, "Paanch sa'ab?"

I said irritably, "*Yaar* call me Siddhartha..."

"You had driven her crazy..."

"I had driven myself crazy. I made a complete fool of myself. You were there; tell me what madness did I exhibit?"

He said lost in thought, "Oh you danced for a long time and with full energy! The best part was you taking her in your arms and going round and round carrying her. You must have danced with her for a long time! You both looked like an Indian hero and heroine."

I wanted to hide my face in my boiler suit. I groaned, "Oh God! I was doing the stupid 'dancing around the trees' routine that we see in our movies! And I don't even remember this part!"

"Oh but you were doing it well."

I was shaking my head in disbelief. I said, "I hate that dance...how could I...unbelievable!"

"We have grown up seeing those movies. We love that dance..."

"Tengalkar, please don't include me in your fan-group."

"She's such a lovely girl. She was dressed modern and when you lifted her she was making sure her dress was in place...just like an Indian girl."

"She doesn't drink like an Indian girl though!"

Tengalkar didn't like my comment, "How can you be rude to her? She was uncomfortable when you carried her and her hands were constantly on her dress but she never told you to stop. She let you do everything...actually she made you look good. You were dancing like Govinda and she matched steps in all that you were doing and it looked so good. Even the *goras* sitting in the bar were cheering you guys."

I didn't say anything but was surprised. She did like me a lot but why?

I asked Tengalkar, "Do you know why she beat up Param?"

"Yes I saw him kiss her and she beat him. He deserved it...I'm telling you, she's a good girl."

"I know she's a good girl Tengalkar...never doubted that; except for the push I did treat her right, didn't I?"

"I think so...and do you know how you climbed the pilot ladder? I was on the boat looking at you...your foot missed the plank twice and I thought you would fall. I hope the AB doesn't report it to Captain."

Sam reached ECR at 0800.

He said, "5th I heard you had fun last night."

"You heard already?!"

"Galley, you see, is the hub of the news. It's between you and Param...it's become an E/R vs Deck thing now."

I took leave to have breakfast. I feared going in there but then I had a hangover to take care of...and for that, eat I had to.

Chief and 2nd cook were busy preparing eggs for people sitting in officers and crew mess. They both looked up and smiled mischievously.

"Kya Paanchu! You are a surprise package! We were lucky to see the fireworks in person!" said Chief Cook excitedly.

2nd cook added, "She is beautiful...you should have slept with her."

I wasn't amused, "She's a student...not a bar girl."

Bosun and his deck team were eating and chatting about something. I saw Tengalkar too come in. Bosun was calling me so I went to the crew mess.

"Good morning everyone." I said.

Bosun smiled saying, "How are you?"

Before I could reply AB said, "Who will get the girl? I think Param will finally. What do others say?"

I couldn't believe what I just heard. I looked at Bosun who chose to stay quiet.

FC spoke next, "Param deserves her...he must have appeared proud to her but he actually isn't like that. Paanchu took her just because Param wasn't competing. But how could you steal your friend's girl? He saw her first."

I shot back at them, "I didn't steal her. I gave Param all the chance but she chose to be with me. I just danced with her and got drunk...that's it!"

Same instant Param walked in, head high, shoulders squared and confident smile on his face.

People all around welcomed him as if he were some hero.

OS said, "Param we were telling Paanchu, he shouldn't have stolen your girl."

Param replied proudly, "Girls come and go in my life...I don't give a damn."

I felt pathetic that I had misbehaved with Veronica for the asshole.

FC spoke now, "Paanchu was so drunk...he must have misbehaved with the girl. But poor Param got beaten up."

I looked at FC, "At least I don't fuck on other's money!" I then turned towards Param and said, "Ask your hero what he did because of which he got beaten up. I'm sure many here would have seen the act. He deserved it totally."

Param replied with a fake smile, "I forgive you for ditching me. I would sacrifice thousands of girls for friends."

Tengalkar, who was sitting quietly till now, spoke, "Bosun your people get drunk on smelling alcohol or what? The whole world knows what happened last night. Why are your guys cooking up a story? Just because your deck *wala* lost to an Engine *wala*... and that too from someone who's just joined the ship?"

The senior AB spoke this time, "Cadet has gifted that girl to paanchu." Param had a smirk on his face.

I was livid, "People who were not even there are passing judgement over here. You all can say what you want to..." I looked at Param and continued, "...at least you get to know people better after incidents like these."

Tengalkar who was nodding added, "Param? You keep telling us stories about your conquests. After your performance last night it's quite obvious how true your stories were."

Param looked at Tengalkar, laughed, and said with eyes half-closed, "I would have taken her if I wanted to. But I let go of her when I saw Paanchu was interested."

I had listened to enough bullshit so I walked out of there, entered the galley, took my breakfast and sat in the day mess. I felt sad for poor Veronica. She must be waiting for me at the jetty...perhaps she may stand there whole day waiting for me, I thought. In ten minutes I was back in the ECR. Batti, 4th, Satya the fitter were discussing something. The conversation stopped as soon as I entered.

4th spoke first, "Tch...tch...what am I hearing?" I looked up in the sky; I didn't want to hear it again.

Batti began, "5th was fighting with a cadet over a girl! You should learn to treat people on board as your family members."

I finally found my words, "Batti sa'ab you were there...it was happening in front of your eyes! It wasn't so difficult to understand, yet you speak like this?"

Satya spoke next, "I agree with 5th. Batti sa'ab you should support the Engine Room. Moreover that sycophant cadet doesn't deserve support. Param got what he was asking for. She would have killed him if Paanchu hadn't come in."

Batti wasn't convinced, "Param saw her first then why was 5th dancing with her? I can't forget 5th stole his girl rather than helping cadet get the girl. I'm a romantic."

Sam added, "You have a point."

Batti was unstoppable now, "The problem is with this generation. In my days people would give their lives for friendship."

I couldn't stop myself, "For a person as exquisite as you, lot of people would have sacrificed their lives."

He didn't understand I was screwing with him. His stupid smile was back on his face. I looked at him; head tilted to one side, eyes closed and lips tightly sealed together in a clumsy looking smile. It looked as if he was experiencing happiness, pain and possibly constipation all at the same time.

He then looked at me teaching me the essence of life, "See 5th, girls shouldn't be given importance...yes, she is beautiful but that doesn't mean you'll forget your ship colleagues. There was a time when girls would stand in front of my house just to get a glimpse of me...I go to my wife when I have a hard-on, apart from that I don't show love to her all the time. Cadet treated her right while you were overdoing things."

Satya, "Cadet thinks he can woo any girl on this planet? Our 5th is my hero, cadet the villain who got beaten up by the heroine. Period."

With that he walked out. 2nd came in with the manual. Batti continued giving his point of view to 4th, who listened quite attentively.

2nd listened to the crap which was going on for a couple of minutes then interrupted their discussion, "I've got the main engine overhaul today and I've several work listed for you Elec. So if you can join me to the store, I'll explain your work for the day."

Batti got up instantly...I too came out with them. 4th remained seated in ECR. He was still there when chief came in.

"Good morning sir."

Chief asked, "What's happening?"

Sam told him, "I'm going out for couple of hours today. Will get your *guru dakshina*. What do you want sir?"

"Johny Walker Blue label should do. But get me two bottles this time. One doesn't last too long."

"Sure sir. You heard the latest news?"

"No, what happened?"

Sam said smiling wickedly, "Paanchu went out last night, got drunk with a bar girl and got the cadet beaten up by her."

"What?"

"The whole ship is talking about it. Batti sa'ab was there, he says, 5th was the trouble maker."

"Call 5th."

4th turned the calling alarm thrice. Ali came running up.

Sam said, "Ali call 5th. Tell him bada sa'ab is calling."

I was working with 2nd and the fitters on the main engine. Unit #2 overhaul was due for piston replacement and regular checks. 2nd, Satya and I were in the crankcase. We had entered from the huge manhole doors. Satya went in, kept one leg on the crankshaft and then moved ahead towards the short iron steps on the inside body. There were two such steps. He motioned me to come in and climb onto the one on the left side. There was still a lot of lube oil everywhere. I climbed up carefully. 2nd wasn't visible, he must be inside other units inspecting the general condition, I thought.

When we reached the top I said, "Satya...thanks for siding with me."

"Hey don't mention it. I took your side because you were right."

"And...you know I didn't mean to be rude that day. I know I was...but I was told that paanchu was a demeaning name. I'm sorry *yaar*."

He said with a smile, "Hey man, don't say it. I know it happens when you are new here. I don't even remember that incident."

We began detaching the piston from the connecting rod. Like so many other things I never tried to learn the main engine in college. Now that I was seeing it, I understood everything about it. Starting Air moves the piston down to the Bottom Dead Centre (BDC). Since all the pistons are connected together by the crankshaft, the other 5 pistons are either moving up or down. In the unit in which the piston is moving up: by the time it reaches the Top Dead Centre (TDC), the air is compressed to such an extent that it ignites the injected fuel in the chamber. The combustion is like an explosion and it generates enough power to push the piston down. This ignition keeps happening cyclically in different cylinders one by one depending on the timing of the engine. Connecting rod connects piston to the crankshaft. The piston rod and the connecting rod are connected by the crosshead bearing. This bearing plays the vital role of converting the vertical motion of piston into the rotary motion of the connecting rod and in turn the crankshaft.

Satya was pointing towards the bottom part of piston rod saying, "After we have lifted the piston, don't forget to see the cooling oil inlet and outlet." The bottom part wasn't visible now since we hadn't separated it from the crosshead; the large nuts hadn't been removed completely. They would be removed just before the piston is ready to be lifted up. Satya would come down and guide the rod as it goes up.

As we stood inside the crankcase Tengalkar and Osman were working on the topmost part; they were removing the different fittings from the cylinder cover. 2nd went up and instructed them to fit the hydraulic tool to remove the special nuts on the cylinder cover. I was up as I wanted to see how the operation was done. After the nuts were removed, the cover was lifted by the E/R crane. I climbed up to look down at the combustion space. The piston had turned black because of the carbon deposition all around it.

The cylinder liner looked clean; it is made of alloy cast iron, which can sustain its finish at high levels of pressure and temperature. In the next fifteen minutes the piston was airborne. There was considerable amount of carbon deposition on the piston sides as well. Piston rings, which act as a sealing mechanism, and should be freely moving, were stuck because of the deposition. Leaky piston rings have caused major disasters like fire in the scavenge space. A lot of oil and sludge normally gets deposited in the scavenge manifold. Tengalkar had already opened the entry to this space and had started purging the space with flexible ducts; one of them would be cleaning the space. After the cleaning is done 2nd would come in to inspect and then we would be ready to assemble the unit.

Tengalkar was getting ready to go in. He had brought his cleaning equipment: bucket, wooden scrapers of various sizes, scoops, rags, and a bucket with cleaning liquid. He wore his gum boots, wrapped his head with a rag, switched on the lamp and went in. Ali came running.

He spoke even as he tried to catch his breath, "Bada sa'ab is looking for you. Where were you? I've been searching you all over the engine room?"

I said, "I was in crankcase and now came to see if Tengalkar needed help before going in. I'll go meet him."

I was climbing up thinking the last couple of months had made me more of an engineer than I could after four years of my college. Four years spent just to get a degree!

In ECR, chief was pacing around frantically and 4th had a concerned look on his face. They both looked at me as I entered.

Chief shouted, "What were you doing? Why did you take so long?"

I said calmly, "Chief, I just got your message…"

He shouted again, "Where were you?"

I said, "Helping 2nd in unit #2 overhaul." I realised me tone was a notch higher this time.

He said insultingly, "What help can you be? I'm sure they can manage without you!"

I said coldly, "2nd told me to…"

He ordered rudely, "Next time onwards when I call, leave everything and come, ok?"

I said putting on a smile, "Chief, in that case, you should instruct 2nd. If he tells me to complete something, I have to. I'm just a small fish."

Both of them couldn't believe I had said that.

Chief looked at 4th and said, "How's his progress?"

4th was about to complain when I interrupted, "2nd is my boss. You should discuss my progress with him not with Sam."

Chief said after staring at me for sometime, "Ok I will do that. Is the scavenge space open? Did you go in?"

"I was about to when Ali informed that you had called."

He asked, "Has the cleaning started?"

"Yes, Tengalkar is in."

He said smiling wickedly, "Tell 2nd that Tengalkar need not clean it. I want you to clean the space all alone. That's how you would learn."

I went down to find 2nd. He was standing in front of the overhauled piston and instructing fitters as to how to remove the rings. I told him about the Chief's wish. 2nd threw the screwdriver on the floor and turned around swearing as he climbed the stairs noisily.

He barged in the ECR and asked angrily, "Yes Chief?" He stared at 4th for a good few seconds before he looked towards Chief again.

Chief said cautiously, "2nd, I want 5th to learn about scavenge space and for that he should clean the space all alone. Tell Tengalkar to go rest."

"Chief, motorman is working overtime to get extra bucks plus he gets an extra for scavenge cleaning. I'm not sending him before he cleans the space." 2nd looked ready to kick Chief's face.

"Oh then send 5th also inside to clean. That will speed up the process. We need to move out tonight afterall."

Before 2nd could react I told 2nd, "Actually I wanted to request you to send me to help Tengalkar."

I was in the space in five minutes. I could see Tengalkar around fifteen feet away, cleaning on the other end. There was enough space to crawl ahead in this circular cave like space. On my right side I could see a portion of the cylinder liners with the scavenge ports. Through the scavenge ports I could see the piston or the piston rod of the units, except unit #2 which we had just overhauled. I flashed the torchlight through the ports and I could see the lubricating oil holes arranged in the liner.

There was thick layer of oily sludge all over the walls, on the floor that I crawled on. It was a big job; I definitely would have taken all day to complete it. Tengalkar was busy cleaning and he chose to not notice me.

"2nd has sent me to help you," I shouted.

"Go away! I don't need to increase my work! Let me work in peace," He shouted back.

"Don't talk like my mother. Give me work, I'll help. Moreover, I'm not sharing your scavenge cleaning money. I'm working for free!"

He said explaining the work, "Ok, come here. I'll remove the heavy sludge, you take this rag dip in this liquid, scrub the surface where I've removed sludge and then wipe it with this clean dry rag."

It was hotter inside and very difficult to breath. But it was fun cleaning as I kept wondering about how absolutely fantastic this system was. The scavenge manifold provides fresh air to the main engine before combustion happens. The main engine was 2 stroke, which meant two linear motions of a piston (up and down in this case) completed a cycle of the engine. That meant the crankshaft and hence the propeller would have completed one rotation in the 2 strokes. These 2 strokes completed the four stages of the normal combustion cycle- air intake (from the scavenge ports), compression (of the fresh air), combustion (after the fine particles of oil have been injected in the super-compressed air) and exhaust.

It took us six hours to clean the whole space. I remained inside to see 2nd inspect the space. He had brought with him remote device to operate the turning gear. The turning gear, turns the crankshaft and hence the pistons. One by one he went to all the units, turned the gear so that the piston was visible from the scavenge ports. With a screw driver he checked whether the piston rings were moving freely. He also checked the condition of the liner.

In the next two hours the unit was assembled back. We all came up when 2nd was sure everything was ok. I could sense the change all around me...even 2nd chatted and joked with me now; I had been accepted. We all went to the wash basin outside the ECR. I looked at myself; I had sludge on my face, eyelashes, hair and in the nostrils. I needed a good shower. I looked at the time, it was 3 pm. I had to come down for my watch at 4.

I went in the ECR to take leave. Chief was still there, he looked happy to see my condition.

He asked smiling, "Learnt anything?"

"Yes Chief, a lot. I'm thankful to you."

Chief demanded rudely, "Do you understand the scavenge air's importance?"

"Oh yes. I also understand cycles of main engine, exhaust valve functioning, aux blowers, etc...but now please excuse me as I have to take shower and come down again for my watch. See you 2nd." I said completely ignoring Chief.

"See you 5th," he replied while making his coffee.

18

The Reluctant Hero

I came out the engine room. The steward was mopping the floor. He waved at me and said, "Paanchu, there's an agent on board. He's looking for you."

I looked at my black boiler suit. There still was a lot of grease on my face and in my hair. I asked, "Where is he?"

He replied, "In crew mess...and there are letters in CCR. I don't know if any have come for you...go and see."

I decided I would go change in clean overalls before I met the guy. I came down to the CCR in fifteen minutes. Param was holding his letters. He saw me enter and looked at OS and said, "I got only fourteen this time!"

I ignored him, went to the table and hunted for my letters. There were none! I looked again. Not a single letter for me!

I went in the mess totally dejected. This guy was having coffee while Bosun was making a call from a cell phone. The guy was around five and a half feet tall, athletic, and he looked much younger than his actual age. He wore a polo neck T-shirt and rugged jeans. He saw me approaching and gave me a warm smile. His smile made me forget the unpleasant mood I was in.

I smiled, extended my hand and said, "Hi, I'm Sid."

He said warmly, "Oh! Mr Sid! Nice to meet you! My name is Henry. I am Veronica's distant relative."

I was happy to meet him too. I exclaimed, "Oh great! Mr Henry pleased to meet you! How is she?"

He smiled sadly, "She wants to speak with you. Can you now?"

I said enthusiastically, "Sure that would be great!"

He took out another mobile phone and dialled a number.

"It's ringing," he said and gave the phone to me.

I took the phone, my heart suddenly beating faster. I didn't know how I would face her questions but then I wanted to talk to her.

"Ola Henriii!" I could picture her beaming face.

"Hey...Veronica!"

She shouted happily, "Sid! I am glad to hear your voice!"

I said apologetically, "I am sorry I couldn't come today...lot of work...Did you wait for me?"

"Of course I waited. But it's ok...I knew you wouldn't come today."

"You knew? How?"

"Don't know, but when I was coming to the jetty today...I felt I wouldn't see you. But its Ok, I know I'll meet you again."

"You think so?" I said feeling surprised.

She said confidently, "I'm not getting that sinking feeling though I know you are leaving. Maybe because we will meet again. You don't feel anything?"

I thought about it and then said, "Frankly no. I'm not as intuitive...but I've been thinking about you while working today..."

"That's enough for me...there's one more thing...last night when I was going to sleep I feared that when the effect of alcohol goes away I'll not feel the same for you..."

My heart was beating faster. I spoke eagerly, "And...?"

She said cheerfully, "And I realised I do feel the same way...actually I don't know if you have a girlfriend...but it doesn't matter. What I felt was special...and today when I am in my senses I know I will love you all my life."

My mind went into a tizzy; I didn't know what to feel, happiness or anxiety. It was so strange. I wanted to tell her that I liked her a lot but I didn't know to what extent I did so. I wanted to tell her that I had someone in my life, but I also wanted to hide it from her. Above all I wanted to believe that I would meet her again...I was so bloody confused. But I knew it was good to hear her voice; it was reassuring to know that I had not broken her heart... I said with a heavy heart, "Veronica I would love to meet you and know more about you and tell you about myself. You take care..."

"*Muchos amor*! Bon voyage and good health." Her words kept echoing in my mind. Her smiling face flashed in front of my eyes. I remained standing there for a while.

When I came to my senses I realised I was still holding the phone close to my ears. There was no doubt that I was in love with Anoushka but I couldn't understand the effect Veronica had had on me.

"Here Henry, thanks for the phone. She's a great girl."

Henry was looking into my eyes and then he smiled warmly and shook my hands. I didn't understand his behaviour. He said affectionately, "We love her...everybody who knows her does. When she was five she fell very ill. The doctors had given hope but we prayed and she recovered. It was a miracle! For us she's God's only child."

"Yes, she is."

I took a different cellphone from him and called home. I called Anoushka next, "Hi Noush!"

She said in a flat tone, "Hi Sid, nice to hear your voice."

"Noush you ok?"

"I'm ok Sid..."

"Is your mom around? Why do you sound so low?"

She said sadly, "N-no, no one's home. Just one of those days, you know..."

"Last letter from you was dated 2 months back..." I pointed out.

She didn't say anything for a while. She then said carefully, "I've been thinking...about my parents. I've not been fair to them."

"Is it because of me?"

"No, it's not about you...it's me. I tried telling mum about you, but couldn't..."

I had begun to get the familiar sinking feeling. I said desperately, "But Noush, I can make it work...I'll talk to them. I'll make everything alright...am sure about this."

"Sid...I'll need sometime. Let me sort this out please..."

"Noush, you know I love you, right?"

"Sid I love you too. I'm messed up right now. It'll be ok when you're back."

"Yes, Noush. Once am back, there will be no confusion. Just us together."

There was something not quite alright...

I called Garu next.

On hearing my voice on the other end he said excitedly, "Siddhartha! Baba, what a surprise! Man I'm so bored...no tennis, no *sutta*. Sachin's here but he's so lazy... he doesn't smoke either!"

"Though you've not asked, let me still share, I'm doing ok here." I said and then asked, "Sachin? Leave? Didn't the war break out at the border? How did the bastard get leave now?"

"He was here a week after you left. And the war had started before you had gone. All the leaves were cancelled, officers were being called back and our hero managed to take leave during war!"

I exclaimed, "Don't tell me the bastard ran away because of war!"

"What do you think? Of course he ran away! You should see the news these days. So many young guys have lost their lives!"

I shook my head with disgust; these were my friends. I asked, "And have you met Anoushka lately?"

He answered, "Sid, everything alright between you two?"

"You've begun to answer my question with a question!"

He said sternly, "I told you to stay away from her! Girls are trouble."

"Come on...tell me what happened?"

"I've seen a guy...he comes on a Yamaha, stops near her house and they signal to each other."

I asked, "So? Is that it?"

"Nope, I've also seen her go out with this guy on his bike. I enquired about this guy. He's her classmate. They were going around before she started dating you. I'm sure she would have told you about him?"

I felt as if the rug had been pulled from beneath me. I extended my hand to the wall to support myself...I realised she hadn't told me anything about her ex-flame but I remembered Sonu mentioning it once.

He said comfortingly, "Listen Sid, don't think too much about this now...I didn't want to tell you *yaar*! Anyway you come back we'll sort it out."

I said, "I'm OK, don't worry."

"I miss those days when you were here."

"Yes Garu, for me too it's the same...smoking isn't fun anymore."

We sailed out at 2100 hrs. My watch was over and I was standing out, looking at Esmeraldes lights become distant. Somewhere amongst those lights would be Veronica's house. She would be out there somewhere...smiling and lighting up lives around her.

A few days later I met Bosun.

He said warmly, "Paanchu what's up?"

"Nothing much Bosun. Your people still talking about me?"

He laughed and said, "Don't get me wrong. And don't get my guys wrong either...we sailors are an unhappy lot. This incident involved my people to such an extent, almost as if they had found a purpose in their lonely lives. I obviously wouldn't stop something like that."

"You amaze me yet again Bosun."

"What happened in Esmeraldes is like a movie for them...some saw it and some heard about it. Veronica is a great girl...they have put her on a pedestal. And you are the hero."

"Thanks Bosun but I know your guys are supporting Param and not me. I'm sure Param is their hero."

He said smiling, "Everyone knew what had happened. They were supporting Param just because it had become an Engine vs. Deck thing. You stopped reacting to the false stories even though you had all the right to. Truth wins eventually. I didn't expect it to happen so soon and to happen in this way...you rose in their eyes. You are their unlikely reluctant hero."

"Wow, I don't care about being the hero. I'm just glad that the truth is out finally. By the way how's everything at home?"

"OK...my son's not so happy. He's forcing himself to complete studies, and he misses his dance."

"So what will you do? Thought about it?"

"I haven't till now. Will give it a thought on the long flight back home."

"Nightmares? Still getting them?"

"Yes," he said slowly.

I said reassuringly, "I don't have the answers Bosun, but I think everything will be alright."

We crossed the Panama and though I went out on the deck several times I didn't see Frank again. But I felt a change...I could sense the difference in myself from the last trip.

The next few days were spent taking on new assignments. 2nd had started trusting me with new machineries and I had started working on 4th and 3rd's machinery independently...and with the work off their shoulders these two had nothing to complain.

CHAPTER

Marseilles

We reached Marseilles in ten days. I wanted to make some calls and wanted to go see how this sleepy town in France would be like. While having breakfast I came to know that Bosun was going out shopping for family and friends back in India. I called up Bosun's cabin.

"Hey Bosun you going out? I'm coming with you."

"Who is it? 5th?"

"Yes, when do you plan to leave?"

"Forty minutes?"

I said, "Perfect. Meet you at starboard lifeboat deck."

Bosun had arranged for a cab. Nobody else wanted to go out as there were no bars here. The journey to the city was beautiful and short.

The weather was perfect, there was no traffic, the roads were perfect, and roadsides were lined with huge trees. The weather was changing and with that the trees were green again and the grass on open territory around us had grown tall. We reached the city in ten minutes.

I said, "Bosun can we come back walking if we have time? Our ship's not too far from here."

"Sure if I don't shop too much."

I insisted, "Don't worry I'll carry your stuff. The

scenery is breathtaking and we can enjoy it the most if we walk."

We crossed the beautiful church. The buildings had an old town charm about them, the houses looked elegant, cosy and very beautiful. This city had gone through major transformations in the past and that was the essence of the rich culture of this ancient city. The town was ruled by the Romans and the Visigoths before the French kings captured it. The town had seen two major plagues and it was bombarded during the WWII by the German and Italian forces. But nothing could stop this place from evolving. The rich culture of the town was also because of its importance as a port. Historically it had been one of the main entry points into France because of which several immigrants were attracted to this place. Today one-third of the population had their roots in Italy and then there were Africans, Corsicans, Armenians, Turks and even Chinese who lived in Marseilles.

We reached a shopping mart which was located at the beginning of the town. The area surrounding the hyper-store looked like a well maintained park. The grass was freshly cut, dense green trees were all around and then there were wooden benches at regular intervals. I already felt rejuvenated.

Bosun bought a lot of stuff and I bought two litres of the famous French red wine and some chocolates. There was a phone just before the entry to the park area. Bosun sat on one of the benches as I called Anoushka.

"Hi Noush."

"Hi Siddhartha!"

"Have you thought about us?"

She said sadly, "Yes..."

I somehow knew what she was about to say. I asked worriedly, "And?"

She said slowly, "My parents don't approve of our relationship."

I pleaded, "Tell me the truth Anoushka."

"This is the truth..."

I confronted her, "I know about the guy visiting you..."

She said sobbing, "He isn't the reason...it's a difficult phase for me."

"Noush I know you are not so sure about me...how could you? I've been surviving the hardships here in the hope of seeing you again...waiting for the day when I can see you and touch you again! You came in my life and made it beautiful...now you want to go?"

She said crying, "No Sid...I'm very fond of you."

"That's not enough Noush. I always warned you not to rush into this relationship. Everybody told me to stay away from you but I didn't listen to them..."

"I'm sorry Sid...please give me time to think. I'm so confused," she pleaded.

"No Noush. There's no mid-way...I know you're not on my side. There's no confusion."

"But I do love you...I don't want to lose you!"

I said firmly, "You can't love too many people at the same time. Doesn't work with me..."

"Will you see me when you are back?"

I said as my voice choked, "Noush...it's over."

"Can we meet once at least?"

"I don't think we have anything to discuss. Goodbye."

"Bye Sid..."

I kept holding the phone long after she hung up, wishing that she would not hang up and say, "I want you back Sid..." But the loud click kept echoing in my ear as I stood holding the phone trying to come to terms with the harsh reality. The girl I had loved with all my heart didn't love me anymore. I wanted to cry but this wasn't the right place. I took a deep breath, and said to myself, "Ok it's alright. Control yourself...you are a strong person...it's ok!" And with that I left the booth with a smile on my face.

Bosun said, "All well?"

His question took me by surprise. I tried to smile as I asked, "Of course, why do you ask?"

"Speaking out would make you feel better."

"I broke off with my girlfriend."

He asked, "What happened?"

"She doesn't need me."

234 Eagle Spotted, Message Decoded

He said angrily, "That is her loss. She's lost someone who would have loved her till eternity."

"Thanks, but I am not that good."

"Is it? Ask Veronica!" he said with a mischievous grin and then added, "Next time you come to Esmeraldes, tell her you love her and make love to her."

"No idea if I will ever see her again..." I said thinking sadly.

"You will Siddhartha."

I smiled and said, "I'll miss you...you are a good guy."

"You wouldn't have heard this, friendship on a ship lasts till the sign-off. It's an old saying and I've seen numerous examples all through my career. The best of friends on ship fail to connect once they reach home."

"Strange that it would happen this way...will you want to meet me?"

"I believe in this theory, so I will not even try..." he said nonchalantly. But it made me feel sadder.

I wanted to change the topic, "You must be excited to go home?"

"Yes," he said in an excited voice but he didn't look so eager.

"You see challenges ahead?" I asked.

"Maybe."

"Bosun I think you should also talk about it..."

He thought for a brief moment before saying, "I fear I'll see her again."

"It'll work out OK. I'm sure you'll find a way. But I still believe you should find happiness in what your son has chosen."

He remained quiet.

I had to call Garu and Bosun wanted to call his wife to make sure he had shopped for everything his wife had asked for.

I called Garu. He picked the phone, "Hello?"

I said happily, "Oye Baba!"

"Siddhartha! Baba you must be missing me too much!"

I shared the news, "I broke off with Anoushka."

"Good news! And good for you."

I said smiling, "I know you are happy because now I'll spend all my time with you."

"Come on. She isn't your type...I told you."

"You were right. What's up?"

"Sachin's here for two more months...so meet him regularly and then you would be here in three months..."

"And what about studies?"

"Oh the classes are on...final year exam and then I would be an engineer like you."

Like always he was lying again. I said, "Sure hope so."

Garu asked, "Can you guess who is with me now?"

I exclaimed, "Sachin? Give the phone to that spineless mongrel."

"No it's not Sachin..."

I asked, "Who is it then?"

"Vikram."

"Vikram? Put him on the line."

"Hello Siddhartha."

I asked curiously, "What are you doing there? You should be on..."

"I came back two months ago..."

"What happened? You came back within a month?"

He said, "Chief Engineer was a bastard. He slapped me once."

"What? And you beat him?"

He paused for a while and then admitted, "Actually no. I quit...wasn't able to adjust."

I couldn't believe it...the stud quit because he was slapped! I asked, "So what's your plan now?"

"For now I'm not thinking of anything. Will join when I think I am ready. How's it going with you?"

"I faced similar situation here...no slapping, but lot of mental torture. Things are getting better now."

He observed, "You're a tough guy."

"Well not as tough as you."

He said decisively, "The truth is I ran and you stayed. If I had I would have been comfortable too like you..."

"You will bounce back."

"Sure I will."

I offered, "If you are still around when I come back

we can go for another round of meditation at the stadium. But this time I'll make the crickets quiet without your help."

He said promptly, "You don't need my help."

I asked surprisingly, "You think so?"

"You don't know? You've done it already."

I asked sharply, "What have I done already?"

"That day at the stadium…I had gone out to buy cigarettes. When I came back you were in a trance and the crickets were quiet."

I exclaimed, "You mean to say, you didn't do anything?!"

He said admiringly, "You're a freak show man! You did it!"

So I hadn't been dreaming…I had actually had a conversation with a cricket! I wasn't sad anymore and the world seemed like a beautiful place. I was still sad that Anoushka wasn't in my life anymore but then there were so many things to look forward to…and then there was life, which was inviting me to look at it in a completely fresh perspective.

I was sitting on the comfortable wooden bench waiting for Bosun to complete his call. A squirrel came running from a tree ahead towards me. It came close and then realised I was sitting there. It stood still for a while and then looked right then left and then at me again. I stood still.

The squirrel ran around the bench and climbed up the tree behind me. It kept running from branch to branch, searching for food. A squirrel back in India would have behaved the exact same way and would have looked the same as well. I thought, "Does it hold true for humans as well? A person from France and a person from India are they connected to each other? Are all humans inherently the same?" My thoughts were interrupted by Bosun's footsteps.

I looked at his worried face and said, "Bosun…I was thinking…I think you have the capabilities to make everything alright in your life."

He said sadly, "Thanks for trying to cheer me up but I

know that reality is quite different and she is far stronger than I am."

"Look Bosun I just know that if this problem can be solved, it can be done only by you. That's my belief."

He said, "You know, I feel cornered now. Till now I've been trying to push out the negative thoughts..."

"I understand Bosun. In a way it's good that you feel cornered. Sometime back I felt cornered too and it made me think and act beyond my own limits. Another strange fact I have begun to realise lately is that people around me have always believed I can do a lot more but I always underestimated myself. Now, I have become aware of my strengths and I know that they are enough to make me successful in life."

"Hmmm...I get what you are saying. I have been running away all my life. Not anymore. I think it's time I proved my worth to the world."

I added with a smile, "And prove your worth to yourself!"

He looked at me smiling, "Let me share something with you...I had underestimated you. Your body language in initial days...I thought you would not last long here. I am a very shrewd judge of people and you've proved me wrong."

"I'm glad I stayed...I've begun to like it here..."

He observed, "You do love her."

"Not anymore Bosun. If I hadn't come to the ship I wouldn't have known. I'm not as smart as others think I am...I feel like a fool."

He said vehemently, "It takes strength to give yourself completely to someone...that is not foolishness. She's betrayed you. And why do you worry? The most beautiful woman in the world is in love with you!"

"Bosun, give me your phone number. I'll call when I reach Boston."

He scribbled the number at the back of his shopping bill and gave it to me.

"How's everyone at home?" I asked.

"They are good. My wife was scolding me for doing last minute shopping!"

"Married life...!" I said philosophically.

He looked at me, then away, and again at me as if he was contemplating whether or not to share something with me. He decided to share, "My son had a strange dream last night."

I looked at him with interest. He continued, "He sounded tense...the dream was disturbing. He said he saw that he had gone to a temple, which was on the top of a hill. It was early morning and he was barefoot climbing the stairs. He knew this place was the purest place on earth, as if God resided here. He remembered the temple was made of marble...the sun hadn't risen, yet there was this brightness around the temple...an aura because the place was so holy. He had never been to a temple like this in his life yet after he woke up he remembered minute details as if he had been there. When he reached the top he closed his eyes as he folded his hands before the idol. When he opened his eyes he saw it was *Durga Ma*'s temple! Now he's never been to the deity's temple, he doesn't even know what she looks like except that he saw Her in the dream."

I was surprised too, "That's strange!"

He continued, "He closed his eyes to pray and when he opened them he was not in the temple anymore. He was standing outside it and the vision to the Goddess was being blocked by a priest who was standing in front of him. He looked into his eyes wondering why the priest was staring at him. This man looked very powerful...there was this magic in his eyes. He greeted the priest with folded hands. The priest spoke, 'Devi Ma has chosen you. She wants to bless you and for that you would have to accept a gift from her for two weeks and then come back and return it to me.' The priest extended his right hand and in his palm was a doll's head, the body was missing and *sindoor* (vermillion) was smeared all over her face and hair. He was frightened to take it and moved back a step but the priest moved closer and brought the head near his eyes. My son looked at the doll's face and it opened her eyes and looked at him. My son began to shiver, 'Please...what is this! I can't accept it...she looks evil to me. It can't be from the God'. The priest then became angry, 'You can't ask questions! If you refuse the gift, it means you are refusing God's order. You would be finished.' He ran away from there but he could still listen to the priest, 'You have committed a sin. No one can save you now!' As he ran down the stairs morning turned into night. He noticed his white *kurta* had *sindoor* on it. He ran towards the taps. The stain wouldn't come off. He looked up in the mirror...to his horror his face and hair was covered in *sindoor*. He started washing it frantically but it wouldn't come off. His eyes had started changing shape and they began to resemble the doll's eyes! The dream was so real that he actually screamed out aloud. My wife had never seen him so terrified. I just hope it's not the ghost which is doing all this to him."

I blew out a whistle and said, "It was a scary dream, but it doesn't mean she's after him. We don't analyse every bad dream of ours, do we?"

"I just hope somehow everything becomes OK."

"It will be, Bosun, it will only get better. The sufferings don't last for long. And I will call you as I don't care too much about your old wives tale!"

Bosun was laughing, "Old wives tale! Have you ever seen such an ugly wife before?" he said pointing at himself.

I was shaking my head with disgust, "You refer to yourself as wife one more time and I will take an eternal vow not to get married!"

"What will happen of Veronica then?!"

"Come on Bosun! Marry her? I don't even know if I'll ever meet her again."

"So you do want to meet her..."

"Maybe..."

We spent sometime in the park and then we walked back to the ship. The walk back was one of the most memorable events in the last three months. We talked about things which weren't important, things which I knew we wouldn't remember after an hour...but I felt nice and I could see Bosun looked happy too. We strolled as we breathed in the fresh air and enjoyed the scenery; it was one of those rare moments.

We reached the port in half an hour. I kept looking at the ship, it looked different today and as we climbed the gangway ladder I felt different too. It was as if the gangway ladder had brought me to another world, a world where work was as important as life itself, where machinery were considered companions, where no work was considered lowly, where strangers suddenly became family, where inspite of difficult conditions you know you'll survive, maybe because you are being taught to be a fighter. I found it very strange that not so long ago I had a completely different opinion. And now I could feel it, I had been transformed into a different person. The ship looked beautiful.

As we walked by the pipeline manifold Bosun kept looking at his ex-team working with the new Bosun. The team looked towards him, some smiled, some waved but nobody came to him. 'Shippies' are a strange bunch of people; they adapt so easily to change; different bosses, different colleagues, different ships, different equipments, different nationalities, different food...different everything.

Bosun was to leave the next day and though he would be missed, people would forget him eventually. Going by what Bosun told me, I too would forget him. It seemed unlikely that I would...

I left Bosun where he was and started going ahead. But I stopped after a few steps turned around and said, "My watch starts in ten minutes. And you have a safe journey back home."

"But I'm leaving tomorrow!"

"I know...am not too good at goodbyes. All the best for your life and I'll call you."

He looked surprised for a moment but then he smiled and said, "You'll do great in life. But I won't wait for your call because you know what I believe in. Goodbye."

His eyes were moist. I turned abruptly and started walking towards the accommodation. I quickly went up the stairs to the lifeboat deck and opened the watertight door. Before I went in I looked at him one last time. He was still standing there looking at me. I didn't want to feel emotionally attached to him...I couldn't afford to feel bad. Was this the reason why relations on ship never work once people reach home? Is it because we learn to detach ourselves so that we can move on? I ran up to my cabin, threw the shopping bags on the bed, changed into overalls and looked at the watch. I had five minutes before my watch. As I ran down I had forgotten all about Bosun.

In the ECR, 3rd was awake for a change. He was standing and looking at the control panel. I looked at the guy standing in front of me. He looked old and tired. A lot of people his age would be chief engineers by now. He had always been quite negative in his criticism of me but then it did help me grow as a person.

"Hello 3rd," I said smiling.

He looked confused. He just said a gruff, "Hi."

I persisted, "What's new 3rd?"

"Keep an eye on the Cargo Engine #2. We're losing the gear oil so instruct your motorman to keep filling it at regular interval. We can't stop the leakage as we are in the mid of discharge."

I looked at the alarm console. No red light. I was making coffee for myself and turned around when I realised 3rd had not left. I was surprised he was in no hurry today.

I thought I should strike up a conversation. "Who all are there in your family?" I asked feeling quite awkward.

I was relieved to see him smile as he answered, "My kids...three of them and my parents."

"It would be good to have your parents around when you are sailing...kids and wife need that support system."

"My wife didn't survive the 3rd delivery."

I wasn't prepared for the answer, "Oh God! I am sorry 3rd..."

He had the sarcasm back on his face as he said, "It's strange that I'm sharing such a personal thing and that too with you!"

"Sharing helps take off some load. I can only imagine how hard it would be for you and the kids."

"It is...anyway I can't stay here throughout your watch entertaining you."

I said warmly, "Anytime you want to share, I'm all ears."

He went away slowly nodding his head.

The following morning after watch I went upto the galley for breakfast. The cooks and crew were still discussing about the Esmeraldes event. I quickly ate whatever was available and came down. Sam was still in ECR when I came down again.

He said, "When I took over watch from you I noticed a change in you."

"What 4th?" I asked.

"You look fresh...your body language has changed too, for better."

I said with a nod, "I feel good."

2nd came in, "Good morning!"

I said warmly, "Hi 2nd."

He explained a job to Sam and then came to me, "5th today onwards you do only two hours of overtime like other engineers. And Sunday would be no OT for you too."

"Wow thanks 2nd," I was going to have a lot of free time then on.

I finished routine maintenance work on compressor valves and came up to wash my hands and take leave. It was 1030 and Chief engineer was in ECR with Sam. They had not seen me and instinctively I felt like leaving E/R without their knowledge. But I didn't. I wanted Chief to be aware of 2nd's decision so I went into ECR.

Chief was all eyes. He complained, "You don't visit me these days."

Since I had no reply I kept quiet. He asked, "What's happening?"

I wanted to tell him to ask the duty engineer. But my reply was different, "I was lapping compressor valves."

He demanded, "What next?"

I said, "I'm off now."

He looked at his watch and shouted, "Off?! Who gave you an off?"

"2nd told me that I don't need to do more than two hours OT daily."

He said annoyingly, "What does the Filipino know? You have a lot to learn...continue working, I'll speak with him."

"Chief, the reason for me spending extra time was that I had to pick up basics of watch keeping. I've learnt more than that. When required, I'll be here 24 hours non-stop."

"I will have to mention that in your report."

"Chief, do you think I care about the report?"

Sam couldn't believe the exchange he was witnessing. Chief's mouth too remained open for a while. I said, "I have come here to work and to learn and not make you happy."

He said unhappily, "It's for your good. It's up to you whether you want to listen."

"I'm just asking for my personal space after I'm done with my work. I give my hundred percent in engine room."

He added seriously, "Think about my advice. I want you to be a good engineer."

"With all due respect, when I need advice I generally ask."

"I've warned you already...it won't be good for your career!"

"I'm glad we had this discussion. This is what my take on this is. If in my place it was a Yugoslavian or Turk or a Filipino you wouldn't be having this discussion. You're taking me for granted because I am an Indian. But as would be obvious to you, I'm not afraid. You do what you think is right and I...will do what I think is right!" and with that I walked off from there.

That night after my dinner I went to the officer's smoke room to have a chat with whoever was there. In an hour I was lying in bed thinking about pleasant memories. I wondered what Veronica must be doing...I wanted to meet her again. It would be tragic if I never see her again. For a moment Anoushka came into my thoughts but I forgot about her immediately thereafter.

I was sipping my evening tea in the verandah of my home. The sun was about to set, the breeze as refreshing as the tea. I looked around feeling comfortable and secure.

I looked out to see the dense trees around the house and could hear the leaves rustle in the wind. I heard some noise outside. I stopped sipping my tea...nothing for a few moments and then I heard it again, the unmistakable sound of somebody stepping on a twig. In a moment I could hear them inside the house, they didn't care to hide themselves anymore. I dropped my cup and ran out from the back door. They had spotted me and started coming after me. I looked around to see the faces of the people chasing me. They wore long black robes, their heads were covered and they were armed with swords, daggers and pistols. They had started shooting at me. The sky had become overcast, the trees looked ominous and the whole place looked dark and demonic. I had reached a hilly terrain. I jumped over the rocks, tumbled, got hurt but continued to run for my life. And then I came to a dead end...it was the end of the terrain. I looked down into the ravine...I could not see the bottom. I could hear them but I didn't dare turn around. I was contemplating jumping down to my death. I was about to leap when I felt a hand on my shoulder. My eyes were shut tightly...they had gained in on me and I would be dead soon.

But nothing happened, and I was surprised to be still alive. I heard a movement next to me...my eyes were still shut tight. I was waiting for my death...I was expecting a bullet to hit me or a sharp cold blade to pierce my heart. But none of that happened; instead there was this familiar voice, "Open your eyes Siddhartha."

It was Frank! He was standing next to me on the cliff. "Remember what I told you...you are capable of handling your problems. Turn around and face them. Believe..."

I slowly started turning around. Apprehensive at first but there was a change I felt in me...I felt more and more confident as I turned. I looked towards them. They stopped in their tracks. My enemies looked confused. The air was filled with the noise of crickets. Everything was going in slow motion. I could see everything...I was in control. I raised my right hand up in the air slowly and brought it down suddenly and the crickets became quite...there was pin drop silence all around. The black shadows started bursting one by one...like black balloons being pricked. I had got rid of them. I smiled as I turned around. But Frank wasn't there now...in his place stood the *Baba* from Shirdi.

He smiled as he said, "You seem to have found your way. Do meet me when you come to Shirdi. You can find me at the temple's kitchen. I am in charge of the F&B."

For the first time in months, I did something I had forgotten to do...I woke up smiling.

CHAPTER

20

Naeem Chacha's Gift

Bosun flew from Marseilles to Amsterdam to Bombay. He had around eight pegs of Glenfiddich. He still couldn't sleep. He knew this time he may have to make difficult choices...he knew he may have to confront her. He remembered how Naeem *chacha*'s spirit had saved him last time. Thinking of him brought back the good memories. Now that he was thinking about it, his childhood didn't appear that bad. He remembered what he had told him, '...why are you running from here? This place belongs to you...' One day he will have to stop running away. He was in Cochin the next day.

Like always when Bosun came home there would be a party the same night and like always Bosun had brought with him scotch for his friends. Bosun's wife and mother were busy preparing snacks for the evening while Bosun chatted with his father and his son. After evening tea he went out for a stroll with his son.

He asked, "Did you have a nightmare again?"

"No papa."

"Anything else disturbing you?"

"Nothing papa. All well."

"Hmm...it's strange that you dreamt of *Durga Ma*...but then it's a good sign if God comes in your dream."

"I think so too papa," he said not too sure.

Bosun had made up his mind to pay a visit to Naeem *chacha*'s son, Afzal. He was his childhood friend but since the day Bosun had left home, his interactions with his old friends had lessened and slowly he had cut himself off from everyone. Afzal lived in the other part of the village and though Bosun wanted to meet him, he never went there.

Bosun's son asked, "Where are we going papa?"

"To that shop over there."

"Afzal uncle's shop. It's been there forever."

"Yes son...it's been there forever!"

Afzal was arranging stuff inside the small cubicle. It was strange to see the shop without Naeem *chacha* in it. He suddenly felt like crying...he never had time to realise that he was fond of Naeem *chacha*. He was feeling bad that he never visited *chacha*. He spent some time quietly looking at the shop. Afzal realised someone was standing outside his shop.

He kept staring at Bosun for a while and when he saw Bosun smile he exclaimed, "Govi!"

"Afzal *mian*!" Bosun exclaimed.

They shook hands very warmly. They talked about childhood spent together climbing mango trees. Afzal admitted how jealous he was as his father was very fond of Bosun.

They had tea together. They were sitting outside the shop when Bosun saw it. After all these years, it still moved about in the same way. The yellow beak, white chest and golden-brown body...though the colour had faded, it still looked majestic.

Afzal followed Bosun's gaze and said, "It belongs to you."

"What do you mean?"

"The eagle...a week before he died he used to remember you a lot. One day he came to see his shop. It was the last time he visited it. He sat here for a while. He looked up at the eagle, smiled and said, 'One day Govi would come here. Give this eagle to him and tell him not to forget his roots. Tell him to accept this place as his home and hence be accepted.'"

248 Eagle Spotted, Message Decoded

Bosun took it from where it hung. He wondered whether Naeem *chacha* had made up the story about the eagle. He wondered whether it actually had magical powers. He closed his eyes as he felt the bird...he felt calmer. He was happy to be home.

Bosun got up to leave. He said, "Afzal tonight there's a party. I want to invite you and your family."

Afzal looked hesitant, "We'll not be comfortable there."

"I insist. It would be good re-union for us all."

"Nobody from your part of village comes here. And we don't go to that side anymore..."

"Afzal, in that case tonight things would start to change. Promise me you'll be there."

The party began two hours after Bosun met Afzal. Afzal, his wife and daughter Izaana attended and were comfortable at once. Bosun's son fell in love with Izaana the moment he saw her. After dinner the party was still in full swing for the ones who were drinking. Afzal and family expressed their desire to leave and Bosun's son offered to see them home. Women and children too had left for home.

Around midnight, the last bottle was over so the remaining people said goodnight to each other and left for their home. For Bosun it would be a fifteen minute walk back home. The scotch was great and so was the company. The music of the latest *Malayali* flick was still playing in his head as he walked. It was an abrupt change from the party and the silence and the loneliness made him uneasy. He saw a movement at a distance. He focused his sight and realised someone was sitting on the old wooden bench at the side of the *kuchcha* pathway. He looked at his watch. He thought, "Who could be out here at this late an hour?"

On reaching closer he realised it was a woman as he could make out that the dress worn by the person was a *sari*. His old doubts were back and he was afraid to go ahead. He slowly approached the bench. He wanted to run away but then there was no other way to reach home. He didn't look towards the bench as he crossed it and he immediately quickened pace when he heard the voice calling out his name. It wasn't Mrs Kavita...he sighed with relief, it was his wife!

He grumbled, "What are you doing here?! What if our drinks lasted longer?"

"I knew your drinks wouldn't last long. We don't get time to talk...and today I was feeling uneasy."

"What happened?"

"It's Yudi I am worried about. He's not studying properly...his grades are going down."

He asked, "So should we force him into studying?"

"But studies are important! He doesn't listen to me. You tell him to concentrate on education. Be stern with him."

"It's strange but I am not too sure..."

"Not sure about what?"

"About our attitude towards him."

"I don't understand...you wanted him to study!"

He said thinking deeply, "Yes but till now you always objected when I forced him to study. And today I think you were right. Is it the drink?"

"I guess so..."

But Bosun realised something...the dream...he realised the meaning of his son's dream! He said, now sure of himself, "Actually no. I couldn't live my life the way I wanted to. I always wanted to go to sea to catch fish. This life was not chosen by me...it happened because I ran away. Nevertheless, I am happy with my career... but then I would love to come back home every evening to you and Yudi. I know what it feels if you are not able to do what you want to. Today my son has realised the path he wants to take but I am not letting him take it because of my selfish reasons..."

His wife started coughing and when she spoke her voice had changed as was her face and body. Bosun watched in horror as he saw he was sitting next to Mrs Kavita. She said in hoarse voice, "I knew it...you need a lesson. I shouldn't have let you in peace. Now you are thinking of spoiling your son! You will have to come with me now!"

Bosun was paralysed with fear. He wanted to get up and run but his legs wouldn't respond to his command. He tried again as he saw her reaching out for him but he fell down. He bumped his knee into a stone as he fell. He was in pain and he looked down to see if everything was ok; he needed his knees in perfect condition as he had to run for the next five minutes. Something had fallen out of his pocket as he fell. He looked at the eagle by his side. He picked it up. His breathing became stable and he could feel his legs again. He stood up but he didn't run. He confronted her and said, "I'm not going with you."

She whispered eerily, "You think you have a choice?"

"Yes, you always have a choice. I am sure about what I want. My son would leave school and pursue his interest."

She started laughing but Bosun wasn't afraid anymore. He said, "I'm better off without your education. I have learnt my life's lessons on rough seas. The work that I have done has shaped my life in a way your classes never could have."

"But you admitted that you had no choice so you opted for this career. Now you say it has shaped your life?"

"Yes, I ran away and hence came to do this job...I admit I didn't choose it but then it has made me a better man. I am respected on the ship and in my village. And yes I still admire the job that my father did all his life...my heart lies there. I didn't have the courage to take that job but I wouldn't make the same mistake with my son!"

"If you make a wrong decision for your son I will kill you."

"I will not take any decision regarding my son's life. I will let him take it. And I'm sure it is the right decision."

"If your son doesn't attend school I will kill your whole family."

"The decision about my son is made. I do not need your advice. Get lost from here and never come back again."

She didn't move from where she was. Bosun looked into her eyes as he said, "And I'm not afraid of you anymore." As soon as he said this she disappeared without a word. The night sky appeared clearer. The silence wasn't deathly anymore. He felt relieved and happy as if a heavy weight which was bearing down on him for so many years had finally been lifted off him. He breathed in the fresh air and walked back home. His house looked beautiful; the cracks in the wall and the peeled off paint not visible in the moonlight. The night had hidden the flaws of his house.

He opened the gate and walked towards the door thinking of his fishing trips with his father. He would watch his father as he worked on the nets with full concentration. He would tell him, "Pa when I grow up you rest at home and I'll give instructions to your men the same way you do now."

And he would reply, "Govi you would own a bigger boat and would command better men."

"No Pa I want this boat and I want to command the same men you do!"

And his father would laugh heartily.

21

Solution from the Solution

After Marseilles Tengalkar was brought back in the 8-12 watch as most of the important jobs were planned during this period and 2nd needed an experienced hand. 2nd was also confident that I could manage the watch with Ali. Ali still was the quietest of the lot. During watch he would not waste a single moment; he would either be taking rounds or cleaning the engine room. I tried to strike up conversation with him but he would always give me short answers.

Three days after we left Marseilles I was looking out for Ali in our early morning watch. He was down somewhere hiding from me...the same way I used to from everyone else in engine room. I knew he needed help. I rang the calling bell thrice. He came few minutes later wiping his hands with a rag.

"How's it going Ali?"

"There's a little leak from the outlet line of the sludge transfer pump...was cleaning the floor beneath it..."

"Ok Ali and what about you. How are you?"

"Oh? I am good."

"Sit," I said motioning him to a chair.

He sat down reluctantly. And when he did, he sat very uncomfortably.

I took out my packet and offered him one, "Do you smoke?"

He looked at the cigarette and then at me. I nodded gently signalling him to take it. He took it finally. I looked at him drag a puff. It hit him instantly and he ended up coughing.

He looked embarrassed, "I'm smoking after a long time..."

"You aren't regular?"

"I am but am not comfortable smoking on ship."

I asked, "Why?"

"I don't go to the crew smoke room very much, as people are quiet rowdy and then they either watch non-Hindi movies which I don't understand or they watch porn which I don't want to watch."

I nodded and said, "You can smoke here."

I saw him smile for the first time, "You are not like they say you are."

"No Ali, I am not like they say I am!"

In the next few days Ali told me about his children. He was opening up slowly. One day while smoking he said, "I offer *namaaz* everyday, I don't drink, I'm faithful to my wife, I don't think evil of others, I don't use foul language...I'm a good Muslim except that I smoke."

I took a drag saying, "Yes it is an evil thing. I have quitted so many times you know... but I always start smoking again. Now, I've quit 'quitting smoking'."

By the time we reached Boston we were good friends.

After our evening watch was over I told him, "I'm going out to make some phone calls. Want to join me?"

He said hurriedly, "Ok will go change."

I signalled him to stop and said, "Not needed. I'm sure there would be a phone on the jetty."

We came down from the ship but couldn't locate any phone. I could see a lit cabin at the corner. I approached the cabin to ask for directions from the uniformed personnel sitting inside. He was watching baseball. I asked, "Hi! Where can we find a phone?"

At first he looked at me as if I was from some other planet but then he smiled and told me, "Keep following the lit up path...you will hit the road. Cross it and you'll find a couple of booths."

I thanked him and went to Ali, "Bad news. We'll have to go out of the jetty dressed like tramps. Hope we don't scare the city folks!"

Ali said in a tense voice, "Look at me...my hair is unkempt, I haven't trimmed my moustache and beard for the last six months and I can't even speak in English! And on top of that I am wearing oil stained boiler suit!"

The lit path led us through a small patch which was so green it felt we were taking a hike through a jungle. We suddenly hit the road. The road as expected in the US was wide, well marked and very clean.

Ali said, "I can sleep on it!"

"Me too," I said smiling.

On the other side of the road was Macy's in front of which were a couple of booths. To the right of the Macy's was a huge compound where hundreds of colourful trucks were parked. I looked at the name plate affixed to the netted boundary 'Boston Freight Lifter'. Crossing the wide road was a piece of cake as there was no vehicle on the road. We reached over to the other side and I still couldn't take my eyes off the beautiful machines.

I took out Bosun's number and the calling card as I dialled the required codes. The phone was ringing.

"Hello?"

"Bosun?"

"Oye Paanchu! You called me!"

"I told you...I don't believe in your old wives tales."

He was laughing.

I asked eagerly, "Hey Bosun how's it going?"

"It's never been better. My son has joined his dance classes and he's also completing his studies through correspondence. I didn't tell him to...he himself selected this option. He says going to school was such a waste of time...and I agree with him."

I said happily, "That's good. And what about the ghost...?"

"She's gone! I confronted her."

I exclaimed, "What are you saying? She came? And you confronted her? You are a brave man!"

"I got my strength from the gift Naeem *chacha* gave me...the eagle from his shop."

"So it does have magical powers?"

Bosun replied philosophically, "Magic is where your mind finds it."

"I get it Bosun. You mean to say there was no magic in the eagle...it's just that you believed that there was."

"Exactly, in fact I think there was no ghost either...it was a manifestation of my fears and weaknesses which had taken the shape of Mrs Kavita. I didn't have to fight the ghost, I had to face my own issues and resolve them."

"It makes sense Bosun."

"And you were so right about me letting my son choose his own path."

I said grinning, "I'm glad it's turned out this way..."

"And do you know, it's when I was talking to her that I realised what my son's dream meant."

"Your son's dream was related to your problems! That's interesting..."

"Yes, it's strange but true. My son going to *Durga Ma's* temple is similar to trying something that no one in our family has done before...he chose a career which I or our forefathers would never even have dreamt of. I unfortunately was the priest; the person my son respects and loves. I too was imposing my beliefs on him. I realised I was doing the wrong thing. I didn't want my son to run away from me. I would have failed as a father!"

I agreed completely, "True! Wow Bosun, I'm glad you solved it!"

"You helped me too Paanchu."

I said thoughtfully, "Well actually it's you who's helped me. The way your life turned out...the way you solved it...answers a lot of questions for me."

"I'm glad to be of help. You know one of the most important learning for me was to not forget my roots...one should never disown the place they belong to. The roots define who you are."

"I agree Bosun."

"And the other point is...I needed to believe in some magic. What about you Paanchu? Have you met your eagle yet?"

I thought of the saint, the cricket and Frank, "I think I have..."

Bosun said, "I don't need the eagle anymore...because now I have started believing in myself."

"So very true. I am glad I called you! Thank you Bosun."

"So will you call again?"

"To tell you the truth, I don't know...I still have a lot of sailing left. You never know, I too may start believing in your old wives tales."

Bosun was laughing again, "All the best to you son."

"All the best to you too," I said smiling.

I hung the phone and came out. Ali was still talking, so I sat on the pavement and started singing 'Wish you were here'. I was thinking about what Bosun had told me, 'The roots define who you are'. My parents had always questioned why I spent time with a person like Garu, who according to them was a loser. I didn't know whether Garu was going to have a successful career, but I did know that he was a part of my 'root'. He may do absolutely nothing in life but he will remain my friend. Manish couldn't speak nor could he hear and he would spend his whole life living in the same locality, spending all the evenings of his life playing snooker and working in the same cubicle...but for me he would always be a bigger 'Hero' than Vikram could ever be.

We were walking back to the ship. I felt great. I had lost in love but I had just begun to find myself. I was still not sure what I wanted to do in life, but I knew life had unlimited possibilities and that I was ready for them now. Who knows, one day I may actually learn to fly, I thought.

Ali broke the silence "Paanch sa'ab?"

"Yes Ali."

"You called home?"

"I called Bosun."

Ali exclaimed, "Bosun!"

"Yeah, I wanted to prove him wrong!"

Ali chuckled as he looked at my overalls and said playfully, "Will anyone believe us if we told them that we went out in US dressed like this?"

I laughed with him. I looked at my boiler suit and my dirty industrial shoes. Times had changed and for the better too; there was no room for stuffy etiquette in today's no-nonsense world. To be in uniform was to be in shackles and talent was way more important than a pair of polished shoes! I looked at the night sky and smiled.

There was a moment of silence and then Ali asked, "Paanch sa'ab, where you from? Bombay?"

"No, Ranchi."

Afterword

I began work on *Eagle Spotted, Message Decoded* (*ESMD*) in January 2006. I wrote a few pages on and off and eventually forgot about the book. I became so busy in business meetings, marketing plans and presentations that in the following three years, apart from the book, I also forgot to live.

But I got my wakeup call in January 2009 — it was through a phone call which I got while attending a conference. I was told that my wife's MRI report indicated there was a tumour in the brain. She underwent an eight-hour-long surgery. But there was more to come; the biopsy report on tumour tested positive for malignancy. And then began the search for answers to the many questions which kept cropping up. What is this disease? What is the right protocol? What is the efficacy of a particular medicine? Where should we get the treatment done? Life expectancy...? Well, we went ahead with the year-long treatment of radiation and chemotherapy. The ill-effects of the treatment, clubbed with the side-effects of the steroids, brought with them their own set of problems.

Our so-called perfect world had crashed before us. But in spite of the numerous vomiting, severe pain, depression attacks, hormonal changes, hospitals, surgeries, doctor appointments, etc. she stood her ground bravely, smiling and looking forward to life. The least I could do was to be by her side in this battle. I took leave from work and when it was not extended I decided to resign. Ironically, this was the time I realised what being alive was.

I would tell her stories about the time I spent working on ships. One thing led to another and one night I started penning it down. It became a ritual — every night I would tell her a story and when she would fall asleep, I would start writing. Writing to me was like a door which led to the perfect, happy and magical world. It was a means to connect with the universe.

ESMD, however, is not a story based on cancer. It is a story about a world very different from ours — where strangers come together to work and live like a family. *ESMD* is based on life on board a merchant ship.

And as they say on a ship — "Problems come and go...but nothing can stop the ship from reaching its destination. It keeps sailing." Life, too, goes on...

Acknowledgements

I would like to express my gratitude to all the magnificent people I had a chance to work with during my brief career spent on various ships.

To my parents, for making me what I am.

To my brother, for showing me the direction.

My wife, who believed in the book more than I did. She forgot her pain, stood by me and convinced me to go on when I had lost hope.

To Sunil K Poolani of Frog Books, for believing in *ESMD*. To Sadhvi Sharma, for her patience and time and who brought the best out of the book by her editing.

To my friends, for the wonderful memories and support.

www.ingramcontent.com/pod-product-compliance
Lightning Source LLC
Chambersburg PA
CBHW022157170626
46807CB00005B/2239